I0461089

CHASING
LOVE'S
WINGS

CHASING LOVE'S WINGS

Zoey Derrick

Cover completed by Rachel Rivera of Parajunkee - Parajunkee.net with the help of BigStock Photos and Rachel's MAD MAD Skillz!

This book was edited with the help of Sione Aeschliman, Owner of Sione Aeschliman LLC out of Portland, Oregon. Sione has been my rock, my constant and the light that has kept this project moving forward, without her, this book would not be in your hands. You can visit her on Twitter at www.twitter.com/writelearndream or on her website http://sioneaeschliman.blogspot.com

Copyright © 2014 Zoey Derrick

All rights reserved.

ISBN-13: 978-0990326427

All rights reserved. Without limiting rights under the copyright reserved above, no part of this publication may be reproduced, stored, introduced into a retrieval system, distributed or transmitted in any form or by any means, including without limitation photocopying, recording, or other electronic or mechanical methods, without the prior written permission of the publisher, except in the case of brief quotations embodied in critical reviews and certain other noncommercial uses permitted by copyright law. The scanning, uploading, and/or distribution of this document via the internet or via any other means without the permission of the publisher is illegal and is punishable by law. Please purchase only authorized editions and do not participate in or encourage electronic piracy of copyrightable materials.

For permission requests, email zoeyderrick@gmail.com

For Barb & Walt – may all your dreams come true

together.

A Back Story...
June 20th, 2012
While in Tarah...

"How long are you planning to keep this up?"

"Keep what up?

"Are you ever going to tell anyone else?"

"No, things are just fine the way they are." Little does one of the men on the phone know, it's all about to come unraveled, at least in one aspect.

"She's your daughter, you can't keep doing this forever."

"I don't see any logical reason why not, isn't it better this way?"

"I highly doubt it's better this way. You should've seen her two weeks ago. She was a complete mess. She kicked your headstone, for crying out loud. She deserves far better than this. For the life you put her through, she at least deserves an apology."

"Enough, Vincent!" His voice is a harsh growl crackling over the phone.

But Vincent knows he can't stop now; the man needs to hear this. "She's taking over the business."

"Dammit."

"That's what you wanted, isn't it? You left her no choice in your will, you forced her into it." Vincent is losing his patience.

"It was, but I expected her to find some loophole out of it. She never expressed any interest in what I did, at least not until college."

"Wake up and smell the damn roses. You pushed her away for so long, and she fought and fought hard for you to see her. She got a degree in public relations, exactly what you did. She followed in your footsteps whether you wanted her to or not. If you can't see that—"

"I get it," he snaps. "What makes you think that I have any chance of making this right with her? She is going to be even more angry with me when she finds out I'm alive after all this time."

"She doesn't have to find out, but dammit, Bobby, the guilt I feel, knowing this secret, is beginning to weigh heavily on me," Vincent says. He is doing this for Bobby because he owes Bobby his life and everything it has become. Robert Enders sees something in him that no one else has seen, has offered him an opportunity that he would've never had. Bobby has given him a career that he loves more than anything in this world. He lives and breathes his job. But something about the way Bobby is talking is nagging at him. "She's already going to find out, isn't she?"

"She's turned twenty-five, Vin, that package is on its way to her. I may have added a few things, so yes, she is going to find out. It is just a matter of when." Bobby's voice comes across the line with a sadness in it. "I can't make her open the package, I can't make her read or watch anything in it, so it could be days or years, if ever, before she figures it out."

"She's been in Tarah, how is she going to get it?"

"Mick."

"Mick knows you're alive too?" Vincent can't hide the surprise in his voice. When he committed to doing this, it was on the grounds that no one else should know about it. If Bobby'd had his way, Vincent wouldn't know about it, either. The fewer the people who knew, the less likely it would become public knowledge.

"No. The estate lawyers received a package from an Enders family friend, to be delivered to his next of kin. Mark was very clear that he wanted nothing to do with anything, which is why Cameron was named next of kin and head of the estate. The package will go to her."

"I hope you're right."

"I have a duplicate if it doesn't."

Vincent rolled his eyes. "Why am I not surprised."

"Just relax and give it some time. Nothing in that package indicates anyone else's involvement. Everything that happens at this point is between her and me, no one else. End of story."

May 26th, 2011
A Year Ago...
******
Robert "Bobby" Enders
******

"Mr. Enders, thank you for coming in," the tall, fit man says to me. A pathetic apology for the way I've been treated, considering.

"You didn't give me much of a choice."

"This is true, we didn't, and I apologize about that. I'm Special Agent Markensen. We understand that you have some information that pertains to an open investigation regarding the Mendoza family." The man is dressed in a white shirt and blue tie and is wearing an FBI jacket.

"I just came here to talk to the LAPD."

"I understand that, but the information you have uncovered is a very strong lead that we can use against the Mendoza family. Have you ever heard of them?"

"I have. Though I am sure my information is far less accurate than your own."

"They are one of the largest U.S. and Mexico drug traffickers. Your information is more important to my office than it is to the LAPD. Which is why you've been waiting and why I'm here."

"How can you be so certain that the information I've given the LAPD is what you're after? Or, better yet, how do I know the information I repeat for you will be kept safe and my life not put in danger?" I ask the question. I have to know.

"Mr. Enders, we're more than willing to provide you with any protection you need. Whether it be agents assigned to you or other, more drastic measures."

"What would constitute 'drastic measures?'"

"Well, federal witness protection, if we feel it is necessary, but we can't make certain that protection like that is warranted until we know what you know."

"What I stumbled into was purely by accident. I believe that it was very fortunate that I managed to get away, hopefully undetected, but I can't keep spouting off the things that I know without knowing that there is some type of protection that can be put into place. I understood the risks when I got here, though I never expected it to be as dire as you're making it out to be."

"Mr. Enders, let me assure you that we can and will do everything within our means to protect you from any ramifications that arise from your being here."

I begin telling the agent what I know and how I know it. The longer we talk, the more concerned Special Agent Markensen becomes. He's completely blown away by how I stumbled into this mess: compliments of Aaron Iverson, one of my clients, an actor, a very well-known one at that. As soon as I drop that name, Markensen immediately begins to question who I am.

"I am Robert Enders, owner of Bold International."

He really doesn't like my response. "Mr. Enders, you're a well-known public figure in this community. Are you certain they didn't know who you were?"

I let out a strained chuckle. "If they didn't know, I am certain that Aaron and whoever his buddy was will take it upon themselves to notify whoever they need to about the potential for exposure, and in doing so they will reveal who I am, if for no other reason than to save their own skin. It won't take a rocket scientist for this Mendoza to find me. And I'll take it upon myself to assume that Mendoza is a man of action: Shoot first and ask no questions later."

"Well, Mr. Enders, this changes things." He stands up and walks the three steps to the door. "Please excuse me a moment?" He leaves the room without allowing me to answer his question.

Panic starts to set in. This isn't good.

I start to think about all the things that have happened over the last few months. Just when I think I have what I need to get somewhere with Cameron, this shit has to happen. What the hell am I going to do now? I am going to have to walk away, at least if I want to stay alive. But is death really so bad?

I can't shake the memory of watching her walk across that stage in her maroon gown, and I was even prouder when I saw her master's hood. My baby girl, all grown up.

The reality of what Evelyn put me through when my children were younger finally has new meaning and a new purpose. Because of her I've managed to keep my fatherhood a secret, and I have no doubt that there will be no reason Cameron needs to get involved in all of this. At least I hope not. But I'm suddenly scared for her. If I stay here or flee under witness protection, where does that leave Cameron and my family?

If these men are as dangerous as Special Agent Markensen is implying, they will stop at nothing to bring me back to them, including, but not limited to, killing my daughter.

I continue to ponder ways to protect Cameron until Special Agent Markensen returns. This time he is not alone. "Mr. Enders, this is Agent Elizabeth Tod. She is one of our agents who specializes in witness protection." We exchange handshakes. "I've explained to her your situation regarding who you are, and she is going to discuss some options available to you at this time. Due to the nature of witness protection, all the microphones and cameras have been turned off in this room, and I will be leaving you with Agent Tod. She will inform me of your decision and the steps we need to take."

Uh, what? "Sure," I say, despite the fact that my hands have gone cold and clammy and my heart is trying to pound through my chest. Losing my cool is not something I'm used to, but I am no longer in control. I can't control this situation, unless of course I want to end up dead. Which just might happen anyway.

"Mr. Enders?" The pretty Agent Tod is working to get my attention. I look over at her. "I want to first let you know that I do not know the nature of the information you've shared with Special Agent Markensen, only that we need to establish some type of immediate protection. We can give you no more than twenty-four hours to get your personal affairs in order before we need to find someplace for you to go."

"Twenty-four hours? That's it?"

"Yes, sir. We can protect you for the next twenty-four hours, after which point it becomes difficult to remain conspicuous. Given the nature of who you are — and I do know who you are — we need to figure out the best course of action to take. We can protect you as long as you're out of the public eye. After that, we would be hard-pressed to keep you under wraps."

"What exactly are you suggesting here?" I knew I should've just left this shit alone. More than likely, I'm being paranoid and nothing will ever come of this, but dammit.

"You need to disappear. Completely. If you have the means to leave the country, I strongly suggest that you do. We can help you with passports and identification to get you out of here. Unfortunately, if you leave the country, we cannot protect you. However, leaving the country anonymously should help."

"What if I don't want to leave the country?"

"Again, Mr. Enders, I do not know the nature of the information you've shared with Special Agent Markensen, but his recommendation is out of the county, and not to Mexico or any countries within Latin America. Otherwise, the world is your stage to go where you want. Is there somewhere you can go that cannot be traced back to you?"

I don't even need to think about it. "I have a ranch in Montana."

"Do you own it?"

"I do, but it is not now, nor has it ever been, under my name."

"Can the home be traced back to you in any way, shape or form?"

"Look, Agent Tod, I am a man of Hollywood. Everything in my life is subject to the same scrutiny that my clients face. So much of my life is public knowledge, and there are very few things that I have that allow me to maintain some level of my privacy. That ranch is one of them."

"What else?"

"My daughter."

"You have a daughter?" She doesn't succeed in hiding any level of shock she feels in response to that information.

"Yes, but I don't think she likes me very much."

"Will she be a problem for those we are hiding you from? Since that piece of information isn't common knowledge, can she be traced back to you?"

"She can, but the paper trail is very long and I'm not sure there is a vendetta big enough to make that worth the effort. I tried my hardest to protect her from Hollywood and what I face on a daily basis. No one knows she exists." Sometimes I wonder if she even knows I exist, but I don't need to bring that up right now.

"What about your business? What will happen if you walk away? I'm assuming, based on your public stature, that you're an integral part of your business?"

"I am, but just up and leaving my life, personal or professional, will cause major problems. I am a very active contributor to my business; if I just up and disappear, that will not only cause business problems, but it will make the news. Bringing attention to the fact that I've disappeared is not what you or the FBI want to deal with. Not to mention the fact that, because of the news, they — the bad guys — will know that I've consulted law enforcement, forcing their hand to more drastic measures. Agent Tod, let's be frank for a moment. The only way I can walk away from my life and make a clean break from everyone and everything is if I die."

I watch as she considers my options. "Mr. Enders, faking a death is not something we believe in doing. We prefer to pull you away quickly and quietly."

"Agent Tod, my leaving my job and walking away from my life will do a multitude of things. One, my business will fold, and therefore my thousand-plus employees will be out of their jobs. Two, my daughter will be exposed for who she is, my daughter, thereby making her a target for the people you're trying to protect me from. That would be counterproductive, don't you think? Third of all, if one and two happen, all of my assets will be frozen in the big Bold business blunder and my daughter will walk away from all of this with nothing. I have not worked myself thin for the last thirty years to establish a business as successful as mine to watch it fold in front of my eyes, and I would then have—" I stop myself. "I would have someone to blame for that. Do you see where I'm going with this?"

She nods.

"Good. Now, if I 'die,' my daughter gets her inheritance, my business stays afloat, and I can walk away from everything I've just outlined, keeping everyone safe. Now, let me tell you again, if you want to protect me and my family, I need to die."

May 27th, 2011

"Goddammit, Bobby, this is not the way to go about this. There are other options."

"Options like what? Hiding or wandering around wondering if I am going to get shot or killed?"

"Think about her, about your family, your friends, your life."

"Shut up, Vinnie. This is the only way I can do this and you know it. If I die by their hands, they win and my daughter will never be safe. If I die by my hands and within my control, she remains safe, the business goes on, she takes over, and life goes on, just as it would go on if I died without all this bullshit."

"I know, but...dammit, Robert, she's not ready for this. She hates you; she won't take over the business, and she will resent you for the rest of her life."

"She won't have a choice. My final will and testament will see to that. As far as resenting me goes, I'm pretty sure she already does that."

"How did you even get mixed up in all this bullshit?"

"Tick."

"What? How?"

"He neglected to tell me that he changed suppliers. When the new supplier forced the original one out of business and out of town, Tick had no one else to turn to. So he went with Mendoza. Tick failed to tell his clientele that they were dealing with the purest of drugs available."

"You don't think that's what..." Vinnie doesn't finish his sentence. He knows it. The whole reason Bobby had gotten involved in the supply business was to keep his clients' names off police radar and give them a constant supply when they needed it from a reliable source. Tick, of course, was making bank on the markup, but neither Bobby nor Bold ever took a kickback from the drug sales. Leaving their hands clean, but them aware of what was going on.

"So, I figured it out, figured out who to blame for the change, and ended up walking into a drug deal between Mendoza and Aaron." Vinnie can't hide the surprise on his face. Aaron had never been on any of their lists. "Because of that, I have to either disappear or be killed for real."

"There is so much I want to say to you."

"Stop, it's not necessary. We will see each other again one day. Once the world has forgotten about Robert Enders. Or this asshole's bullshit ends."

May 28th, 2011

******

Mick

******

"Mick, it's Vincent." Why on earth is he calling me?

"What's up, Vinnie?"

"Are you still working with Cameron?"

"Yes," I say rather slowly.

"Is she your friend?"

"What the fuck, Vinnie?"

"Look, I need to tell you something, and I need you to pass it on to her. It will be better if it comes from a friend." Not good.

"Sure, what is it?"

I hear Vinnie take a deep breath on the other end of the phone, almost as though he is composing himself to say something serious, but I can't even begin to imagine what it is. "Bobby's dead."

Well that is not what I was expecting. "When? How?"

"Last night. One of his security men found him this morning in his office, crumpled up on the floor." Another deep breath.

I pinch the bridge of my nose, trying hard to figure out how best to tell Cami this. They are far from close, but dammit if this isn't going to kill her.

"They believe it was a heart attack."

"Christ, Vinnie, he's only fifty-seven." I'm trying to wrap my brain around this, trying to understand it, but I can't. Bobby has always been healthy — exercising, eating healthy, everything.

"There is nothing to indicate foul play, though they will be doing an autopsy today to be sure. If it was a heart attack, we'll know right away. If it was something more malicious, that will take time. I just thought Cameron should find out from you rather than from me. She doesn't even know who I am," Vinnie says. There is a sadness in his voice. Sadness for Cami, possibly. Maybe because he didn't find out until this morning that Bobby had a daughter or just a general sadness for his own loss. I don't know Vincent well, but I've never known him to be the emotional type.

"I'll take care of it. Are there funeral arrangements yet?"

"If the medical examiner finishes today, we will have service on Tuesday. With Monday being the holiday, it's easier on Tuesday. The estate attorney has scheduled the open reading of the will for Tuesday morning. Cameron should probably be there."

Not likely. "All right. How can we contact you with questions?"

"Use this number."

"All right, thanks Vinnie."

He hangs up without another word.

I sit back in my chair, trying to figure out how best to tell Cami that her dad is dead. I wish I could do it in person — I should probably do it in person — but I...I'm not sure I can take the look on her face. This is going to destroy her.

I pick up my cell and pull up her contact information. After a minute or two of debate, I press the send button.

"Magic Mick."

I smile, despite the circumstances, at her nickname for me.

"Hi, Cami girl. What are you doing?"

"I just pulled up in front of the Apple store, why?"

"Are you still driving?"

"No, what's going on, Mick?"

"Is Beau with you?"

"No, she's in Portland for a few weeks with her family. Mick, what is going on?" I can hear the rising panic in her voice.

"Do you know who Vincent is?"

"No, should I?"

"Not really, it's not that important." I don't know how to tell her this but I have to. "Cami, I have some bad news."

"Mick, the only bad news you could possibly have for me is that I'm broke, but I doubt that. So what's up?" That hint of panic disappears momentarily and then returns. She doesn't sound at all cheerful or like her usual joking self when it comes to money. But it doesn't seem like she is on the same wavelength as to why I would have bad news for her, so this is going to either go really smoothly or she is going to go over the top.

"Cami, your father passed away last night."

"Well, shit," she says, but then I hear it: the sob I wasn't expecting.

"I have the details, if you want them..."

"How?"

"How what?"

"How did he die, Mick?" she asks, but her anger is coming through.

"Heart attack."

"That son of a bitch." The phone goes dead.

"Cami?...Hello?" Nothing.

ONE

July 2012 - Phoenix, Arizona
******

Cami
******

"How long until your flight?" Tristan and I are in my condo in Phoenix, a place we've only been for a few days, ever since returning from Tristan's New York premiere. That was an experience that I'm not entirely sure I'm ready to do again. But he made it fun by making me feel like I was the only thing that mattered, and that made it worth it. Regardless of what was going on around him, I was more important.

"About three hours." He kisses me gently on the lips. The kiss quickly turns urgent and needy. I can't help my body's response to his lips on mine. My back arches and I feel his erection grow stronger and harder as he slowly moves in and out of me.

A soft breathy moan escapes my lips, and his kisses grow more urgent and his pace increases. I feel myself building toward that cliff we've been dancing on every day for over a month. My hand slides down his chest and I feel the dermal piercings that create the eyes of his dragon.

He's propped himself up on his left elbow, and his right hand glides feather-soft over my hip to my stomach, tracing light patterns until his fingers gently graze my breast. Both my nipples harden in response to the involuntary shiver his touch has caused across my heated skin, and I feel his fingers graze one pierced nipple, then the other. They are hard as diamonds, straining against the stainless steel balls holding the barbells in place.

I moan again, and his pace increases as my body locks down and the climax I've been trying to avoid washes over me in a warm rush of fire. Tristan increases his pace to a fever pitch, pushing my orgasm to limits I've come to love. "I love you," I hear him whisper in my ear as I come floating down. I feel the muscles of my sex spasm, and he thrusts hard, pouring himself into me.

I open my eyes to see the strained look of orgasm on his face and I whisper, "I love you."

Once we finally settle again from our orgasms, Tristan doesn't roll off me. Which is fine. I love having him so close to me, and it's breaking my heart that he is leaving so soon. I can't bear to look at the clock.

He is only going to be gone for a couple of days, but we haven't spent more than a couple of hours apart since we met in Tarah a month ago.

Ever since that Friday night in the hotel bar, everything in my life has changed. I met the man of my dreams — literally — and I fell in love with him. Hard. Okay, I was probably already in love with him before I met him, but the emotions were superficial, as I didn't actually know him for who he is. I know him better now, though I'm not convinced I know everything there is to know about Tristan Michaels. I'm determined to find out anything and everything about him.

"I don't want you to go," I say softly, and I feel him stiffen, as if I've woken him up, but I know he wasn't sleeping because the hand playing with a stray strand of my hair hasn't stopped moving.

"I told you to come with me," he says. It's the same argument we've been having for the last twenty-four hours.

"I know but I need to take care of some things here. We've only been home for a few days." He slides off of me, but it's not a rejection; he pulls me close to his side.

"I know, and I'll only be gone until Friday. Then I'll come back and we can pick up where we leave off." He kisses my shoulder and his thumb begins to move circles across my stomach, something he tends to do when he is thinking about something.

After we left Tarah, we went to New York, where we spent a few days roaming around the city. It wasn't as much fun as I'd hoped it would be.

After Tristan's premiere, we were followed nearly everywhere we went. I was impressed that it only took the media eight hours to figure out exactly who I am. Then of course the speculations about he and I not really being together started to soar through the roof. It was a good publicity stunt, letting the girls swoon a little longer over the fact that their beloved Tristan might still be single.

The tabloids would read things like, *She's just his PR rep*, etcetera. It didn't bother me any, but Tristan was a little miffed that they were going down that path. It was clear to me that he really wanted them to run away with us being together.

I tried to tell him that it didn't matter to me at all, even played the 'It's good publicity' card, but he wasn't buying it. I told him that *I* knew he was with me and I was with him, and that nothing like that should matter. Over the next day or two he calmed down dramatically about it. That was until we were walking of The Electric Room. Tristan pushed me up against the door of our limo, kissing me feverishly, right in front of no less than a dozen cameras. After that, the speculative headlines stopped and the love stories started. The only reason I knew about any of this going on was because Trinity - the PR manager for Bold, my company - demanded that I take over as his rep. I hadn't seen a problem with it, except for the fact that I'm now responsible for all the things that are said about the man I love.

He nuzzles closer to me and I snuggle into him, content to lie here, but as I move, the insatiable man that he is, it doesn't go unnoticed. We've been in bed all day — literally, as I know it's nearly four in the afternoon — and Tristan has been giving me his undivided attention, from head to toe and back again.

I'm truly enjoying it. I'm sure he's trying to wear himself out so that he can survive the next few days without me, and I am perfectly okay with that.

I use my free hand to bring his chin up. He immediately knows what I'm trying to do and he doesn't disappoint me. Our lips meet once again, and he doesn't stop kissing me over and over.

******
Tristan
******

Leaving Cami here in Phoenix is the absolute last thing I want to do, but I completely understand why she wants to stay. She hasn't been home in what feels like forever, and her new condo needs some attention. When she asked me to come stay with her in Phoenix, I didn't hesitate. I want to be near her all the time, and I can't get enough of this beautiful woman whose tongue is dancing with mine.

After our last go-round not twenty minutes ago, I thought for sure I was done, but that is not the case, not today. It kills me to have to leave her after we've spent all of this time together. But Vincent needs me in L.A. Both Cami and I did our best to convince Vinnie that my traveling there wasn't necessary, that we could handle everything from here, but he wasn't having it. Since that conversation, I've had it stuck in the back of my mind that there is a reason he's trying to pull me away from here, but I can't for the life of me begin to imagine why.

Regardless, I will be back on Friday, no matter what. But if I have anything to say about it, I will be back Thursday night to surprise her.

I'm mulling all this over when Cami pushes me onto my back and I feel the scalding-hot wetness of our all-day lovemaking brush across my erection, and he stirs awake once more. I watch Cami give me her all-knowing smile, knowing full well that she has this effect on me, no matter what the circumstances are.

She begins to flick her hips across my hardness and my eyes roll back in my head. I can feel her clit rubbing along each of the piercings along my cock, and it makes me shiver with excitement. The next thing I know, in one quick flick of her hips, I'm buried deep inside her. I watch as the sensations register on her, causing her eyes to roll up and her head to fall back. Her back arches, thrusting her beautiful tits in my face. I take that as my cue, cupping them in my hands, and my thumbs slowly glide over her nipples. She starts coming unglued in only a matter of seconds and I love to watch the transition.

Cami continues to glide her slick wetness up and down my shaft. I can feel when her muscles spasm, but she hasn't come, not yet. One of the many things I love about being inside Cami is that, once she starts, there is no stopping her from achieving orgasm after orgasm, and it makes me hungry to make her come undone whenever possible.

Her hips increase their tempo and the muscles of her pussy begin clamping and releasing me. Her orgasm is crushing her ability to maintain her pace and she begins to slow, losing her rhythm. I know it's time for me to help her out. She raises her hips, as if reading my mind, and I begin pounding up into her, hard and fast. Her fingers dig into my stomach as she starts to come. I squeeze her nipples between my thumb and forefinger, hard. She screams out my name.

Hearing my name across her lips is my undoing, and I explode once again inside her.

An hour and half later we've finally managed to untangle ourselves from the sheets and make it to the shower. Our only mistake is showering together; it's counterproductive when I take her one more time, from behind, while we both watch in the vanity mirror.

We've finally managed to make it into her car, and she is driving me to the airport. In her R8, mind you. This is such a beautiful car, and very fitting for Cami.

This is the first time since coming here two days ago that we've even considered venturing out of the house and, ironically, it is to take me back to Los Angeles. Besides Cami, the other nice thing about Phoenix is that celebrities live here, but there are hardly enough paparazzi to really make a difference. Especially at the airport. But even knowing that, neither one of us has wanted to take the chance and venture out. So far, her condo is a secret, and it would be nice to keep it that way...for a little while longer, at least.

"Call me when you land?" she asks me as we pull off of Forty-fourth Street and into the airport.

"Of course," I say as she squeezes my hand. We've both been quiet in the car — well, ever since we got dressed — neither one of us wanting to discuss the inevitable goodbyes we're going to face in a few short minutes.

"I can come in with you..."

"No need, love. I'll be fine."

She is staring straight ahead, watching the traffic around us. It's Tuesday, early evening, and traffic is rather light, but I can see that she won't look at me. I look over at her. She knows that I'm watching, but she won't turn her head. It doesn't take but a moment for me to figure out why. I watch as a single, fat tear streaks down her cheek.

I release her hand and wipe it away. She tries to smile, but it doesn't go like she hoped it would. "I'm sorry."

"Stop." I can hear the emotion in my own voice. I don't want to leave, now or ever. But we both knew at some point it was going to have to happen. "I'll be home on Friday and we will have nothing in our way for what, six weeks? Before Montana." We haven't talked about Montana, but I'm hoping she will be coming with me. I'm going to be there for three weeks, with little time for a break. If less than three days is like this, three weeks will surely kill me.

"I know, it's just—"

I wipe another tear from her eye and we drive out of the setting sun and into the drop-off area for terminal four. It's another few seconds and she is pulling over to the curb to let me out. I take a quick scan of the terminal; it doesn't look like anyone is here to snap my photo this time. Thank stars.

She pulls the e-brake and we both reach hesitantly for the handles of our doors; eventually we open them and climb out. When I come around the front of the car, Cami is opening the trunk to pull out my bag. I've left nearly everything I own at her place, at her request. "So you'll come back," she said last night. There was never a doubt in my mind that I would come back, but I can understand her logic. We've spent so much time together; thinking rationally hasn't been our strongest ally these last few weeks. She's afraid that my getting away from her will clear my head. But I know that the exact opposite is what's true. I know I am going to miss her like crazy, and I know that when I come back to her, it will be a sweet reunion.

She closes the trunk and sits gingerly against the front of the car. "Come 'ere, you," I say, and she slides effortlessly in between my legs and I wrap my arms around her, kissing the top of her forehead. A part of me wants to tell her she's being irrational with her reaction and that I'll be back in a couple of days, but I can't because this is killing me too. "I love you," I say into her hair, and she squeezes harder. I can feel a small wet spot forming on my shirt and I don't care. I hold her tighter to me, and I don't want to let go but I have to.

"I love you too," she says, standing, then stepping away from me, slow and hesitant, back toward her side of the car. I take her hands and I kiss each one as I slowly step away onto the curb. She doesn't let go of my hands until I turn and one no longer touches hers, and then I take a slow, painful step forward, and another, before our hands fall away from each other. I turn back and I can see the tears in her eyes, which causes my own eyes to water. I give her a small smile and she smiles in return. I slide past the automatic doors and into the terminal. Turning back one last time, I see her wave to me and I wave back.

I round a corner inside and she disappears from my line of sight. I want to run back, climb into her car and go back to her house, but I press on — up the escalator then on to security. Before I know it, my flight is called and I'm on my way to Los Angeles.

TWO

******
Cami
******

I wipe the tears away from my eyes and climb back into my car. "This is so stupid, why am I so upset? He'll be back on Friday." I keep trying to talk myself into putting the car into first. Then finally I see a clearing in the traffic; without thinking, I throw the car into first and peel out.

I decide to take a drive, out of the way, before heading back to my condo. It's been so long since the Spyder and I have had a run on the freeway. Traffic leaving the airport is a bit of bitch, but I know once I get to the fifty-one, I can fly. I pop open the sunroof; it's a hundred and twelve outside, and I know I can't run the car like this for long, but I just want to open her up. When I finally clear the Camelback area, traffic evaporates in front of me.

The Spyder hugs the curves of highway and the wind is whipping through the car, causing my hair to fly wildly behind me. It feels great, just shutting it all out while Tantric's "Astounded" fills the car.

It is nearly an hour later when I pull into the parking lot. I see Beau's car parked in front of the garage, but it's empty so I know they're inside, though I'm surprised that they're parked behind my SUV. They usually park behind the Spyder; I guess they must've known which car I'd take. I pull the R8 into the garage and walk into the condo. I'm on the second floor - technically - and it is empty down here. I haven't decided what to do with the space, more specifically the basement below me.

The condo is technically five stories tall. The bottom floor, the one below me now, is underground — at least on the west side of the house. The garage is elevated half a floor above ground; I have to drive up a small hill to get in and out of it. The bottom floor is pretty much open space. There is a bathroom — a good sized one — a bedroom and a wide-open area that would be perfect for an entertainment room with a bar. Which is what I think it will be, eventually.

This floor, the second floor, has the garage, which is a wide, two-car width but could easily accommodate a small boat, camper or motorcycle, along with plenty of room for a tool bench and other manly things. Once inside the actual house, there is a large laundry room and a small section of servants' quarters. The quarters contain two small rooms — more like closets — a small kitchen and a bathroom. A mini apartment, really. The servants' quarters have their own separate entrance, which runs along the north side of the garage, as well as a door from inside the house. I guess if I ever wanted a roommate, it would be perfect, since I have no intention of having a fulltime house staff live here.

I bypass the elevator. I still roll my eyes at the fact that my condo has an elevator, but due to the long, shallow staircase leading from floor to floor, the elevator might come in handy someday.

I climb the stairs.

This floor, the third, houses the kitchen and formal and informal dining rooms, along with a living room and a den or fourth bedroom. This floor has more furniture on it than the bottom floor, but it is still pretty bland. One thing that did get finished before I moved in was Beau's mural paintings that adorn the walls, and I'm kind of excited to get real furniture in here. I think that I will be making the fourth bedroom into my office, and while I don't see a reason for a formal dining room, I haven't a clue what to turn it into, so it will likely be that: a formal dining room.

I call out, "Beau? Where are you?"

"In the kitchen," she calls back, and I head that direction. Actually, I head straight for the fridge and the bottle of moscato hiding within it. As I come into the kitchen, Beau and Mick are sitting at the bar opposite the sink. Sitting in front of Mick is a big, thick, brown, accordion-style file folder.

"Hi, guys, why the serious faces?" I open the fridge, grab the bottle, then turn, pulling a wineglass down from the overhead rack. "Want some?" I ask them both.

Beau nods.

"Have any beer?" asks Mick.

I roll my eyes at him. "Of course," I say, reaching for another glass from the rack. I pour Beau and myself a glass of wine, and when I return to fridge to put the bottle away, I grab a Sam Adams from the door. I pull the bottle opener off the fridge and pop the cap, tossing it into the hole in counter that leads to the trash can below. Their faces are pissing me off. I slide the beer to Mick. "All right, what is going on?"

"Are you all right?" Beau asks me, and I can see the pity in her eyes and it drives me nuts.

"Yes, I'm fine, but my well-being is not at all why the two of you are here. So spill it." I look at Mick, since the package is in front of him.

"This came to my office while we were in Tarah. I didn't know how you'd react or feel about it if I brought it up in front of Tristan." Mick has a somber look in his eyes and I can't quite understand why.

"An unnecessary worry, but okay." I shrug. "What is it?" I take a long sip of my wine. I have the feeling that the moscato is going to be nowhere near strong enough for whatever this is. I debate momentarily about the bottle of Crown sitting on the pantry shelf behind me, then decide it is probably better to wait until I find out what is going on first.

"It's from your father."

I down the glass of wine in what feels like one big swallow, then turn around for the pantry. I grab the Crown Royal bottle, pulling it roughly off the shelf. I open the bottle and pour it into my empty wine glass. I bring it to my lips, hesitate momentarily, and then I take a big long swig. Oh, the burn. I feel the Crown slide down my throat and into my stomach. When I place the glass on the counter, I just stand there - staring at no one in particular, but Mick is in my line of sight.

"Or rather it is from your father's estate."

"Will this ever end?" I groan in frustration at the two of them. I watch as neither one of them flinches; they've braced themselves for this. Good.

"I contacted the estate attorney and asked him the same question. He said that they have nothing further in regards to his estate, but he also informed me that this was delivered to them the Wednesday before your birthday, with specific instructions that it be sent to his next of kin, care of me." Mick takes a couple of long, large drinks from his own beer, and I can see Beau is uncertain of what to say. That's a first.

"What's in it?" I ask, though I'm certain Mick hasn't opened it.

"I'm not sure. It looks like some CDs, a couple of jump drives and some papers."

I take another long drink of my Crown and reach for the package.

Mick slides it over to me and Beau has managed to find her voice. "Are you sure you want to open it now?" I look at her with an 'Are you kidding me right now?' look, and she raises her hands in mock defense. "I just thought you'd want to do it in private."

"Fuck that." I shake my head at her and begin to unwind the string from the cheap button on the outside. As soon as pressure from the flap lets up, the string unwinds itself and the flap falls open with an audible flop. The movement is jarring to the contents inside, and six jewel cases fall out. Each one of them are hand-numbered: *1, 2, 3, 4, 7, 8...*

"Jesus Christ, what the hell is all this stuff?" I blurt out, trying to wrap my head around what all of this could be.

I pull back the top and look inside. Sitting on top of everything are a couple pieces of paper, and I pull them out. On top is an inventory list of all the things inside. It's not long.

1. CD #1 - containing documentation 1970 to 1975
2. CD #2 - containing documentation 1975 to 1980
3. CD #3 - containing documentation 1980 to 1983

4. *CD #4 - containing documentation 1983 to 1986*
5. *CD #5 - containing documentation 1987*
6. *CD #6 - containing documentation 1988 to 1990*
7. *CD #7 - containing documentation 1991 to 1999*
8. *CD #8 - containing documentation 2000 to 2006*
9, *CD #9 - containing documentation 2006 to May 2011*
10. *CD #10*

I can't keep reading the list of contents, but I can see there is more stuff about papers and a journal. I'm surprised by the fact that there is one whole disc pertaining to 1987, the year I was born. Also by the fact that the 1980s have four discs, when the other decades take up a lot less. But I can't stop the small tear that escapes; I'm already an emotional mess from Tristan leaving, so it doesn't take much to make me lose it again. May 2012 is when Bobby died and the discs' descriptions stop, though there is one more disc on this list.

I flip the page and there, on that page, is a letter. A letter addressed to me. On Bold letterhead, dated May 15, 2011. I can't stop my eyes from scanning to the bottom of the page and seeing that it was signed by none other than my father.

My Dearest Cami,

If you are reading this letter, one of two things has happened. Either I am dead or you've turned 25. I am hoping for the latter, but in this day and age, you can never tell.

Enclosed in this package, you will find various documents pertaining to, but not limited to:

- *Your birth*
- *Your school records*

- *Your mother's death*
- *And Bold International's deepest secrets, dating back to its inception.*

Not everything within this package is Bold-related, though the jump drives contained herein are all Bold business, and on the discs you will find videos and other scanned documents directly from me. Including the reason why you were sent away to England.

I know that this is something that has weighed heavily on your mind, at the very least since your mother passed away. If that is most important to you, then grab disc number 7 and go into the folder dated 1993.

I hope one day we can discuss this package, even if it involves yelling and screaming.

All my love-
Bobby

I can barely breathe by the time I am done reading the letter, and Mick and Beau are staring at me expectantly, wondering and waiting to either see my reaction or for me to share the information with them.

Before I do, I turn to the next page in the package, and there is a much more detailed list regarding what each disc contains.

My eyes immediately scan to 1987.

Cameron's Birth/Birthday/Coming home.

"They're videos," I blurt out, looking up at them. "Well, not all of them, but—" I grab disc number five and head into the living room, wine glass in hand. While putting the disc into the Xbox, I shout back toward the kitchen, "Get in here." I'm trying to be playful, but it's hard. I have no idea what it is that I'm about to watch and it scares the hell out of me, but they are here, and I know Beau will stop me if she senses that it is too much for me.

My phone starts ringing with "Livin' On A Prayer" and I know immediately that it's Tristan. It's the song he sang to me the night of my birthday party in Bora Bora, and I dash to my purse, which I'd dropped on the table at the top of the steps. I take a deep breath as I pull the phone from my purse and answer it, trying to compose myself. I don't need him freaking out because of what's going on here.

"Hi, you," I breathe into the phone.

"Hi." I can tell instantly that something is wrong and panic races through me.

"What's wrong?" I say a little too sharply, and I hear some semblance of a chuckle on the other end of the line.

"Nothing is wrong. I just miss you like crazy. I haven't even gotten off the plane and I wanted to call you."

I can't help but smile. "Will Tyson be there waiting for you?"

"He texted right before I took off, letting me know that they were on their way to the airport and that they would meet me in the first class lounge. You know, that one I saw you in for the first time."

My heart beats a little faster as I think about all of our misses that led to us actually finding each other on the same remote island. "I know the one." I smile again.

"Can I call you again once I'm settled?" he asks.

"Absolutely."

"'Kay." His voice is sweet, and he sounds like a teenager.

"Love you."

"More," he says, and then I hear the click of the line going dead.

I go back toward the couch, and Beau is sitting there while Mick is in the oversized chair, the one similar to the chair in the penthouse in Tarah. I know why he's over there and not with Beau. He knows this is going to be bad, and he knows I will want someone to lean on.

I sit next to Beau, pick up the Xbox remote and scroll through the options. I find June 1987 and open it. Inside, there are a couple of random documents, then "Cameron - Birth." I click it.

THREE

The birth video is uneventful, except for the way my mother acts. I know immediately by her reaction and lack of caring what led to my being sent to boarding school. We watch the next few videos, and it becomes clearer and clearer to me that Evelyn was nothing more than a gold digger, tagging along for whatever Bobby wanted just so she could get hers in the end.

After watching those videos, if she'd been alive when Bobby died, I would've begun to question whether or not she killed him.

We jump to 1993 and the year I was sent to boarding school. The video comes on and Bobby is in his office in the old house; I can tell by the decor in the room. Though I never spent much time in that room, the browns, tans and blacks give it away.

Walking around the desk is Bobby, and it takes a minute before I see me walking over to his desk. It's disturbing because I don't remember any of this. You would think that at five or six I would have.

"Daddy."

"Hi, Cameron." His voice is warm as I climb onto his lap; a warm, glowing smile spreads across his lips. "What can I do for you?"

"I want to go—" My voice is cut off by the sound of a slamming door, and Bobby and I both look toward the source of the noise.

"What is it, Evelyn?"

"Cameron, get out of here," she says very rudely toward me. I watch as the younger me looks to Bobby with a terrified look on her face, but Bobby nods reassuringly and I climb down. I watch as I retreat toward the camera and give my mother a wide berth before I hear the door click closed on the video.

"You fucking whore," Evelyn spats and throws something. It flies with such speed that I can't make it out before it shatters against the wall just over Bobby's head. "All you had to do was fucking keep your dick in your pants, and you couldn't even do that, could you, you...you bastard."

"What the fuck are you talking about, Evelyn?"

"Who gives a flying fuck. I want a divorce, I'm taking the kids and leaving."

"Like fucking hell you are." Bobby is raging pissed; I can see it in his face. He stands and comes around his desk. "If you think for one damn minute I will let any judge award you custody of those kids, you have another thing coming." Bobby stalks toward my mother as he says this. She meets him and slaps him across the face.

I commend him for not striking her back, but suddenly the video is cut off.

The next video is of Bobby, back in his office, this time sitting on a chair or stool directly in front of the camera. I can tell he's been crying. His eyes are all red and puffy. My heart clamps tight at the sight in front of me.

"Cameron, I'm sorry. I am so very sorry. I did what I had to do to keep you safe and out of her hands. It is my hope and my wish that you will one day understand, but it was all I could do to keep her away from you. You deserve so much better." By the end of his speech the tears are visibly streaking down his cheeks and mine.

Beau and Mick leave a little while after that. I can't quite bring myself to watch many of the other videos, but something about the one dated 2000-2006 is nagging at me. When I put the disc in and the folders pop up, there are two that capture my attention. One titled "Coming Home" and the other is called "Amazing Discovery 2004."

I go to the one titled "Coming Home," and inside the folder is only one video. I select it.

Back in Bobby's office, he's sitting on his stool, looking a little older and more like I remember him when I came back after my sophomore year.

"Cameron is finally home, where she belongs. But she hates me. No, she despises me. Which I guess is something I should've expected all those years ago and no less than I deserve. I just wish I knew how to show her how much I've missed her."

The video continues on for a few minutes: he is talking about my being home and trying to work through how he can try and fix the mess he's created, and it pulls harder at my heartstrings.

"I'd have given you a chance, if I'd known," I breathe and pour the last of the bottle of Crown into my wine glass.

I move on to the next folder, "Amazing Discovery." I cock my head at the screen. Tristan and I had talked about the day Bobby discovered I could sing, and Bobby's subsequent reaction, which would've happened in 2004. I open the folder, and again, only one video.

This time Bobby is sitting behind his desk. Someone — who, I can't quite tell — is sitting opposite him.

"I've discovered someone amazing," Bobby says. "Singer, amazingly talented, a great stage presence." I watch as Bobby takes a drink from his snifter; brandy was always his drink of choice.

"So what's the problem?"

I sit up on the couch with interest. I recognize the voice immediately, but the hair threw me off. It's Vinnie.

Bobby doesn't answer him right away. Taking another drink, he stands and walks toward the cabinet to his right, and though he is off-screen just a little, I can tell by the clinking of crystal that he's filling his glass. When he is done, he walks toward the camera slightly and then starts to pace the room.

"I can't sign her."

"Bobby, since when do you not sign an amazing talent? You're by far the best in the business, you know talent better than the talent knows talent." I watch as Vinnie turns in his chair toward my father, and I can see it now; why Vinnie shaves his head. His hairline is receding horribly and he looks years older, and it's been eight years since this video was shot.

"There are two rules for signing new talent in this company. You know them as well as I do."

"No signing someone that you're screwing, or family. So you're screwing—" I watch as Bobby visually cringes at Vinnie's words.

"Dammit, Vin, it's Cami." I feel both shock as he uses my nickname and the shock that stretches across Vinnie's face.

"Make an exception," Vinnie finally manages to say.

"I could, if I hadn't reacted so poorly when I found out." Vinnie looks at Bobby, and he continues. "I hadn't expected what I was going to see. I'd never heard her sing before and I blew a gasket. The first thing that flew through my mind was no way in hell was I going to let my daughter be caught up in this mess, then the other was the fact that I can't sign her, and that someone else was going to profit from my daughter. So I threw a fit."

"Jesus—"

The video cuts off.

Tears streak down my cheeks. After all the years I've wanted that answer, and now that I have it, there is nothing I can do about it. I put my head in my hands as the tears start to roll and the sobs come harder and faster than they have in years.

FOUR

LAX is probably my favorite place to be right now because it means I'm heading back to Phoenix and back to Cami. It is Thursday afternoon and she has no idea that I'm coming home today. I'd told her tomorrow before I left, but I busted my butt to get out of here faster. After being in Tarah and then in Phoenix with Cami, I am beginning to despise Los Angeles.

I spoke with Vinnie about my being able to live in Phoenix and still being able to come here when it's necessary. He said that he doesn't see a problem with it. Especially considering the two movies I am signed to complete by the end of the year are not even in L.A. I am going to have to go to Montana — boring — and New York for the other.

I wonder if I can convince Cami to come with me to both. At the very least I will need her in New York with me because I will be in the city itself and I don't want any negative PR starting up should I decide to go out. This way, Cami can be with me.

"It's time," Tyson says as he stands up. He's coming back with me this time. He wants to go see Jolene and spend some time with her. I can't help but smile at the idea of him and Jolene together. She's a great girl and perfect for Tyson. I think he knows it too.

"Let's do it," I say as we head toward the terminal door of the first class lounge.

LAX is very busy this afternoon and I'm glad Ty brought some extra security along to help with crowd control.

I'm not ten feet outside the lounge and girls are already yelling my name. "Go faster." I grit my teeth and we all pick up our pace. I don't look up in my sunglasses, and I am following Tyson's feet as we walk. The hat and sunglasses, of course, do nothing to hide my celebrity, at least not here in Los Angeles. Maybe that's why I want to stay in Phoenix so bad.

We make it to the terminal, and the three guys Tyson brought with him block the doorway to the jet walkway. Tyson and I immediately, without stopping, walk straight onto the plane. The gentlemen behind us are taking care of my boarding pass.

We step onto the plane, and before we are even seated in the last row of first class, the door is closed and we are on our way. At least being a celeb has its small advantages. I am almost always last to board, and we take off quickly.

The flight from LAX to PHX is quick, and before we know it, we're in a Town Car headed toward Cami's condo. There were a few photographers when we left the terminal, and that, no doubt, is due to someone catching my flight number, airline and destination.

Since New York and the premiere, the press has managed to ascertain that Cami is a resident of Phoenix, so I am sure they were pretty confident that I'd disembark in Phoenix, even though the plane I was on is headed on to Dallas.

"Are you planning on going anywhere this weekend?" Tyson asks me.

I shake my head. "I don't think so, but if that should change, I'll let you know."

Tyson nods his understanding. Jolene doesn't live too far from Cami's, so if we needed or wanted to go somewhere, he could be there.

"I'll talk to Cami, maybe we can have everyone over for dinner tomorrow or Saturday. Travis is still here with Naomi, so..."

"Sure, just let us know," he responds and gives me a half smile.

That's it for our conversation. While we were in Tarah, Ty and I grew a little closer, but I think a lot of that had to do with the fact that he wasn't having to watch my back every second. Since we've come back to the States, things have gone back to business. Though I have no doubt that if we were to all have dinner together, we'd all be right back to the way things were in Tarah.

The car pulls up in front of Cami's condo and I grab my bag. "Want to come up?" I ask Ty.

"Nah, man, I'm gonna go see my girl."

I smile at the goofy expression on his face as I climb out of the car and head for the door.

Cami gave me a key to her condo and I can tell she's here because there are a couple of lights on on the third floor. I unlock the door, but the alarm isn't set. That's weird; she always sets the alarm. But the door was locked, so I don't get too excited about it.

I ascend the stairs two at a time, climbing my way up until I reach the living level. I can hear someone talking, then I hear a rather loud thump that sounds like a heavy bottle meeting the coffee table.

"...I never meant to hurt you, and I'm sorry for what I've put you through over the years, but I'm certain after you see what I've shown you, you can understand why—" There is a pause in the voice and something about it is very familiar, but I can't seem to put my finger on it. I come around the corner to see the back of Cami's head; she's looking toward the blue screen of the TV. I watch momentarily as I see her bring a rather large wine glass to her lips, but the liquid is a dark amber color.

"Cams," I say, and she jumps and screams. I rush toward her, but I am too late and the glass she's holding shatters all over the tile floor. "Don't move," I say as I come around the couch and realize that she's barefoot. And it takes me only a minute to realize that she is still wearing the same clothes as when I left on Tuesday. "Let me get a broom and some towels, please don't move."

"What the hell are you doing here?"

She's angry, but I'm not sure that her anger is directed at me.

"I finished early so I came—" I look at her then, in the light of the blue screen of the TV, and her eyes are completely raccooned and she has streaks of black mascara running down her cheeks. "What is going on?"

She plops back down on the couch. "I'm drunk. Very drunk." Her words slur horribly as she tells me all of this.

"I can tell," I say as I walk toward the kitchen and the pantry where I know there is a broom and dustpan. I grab it, along with the roll of paper towels on the counter, and go back into the living room. I flick on the side table light, and she squints and covers her eyes. "I need to see to clean this up." But I look to the floor and near the TV. This isn't the first glass she's shattered. On the wall on both sides of the TV there are stains dripping down to the floor, and underneath those are piles of clear, broken glass.

Jesus. "Cams, talk to me.... What is going on?"

She doesn't say anything, but lifts her arm, points it at the TV, and suddenly, in sixty-inch glory, is the face and upper torso of none other than Robert "Bobby" Enders.

I'm taken aback by what I'm seeing. She presses another button and the image comes alive.

"Cami, I know this isn't easy for you to watch and I'm sorry that it had to come to you this way, but it is the only way I thought I could get you to listen to what I had to say. I never meant to hurt you, and I'm sorry for what I've put you through over the years, but I'm certain after you see what I've shown you, you can understand why—" Bobby's image freezes on the screen again.

There are no words for what I can even try to say to comfort her, and I can hear her sobbing on the couch, so I forgo the cleanup and go to the couch to sit down next to her. I'm wearing boots, and the glass crunches further beneath my feet. "He's apologizing to you, is that why you're so upset? Because it came in video form and not from him?" I ask her, and she vigorously shakes her head.

"Look," she says and points to the TV. I look, but all I can see is Bobby on the screen. And then it registers what she's pointing at. Down in the bottom right-hand corner is the running time of the video, along with a date and time stamp.

Sat. 06/02/2012 16:36

"Holy SHIT!" I shout and stand up. The image on the screen begins to move.

"I know telling you I'm sorry has come too late, and over a video, but if you'd give me the chance, I'd like to apologize in person." Nothing more is said, but I watch as Bobby holds up a picture in front of the camera.

It's a picture of a very beautiful ranch house — two stories, a rustic brown color with a wraparound porch. Behind the house there is fencing, and a horse can be seen beyond the fence. Beyond the house and the land around it are snow-covered mountains.

"I hope you remember where this is." The image on the screen goes black and then turns blue.

I'm stunned into complete and utter silence, immobilized by what I've just witnessed.

FIVE

"Cami," Beau shouts from down the stairs.

"Shit!" Tristan exclaims. "Does she know about this?" His voice is angry, as it should be. If I hadn't broken my glass when he scared the hell out of me, I'd have thrown it against the wall. Again.

I can't answer him, so all I do is shake my head.

"Jesus Christ, Cameron." I hear Beau from behind me. "What the hell is going on?" She comes around the side of the couch but she stops when she steps on a piece of glass and it crunches under her foot.

I don't look at her. "I need another glass."

"Like hell you do. How long have you been on this couch?" Beau exclaims. My eyes move to hers, and she can tell immediately that I'm hammered. And I could care less.

"Fine, I'll get it myself." I slide to the end of the couch and put my feet down.

"No, don't!" His words come too late and I hear the crunch, but the pain doesn't follow. "Shit, Cams," Tristan says as he picks my feet up off of the floor. I can see bright red blood dripping from my foot.

A flurry of things happen all at once, but I'm too drunk to follow them. Before too long, I have a towel wrapped around my foot and Tristan is bending down to pick me up off of the couch.

"Dammit! Stop, put me down."

"Forget it. You're going to the hospital."

"Fuck that," I say, and I try to squirm out of his arms.

"Stop it. Right now, Cameron."

I look at him, blood-red rage swarming my vision. "Don't you EVER call me Cameron, EVER AGAIN!" I shout at him. But he ignores me.

"Mick, get over here, right now. Cami's cut her foot and she needs to go to the hospital." I turn to look behind Tristan and Beau is on her cell phone.

"I'll drive myself."

"Like hell you will," she yells at me. "Tristan is here. Judging from the fact that I nearly tripped on his bag, I'm assuming he came home and found her like this. She's drunk." She stops talking to listen to whoever she's talking to. I forgot and I don't give a shit. Tristan is taking me around the corner to the elevator.

"Come on, Beau, I need you to show me how to get to the hospital."

"Coming."

"No fucking hospital." I squirm again in Tristan's arms.

"You don't have a choice." He's angry with me.

"What the fuck did I do?" Though the words sound fine in my head, the look of confusion on his beautiful face tells me otherwise.

I start pacing the reception area of the emergency room, waiting for the doctor or Cami to come out. She had several shards of glass in the bottom of her foot. They weren't as deep as the amount of blood had originally suggested, but the pieces of glass needed to come out. She's angry as hell and she kicked both Beau and me out of her room.

"Did you know about this?" I ask Beau.

"Yeah, but not what was on it. We were at the condo Tuesday when she got back from taking you to the airport. Mick and I both thought that whatever was in that package was better delivered while you weren't around. I guess we were wrong." She gives me an apologetic look. "We stayed quite a while Tuesday night. She kind of went through a chronological list of events that happened in her life, and they were not pretty. She got pretty drunk watching the videos and then at one point she kicked us out and said she was going to bed." She takes a deep breath. "Neither one of us wanted to leave her, but she insisted she was fine. Yesterday when I talked to her, she was fine, said she was working on a couple of things and that she'd be busy most of the day, so I didn't question her. I tried calling her more than thirty times between trying to reach her and driving to the condo. I noticed, though, that her cell phone was one of the many shattered things in the living room."

"I talked to her this afternoon around twelve thirty, told her that I would be back in the morning. I wanted to surprise her and come home early. I found her on the couch, drunk. I scared her and she dropped her wine glass, which is where all the glass at her feet came from. I was trying to clean it up when she played a video of Bobby." I pause, remembering the date on the video and finding out that, after more than a year, Bobby is alive.

"What was on the video?" I don't want to answer that question. I'm not sure if Cami really wants Beau to know, but my expression betrays me and she presses harder. "Damn it, Tristan.... She's done this before."

"At first I thought it was just Bobby apologizing to her for all the wrongs he'd done to her. But she paused the video before I could see more. When I pressed her to talk to me about it, she pointed at the TV, and when I look again I realize, Beau, that that video is date- and time-stamped." The image is forever burned into my mind.

"So what did it say?"

"Saturday, June second, two thousand twelve. Four thirty-six p.m."

I don't say any more — I don't have to — as I watch her expression begin to change as she is doing the math in her head. The moment she realizes what I've just said, her hand comes to her mouth and her eyes widen in fear. I nod, acknowledging what's just registered, but her hand comes away from her mouth. "It could be an error." She's trying to rationalize it, but it won't work.

"Of course it could, but it is a very specific time, Bobby looks a little older than I remember, and..." I trail off.

"What?"

"She finally played the video again, and he continues apologizing, then says flat-out that if she wants a real-life apology that she should go to some house. Where that is, I have no idea, and I'm not sure if Cami does either."

"It's in Montana, northwest of Billings."

Beau and I both turn toward the voice. Mick is standing near the doorway to the emergency room.

"You knew about this?" Beau asks. Her voice is angry and sharp with Mick.

"Not until a few minutes ago. I went to the condo before I came here. I noticed that she'd been watching something so I played it."

"So you didn't know he was alive?" I ask him.

"No, I had no idea, but I'm pretty sure who, besides Bobby, knows."

"Who?" Beau and I both say in unison.

"Vincent."

"I knew it! I knew there was a reason he dragged me to California for shit that could have been done over the phone and via email. This is all my fault, I wish you would've waited until I was around." I watch as both of them cringe a little. "What?"

They both look at each other before Beau finally speaks. "Tristan, this isn't your fault, and to be honest, if you'd been here, she would've either tossed the package aside and waited until you weren't around, or things could've been a lot worse between the two of you. Cami has a tendency to be a bit destructive when she's angry, and not just with wine glasses." She looks at me, but there is pain, or maybe it's pity.

"Was she like this after Bobby died? Or supposedly died?" Beau doesn't truly answer the question; she just nods.

After everything Cami has been through with Bobby in her lifetime, he should have just stayed away. "Why did he have to come back? Why now? Why like this?" I mumble.

"Those are the million-dollar questions, Tristan, we may never know the answers to," Mick says.

Beau left a few minutes ago with Mick; they were headed back to the condo to clean up the mess so that there won't be any reminder for her in the morning.

"Mr. Enders?"

Wha? Huh? Oh, that's right; I told them I was her husband. I turn around to find an aging man dressed in green scrubs and a lab coat. "Yes."

"She's ready to go home, though she's rather drunk and I'm inclined to keep her here overnight. Let her sober up."

I shake my head. She'll be furious if she wakes up in the hospital tomorrow. "She won't be alone tonight. I'll take her home and take care of her."

"All right." He hands me a stack of papers. "She has several small lacerations on her left foot. We were able to get all the glass out without too much problem. Her foot is wrapped up and should be elevated, and ice can be used for the pain. Do not get the bandage wet for at least the next twenty-four to thirty-six hours. I will send home extra bandaging just in case, and it should be changed every twelve hours or so. After two days, reduce it to just a light covering, but she needs to stay off of her foot until the stitches come out in about seven days. She'll need to come back to have them removed."

"Okay, doctor. Anything else?"

"Nope, that's about it. I'll have a nurse get her ready to go and bring her to you."

"Thank you," I say, and he turns toward the desk.

I grab my cell from my pocket and call Beau.

"How is she?" she asks as soon as she answers.

"I haven't seen her, but the doctor says she'll be fine. She can't walk on it for at least seven days. They're going to bring her to me shortly, can you or Mick come back and pick us up?"

"Sure, I'll send Mick and then I'll finish up here."

"Perfect. Can you go up to her room, turn down the sheets and set up two pillows for her foot? Then grab some ice so I can put ice on it when we get there. She needs to go to bed as soon as she gets home, and I want all of that shit put away. Not hidden, but not in plain damn sight. She needs to sober up and clear her head before she starts again."

"I watched the video. She's got every right to be angry, drunk and upset."

"I know, Beau, I don't blame her, but she needs to be ready to face tomorrow before she can face any of that again."

"Understood. Mick is on his way. Do you want us to stay here tonight?"

I shake my head. "No, I'll be fine with her. I'll call you if I need anything."

SIX

Ugh! I can't tell what hurts more, my foot or my head. Wait, why does my foot hurt?

I open my eyes and I'm in bed. How did I get here? I look over toward the bedside table and it says 3:17, but my bedroom is full of light. "Jesus." Shit, Tristan should've been home by now, but he's not here. I go in search of my phone, and I don't see it on the table by the clock. I start to feel around the bed and I can't find it. I flip the covers back to get up; I have to pee.

I swing my legs over the side of the bed and my left foot feels really heavy and hurts like a bitch. That's when I notice the crutches leaning against the wall on the other side of the bedside table. I turn around, hoping to see Tristan, but he's not here. Sitting next to the clock are two white-and-red tablets, along with a glass of something sparkling. I reach over and grab the Tylenol and pick up the glass. It's still cool. I take the hint and swallow the pills and return the glass to the nightstand.

"Tristan?" I call out.

"Finally," I hear him say, and he gets up from the couch in the small sitting area between my bed and the doorway out of my room. He comes to stand at the end of the bed. "How are you feeling?"

"Like shit. What the hell happened?"

I try to remember, but nothing is coming to me. I remember sitting on the couch in the dark. I'd talked to Tristan earlier, but...

"You don't remember?"

I try again, but all I can remember is dropping him off at the airport, Mick and Beau being here, and then the package. "Oh, God." Suddenly the images from the last video that I watched, over and over and over again, pop into my brain. When I'd talked to Tristan, I hadn't gotten there yet. I hadn't seen the video, the one that— "That motherfucker is alive."

"That's a start.... Do you remember anything else?"

I look at him. He's scruffy and unshaven, not a usual Tristan look, and I can tell he's exhausted. "You haven't slept?" I ask.

"No," he says with a half chuckle, almost sounding disgusted.

"Why?"

"Because when I came home last night, you were so unbelievably drunk I scared the hell out of you and you shattered a wineglass on the tile. Then you stepped on it. Which would be why your foot is all wrapped up and no doubt hurting like hell."

Oh. "You weren't supposed to come until this morning."

"I came back to surprise you." Well, don't I feel like a bitch. "Beau showed up, we took you to the hospital, brought you home and put you to bed. You've been sleeping for about fifteen hours. I couldn't sleep because I was afraid you'd get up and go back downstairs and start drinking again."

"That sounds like a great idea right now."

"Like hell you will."

Rage fills my eyes and I look at him. "Who the hell are you to tell me what I can and cannot do?"

"I'm your boyfriend, and after what I saw last night, and no doubt how you're feeling this morning, drinking is the last thing you should be doing."

"Go to hell," I say to him, though there is little conviction in my voice and he knows that.

He comes quickly around the bed and stands in front of me. "I'm already there. We promised in Tarah that neither one of us would EVER keep secrets from each other, then I talk to you yesterday and everything is fine. I get home to find you so drunk you can't even see straight, let alone talk straight. Your stubbornness gets your foot cut all to hell because you want more alcohol, then you blow up at me like this is somehow my fault." He kneels down in front of me. I can see the fear and anger in his eyes.

But all I can see is red, pure anger washing through me.

"Get out." He doesn't move. "I said GET OUT," I shout a little louder. This time he stands, but he doesn't walk away. I stand up to push him out of the way, but the pain in my foot shoots straight into my leg and I fall over. His arms are around me in a nanosecond, catching me.

Tears, hot and wet, start streaming down my cheeks and I come completely unglued in a big, nasty, ugly cry.

Jesus, this is really bad. I've never seen Cami like this before and I'm trying to keep it together with the rational thought that her anger is not directed at me. It is at what she's seen over the last couple of days. I take a deep breath and bring her back to sit on the bed. She hasn't stopped her heartbreaking sobbing, and all I can do is hold her close. I begin to stroke her hair with my free hand. I don't say anything. I just hold her, and she seems content to let me do that.

Several minutes go by before she's finally calming down and the tears seem to have stopped altogether. But she doesn't move...other than to bring me closer to her. I try unsuccessfully a few times to get her to lie down, but she just grips me harder. Almost as if she is afraid I really will leave. Which I have no intention of doing, no matter what she says.

"I need a shower," she finally says.

"How about a bath?" I feel her slight nod against my chest, but she makes no move to let me go. "I need to get up so I can start one for you."

"I have to pee, like, painfully bad."

I don't hesitate; I manage to move so that I can pick her up and carry her to the bathroom. She doesn't protest but holds me close. I kiss her forehead.

Stepping into her oversized bathroom, I carry her to the toilet. "I'm going to put you down, but put all your weight on your right leg." She nods and I set her down. She wobbles slightly as she catches her balance. "Want my help?" She nods. I help her lower her sleep pants and her panties, and then she takes my hands so she can sit down.

No sooner does her butt hit the cool toilet seat than she starts going to the bathroom, and I smile slightly; she always kicks me out of the bathroom when she has to pee, but she doesn't this time. I shrug and head toward the tub on the opposite side of the bathroom. The thing is huge, but I start the water, test the temperature and close off the drain. Adding bubbles, I watch as it fills up.

I start thinking about how we got to this point and my own anger at Bobby for what he's done to Cami, not only now, but in the past. She was finally getting better and getting over the fact that he was gone. At least, based on our conversations over the last month, she's seemed to be able to tolerate the subject of Bobby better, and maybe she finally realized that she isn't the unloving monster she once thought she was.

But no sooner does she start to see it than she has it thrown back in her face once again. Whether Bobby's alive or dead, I'm guessing that whatever was sent in that package is just as damaging to her progress as the fact that he's alive.

"I'm done," she says behind me, breaking my trance and thoughts about what's happened. I stand and walk in her direction, remembering the crutches.

"One second," I say and leave the bathroom, skirt the bed, grab her crutches from where I put them last night and return to the bathroom. I place them against the wall of the bathroom, then turn and bend down. I remove her sleep pants and panties from her legs. "Lift your arms," I say and she complies.

I pull my t-shirt up over her head, and she is now completely naked, but with her makeup and hair a complete mess. Though I'd be lying if I told you she wasn't still absolutely gorgeous to me, even in this state. She's not modest and makes no move to try and hide the fact that she is completely exposed to me, and I like that about her. But she has this blank stare in her eyes, almost as though she's checked out on me.

"Cams," I say to her. Nothing. "Cams," I say again, and her eyes lazily meet mine. "How are you feeling?" I ask her again.

"Like shit," is all she says, and I can see that she will say nothing more.

"Come on," I say, putting my hands out for her to take. She does and I help her to stand. "Steady," I say and turn around for her crutches. "Have you ever used these before?" I ask her, and she nods, taking them from me and placing them under her armpits. She reaches for the floor with her left foot. "No weight."

"Ugh," she says, and I move out of her way. She hobbles her way over to the bathtub and then manages to sit on the side of the tub. She jumps when the cold marble touches her skin but turns to put her right foot in.

"Wait," I say as I strip off my shirt and pants. I can't bring myself to get completely naked with her because I have it stuck in my head that if I stay at least somewhat dressed I can control him. It's stupid really, but I don't need her thinking I have other things in mind.

I come up to the tub and she takes in what I'm wearing. "What are you doing?"

"I'm going to help you," I say, and I climb into the tub behind her. I grab a towel from the shelf on the wall, fold it up and put it on the side of the tub, giving her a place to rest her foot once she gets settled in. While holding her up by her waist, I sit down along the bench seat and then bring my right leg up, bracing it against the seat opposite me, giving her a shallow seat on my lap in the massive tub. "I got you, sit down slowly." She does it, and somehow we manage to get her situated on my legs without getting her left foot wet. She puts it on the towel on the side of the tub.

I take the soap and a washcloth and begin to lather it up. I brush her hair to her left and begin lightly washing her shoulders and upper back, massaging gently as I go. I can see her visibly relax as I continue washing her back. I gently nudge her backwards so that she will lay against my chest. She does, and I lather up the washcloth again and begin to gently wash her front.

When I start to clean her breasts, I feel her nipples harden and she moans at my touch. So not helping.

I continue washing her as best as I can, including her legs. All that is left is her sex. I've been avoiding it, but she continues to squirm and moan once in a while, and I've grown completely hard.

I bring the washcloth between her legs, and I begin lightly washing along her clit. Her hand reaches around between us and comes into contact with the head of my erection. "Don't," I breathe. "Not here, not now," I say, and she understands exactly what I want.

We finish up in the tub and, in a reverse process, I get her out of the tub and sitting on the side of the tub wrapped in a towel. I strip out of my boxers and I'm too close. She grabs hold of my cock and pulls me toward her. Before I can stop her, I feel her mouth engulf me and my knees shake. She peeks up at me through her lashes and I can no longer say no to her. I don't want to say no, but I'm not sure if this is the right time. She is not herself, and I'm afraid if we continue, she will regret it. "Cami, stop."

She stops instantly and without hesitation. "You don't want me." She says it as a statement, not a question, and she couldn't be further from the truth. I do want her, very badly, but not at the expense of what we've been through these last twelve hours.

I bend down so that I'm looking up at her slightly. "I want you so bad it hurts," I say.

"Why?"

"Because. This isn't the time."

She doesn't say anything and I can tell that she's hurt, but I can't do this. Not right now. She feels like shit, for one, and for two, I am so worried about what is going through her mind that she's using sex as an escape, and that, to me, is no different than alcohol.

SEVEN

It takes forever to get dressed, but Tristan never once leaves my side nor does he lose patience with me, helping me every step I take.

"Are you hungry?"

Yes. "No."

"You're a bad liar, Cami. Let me make you something to eat." It's not a question.

"I want to go downstairs."

"I'm not sure that's a good idea." His statement pisses me off again, but before I blow up at him again, I take a deep breath.

"Tristan, you can't keep me up here forever. I want to go downstairs. I want to get something to eat."

"I want to talk."

"What is there to talk about, Tristan?"

"I don't know, Cami, a lot of things."

"Tristan, I've never been good at talking about this shit."

"Well now might be a good time to start. What are you going to do?"

"About what?"

"What? You know what. About the fact that your father is alive."

I take a deep breath. "Not a damn thing."

"Bullshit."

"Then why the fuck did you ask the question?" I stand up from the bed and put the stupid-ass crutches in my armpits and head for the elevator. I need to go and clean up my mess downstairs, try and find a clear head, and I can't do that with Tristan hovering over me like I'm going to shatter into a thousand pieces. Which is probably true.

"Dammit, Cami, we're in this together. I will not let you do this alone." I feel the firm conviction in his words and I know he speaks the truth. But this is so hard to even wrap my brain around, let alone explain to him.

"I need to get my own head on straight about all of this before I can even begin to talk to you about it. You won't understand." I manage to maneuver past him and hit the button for the elevator. The doors open immediately and I step in. Hitting the *L* button for the living room, I turn around and see him standing there, watching me.

A few seconds later the doors are opening onto the kitchen and living room level of my condo, which is two floors below my bedroom, and standing there in front of me is Tristan. I smirk. Then I see him take a deep breath, like he's trying to catch his breath, and I can't help but laugh. "I'm impressed."

He laughs too, and the tension between us shatters into a thousand pieces. I know deep down that I owe him an apology, but I'm not ready to give it to him, not yet.

As I come around the wall that divides the living room from the stairs and elevator, I can see that the walls are clean, everything is put in its place, and the brown package is gone.

"Did you—?"

"No, Beau and Mick did while I was at the hospital with you."

"You'd think I would remember that, or even how I got there. But I don't remember anything."

"I don't doubt that. I found three empty wine bottles, one empty Crown, and then the one you had in the living room with you when I came home, which was about half gone. That's a lot of alcohol in two days."

"Jesus, I had no idea I—"

"Beau said that you and she polished off two of the wine bottles Tuesday night."

"Jesus, still."

"I'm afraid to think about what I might've come back to if I'd waited until today." I don't answer his statement. I know damn well what he's thinking, and I'm not sure I'm a fan of the idea either. I imagine that I would have probably been passed out or worse. "I'm surprised you're doing as well as you are today."

"I'm not entirely convinced that I'm not still drunk," I say as I take a seat at the bar in the kitchen. My armpits are already sore and my foot is killing me, though the Tylenol seems to have helped my headache. "How long do I have to walk around on these things?"

"Until the stitches come out." Oh, hell. "In about seven days."

"Ugh! That's too long," I groan.

"Not my orders." He goes over to the counter and grabs something, then goes to the cupboard for a glass. He fills it with ice and water from the fridge door and gives it to me, then hands me two more pills.

"What are these?"

"Antibiotics. You stepped on glass, it's to ward off any infection. You need to take these two now, then two more in a little while, before bed."

I'm really beginning to feel guilty about the way that I treated him this afternoon when I woke up and even last night. He's done everything to take care of me and I was a complete and utter bitch. "Come here, please?"

He looks at me, a little surprised and probably hesitant, and I don't blame him, but he comes to me anyway. He comes to stand between my legs and I wrap my arms around his waist, pulling him close to me, resting my head against his chest. I stay there for a minute, until he finally brings his own arms around me, holding me to him, and he starts to play with my hair. I lift my head and lean back to look at him, but I don't loosen my grip around his waist. "I am so, so sorry," I say, but the words are barely a whisper and my eyes begin to fill with tears. "You've been nothing but caring and supportive and I'm treating you like shit."

He doesn't say anything, but his hands come to my cheeks, holding me between them, and he leans down so that we are nose to nose. "You're going through a lot, and you're in a lot of pain, physically and emotionally, but you need to remember, I am not your enemy, Cami. I am here for you, to support you and to take care of you, so please, please, do not shut me out."

As soon as he finishes his speech his lips are on mine, soft and warm, yet possessive and demanding. He's showing me exactly what he just said. I'm his — to protect and to take care of. I wrap my arms around his neck and he stands up, bringing me with him. I wrap my legs around his waist and I can feel his erection between us. I can't help the flick of my hips that follows the realization that he's right there.

He turns toward the dining room table. I think he is going to take me around the wall to the couch but he doesn't; he lays me out on the table. I can tell without looking that I'm on the corner because part of my ass is on either side of it, and I smile into our kiss when I feel his hands going for the waistband of my pajama pants.

My smile is his cue, and he pulls them down my legs. He breaks our kiss so that he can rid me of my pants and panties.

As soon as they're gone, he brings my legs up to rest on his shoulders. He slides down at the same time, lifting my pelvis to meet his mouth, and before I can stop him, his tongue is buried in my pussy. I shiver at the contact. He doesn't stop the flicking and circling motions his tongue is making. I moan and my hands dig into his hair, holding him tighter to my sex, and he starts to suck on my clit. My legs tremble, heart pounding. I'm so close and he knows it. Alternating between licking and circling, then sucking, it takes another few strokes and I explode into a million pieces.

He stands up, holding my legs to his chest, and I can feel the coolness of his barbells pressed against the heat of my dripping-wet sex, but they don't stay cool for long. He pulls back, and I can see him watching as he lines up the head of his cock with my entrance, and he slams into me, filling me full to capacity in one plunge. I nearly come undone again.

He gives me a moment to adjust before he starts moving — in and out, harder and faster with each thrust.

He leans down and his lips are on mine, hot and wet, tasting of Tristan and of me, and I moan into his mouth.

He rears back. The look in his eyes tells me that he needed this as much as I did, and what he says next isn't a surprise. "I'm gonna come," he says, warning me, but I can feel my own sex tightening around his cock as it twitches. "Cami," he groans, and I explode.

EIGHT

Tristan
******

Though she is walking slower and can't wear her great fuck-me pumps, it's nice to see Cami without the crutches. I haven't minded a single minute of helping her or waiting on her hand and foot for the last seven days. I know she is enjoying her mobility.

Beau and Mick have been here off and on over the last few days, checking on her, and we've been trying to work on a game plan in regards to Bobby and how to handle the situation.

Cami knows the ranch, which was ultimately what led to her drinking so heavily. It wasn't so much the fact that Bobby was alive, though that certainly started the process. The horse in the picture is the horse she used to ride when they spent summer vacations in Montana.

She says that she is going to go but doesn't know when, and she was ready to fire Vincent when she figured out that he's Bobby's likely accomplice in all of this and that he may have known all along.

The only conclusion that any of us can come to in regards to why this happened is far beyond the realm of possibility. None of us — especially Mick, who knew him best out of all of us - can think of any good reason why he would go to such extremes.

We've also watched all the videos that were sent in the package. Most of them were normal kinds of things, but there were three that surprised her more than anything, though I'm not sure I understand why.

One was a video of Bobby and Evelyn, her mother, arguing and fighting. Ultimately, Bobby sent Cami and Mark to boarding schools in Europe to avoid a divorce from Evelyn. She threatened to take everything, including the children, and he wasn't going to have that, considering it was very obvious to Bobby, Cami and even myself that Evelyn wanted nothing to do with her children. Cami also found out that Mark is only a half-brother and that Evelyn was not his mother, but that is apparently something Cami will need to ask Bobby more about, should she decide to discuss it with him.

The next two were videos of Bobby attending what looked like a high school and then a college graduation. Cami lost it because she hadn't even had a clue that he was even there. Which of course made her more pissed off. She said that she might not have hated him so much if she'd known then.

She also understands that, while Bobby is the one that sent them away, he did try, but Cami was too harsh on him and he no longer knew how to get through to her. One of the things that made her see this was the day she went to him about moving to Phoenix to go to ASU. Apparently he'd been making a video diary entry when she barged in on him. She never noticed the camera, and I understand how Cami was so harsh to him — it was all there, right on camera — but it was what happened when she left that made her see it all firsthand. Bobby sat down in his office chair and cried. He cried for so long that he forgot about the camera and the video ran out; at least, he made no motion to stop the tape from rolling, so that was the conclusion she and I both came to.

That video caused another night of heavy drinking and a few arguments between the two of us. I let it go because I knew she needed to handle this in her own way. She paid for it heavily the next day. It was a little bit of bittersweet revenge.

Cami has finally opened up to me about a lot of what Bobby did, though I saw most of it in the videos, and she's also found a newfound reason to take over Bold. I think it has something to do with proving herself to her father more than it has to do with proving it to herself or even me. But I won't stand in her way. If this is how she feels she needs to address him and the issues at hand, she might as well use her anger to her advantage and put it to good use by being the best she can be.

Cami is a very driven woman, and it doesn't take a rocket scientist to see it. When she is determined, nothing will stand in her way. It is one of the many things that make me love her that much more.

Over the next couple of weeks, Cami and I are back and forth from Los Angeles and a couple of times to New York, but I am now getting ready to head up to Montana to start filming a new movie. She's decided that she is going to come with me, and I couldn't be happier about it.

The night before we're supposed to leave we're both busy packing. We're going to be up there for about four weeks, and she's looking forward to getting out of the heat; it is now late August and the weather in Phoenix shows no signs of cooling down anytime soon, so I can't blame her for wanting to get out of town.

We're joining Mick, Beau, Tyson, Jolene, Naomi and Travis for a farewell dinner of sorts. Cami has been bouncing around with excitement for the last couple of days about tonight, but she refuses to tell me why. Travis, too, is leaving Phoenix, the day after we do. He has some business to attend to in Los Angeles. He said that he and Naomi will probably come up to see us in Montana in a couple of weeks.

What I'm really excited about is that Jolene has decided to join Cami's Bold staff and she is now assisting Cami, so that means that she is coming with us, because of course Ty is coming along too. Their relationship seems to be beyond anything either one of them imagined, and anytime I talk to Ty about it he beams with excitement. Which makes me wonder if Ty is planning on proposing to Jolene tonight and if that is why Cami is stupidly giddy about the evening. She shuts me down like nobody's business when I try and ask her about it. It's actually quite cute.

Once we are done filming in Montana, I have about three weeks off before I'm due in New York for my next film. If all goes according to plan, Cami and I will be spending my break in Tarah once again, but that's a secret I'm keeping to myself.

Cami is standing in the bathroom at the mirror. She's just finished with her hair, which of course looks beautiful — pulled over one shoulder and held back by a flower similar to the one she wore in Tarah for one of our dates. Her beauty is something I can't get over. It doesn't matter if she has raccoon eyes or if she is wearing no makeup at all, which doesn't happen often. But tonight I am more interested in the fact that all she has on right now is a black lace bra, matching panties, and lace top thigh highs that are being held up by a matching garter belt.

Her panties leave very little to the imagination and I can't help but stare hard at this beautiful girl. I sneak up behind her and wrap my arms around her waist, my hands gliding along her stomach, and she melts into me.

"Hey, beautiful," I whisper in her exposed ear.

"Hey beautiful yourself." She smiles at me in the mirror and our eyes meet. I love our little greeting ritual and it never ceases to warm my heart.

My hands continue to roam along her body, starting down at her thighs where her thigh highs stop. Her skin is so soft and I can't resist touching it.

"Behave yourself."

I snort a laugh. "Never." And I kiss her on her neck just below her ear, the spot that always turns her to putty in my hands.

"We have twenty minutes before we have to get out of here."

"I can be quick," I blurt out, my erection straining against my jeans.

"Not that quick," she says, and she turns to kiss me. But it is soft and quick. She knows better than to work me up, but sometimes I wonder if it works her up just as much. I can't seem to stop my hand from roaming between her legs.

"See, you're already hot and wet for me."

"I'm always hot and wet for you, but we don't have time." She kisses my cheek. "Now go, before we really are late. I don't want the nasty look from Beau because she will know exactly why we're late."

I huff. "Fine, but you owe me."

She turns so quickly in my arms that it hardly registers until we are face to face. "Behave yourself and I will more than make it worth your while," she promises and kisses me, then playfully pushes me away.

I like her promises of making it worth my while — it usually means that she will do something extra special for me when we get home — so I back away and let her finish getting ready. I head down to the kitchen, pour us both a small glass of shiraz and wait impatiently for her to join me. I haven't seen what else she plans on wearing tonight and I don't really care. I am already starting to feel the ache in my balls, and it is going to be a long, horny night.

NINE

About ten minutes later she comes down the stairs and my jaw drops.

She is wearing bright red fuck-me pumps, the first ones I've seen her wear since cutting her foot. I follow the sleek line of her legs until I meet the hem of a very short, skintight black dress with a lace overlay. Around her waist is a bright red belt that matches her shoes, and the dress is sleeveless, displaying her beautiful shoulder tattoos. She turns so that I can see the back. The black dress dips all the way to the curve of her beautiful ass, but the lace overlay has a high neckline, though I can still see her wings and the silver of her corset rings. Laced through her piercings is a bright red ribbon, visible but subtle.

I make a show of wiping drool from my chin, though I'm not actually drooling, and she laughs. "So I take it you approve?" She smiles as she walks toward me. I can tell that she is a little unsteady in her heels.

"Do they hurt?"

She shakes her head. "No, I just haven't worn heels like this in a while. Takes me a minute." I embrace her as she comes to stand with me. I kiss her neck and then down her shoulder. "I told you to behave yourself."

"Yeah." I snort. "Like that's gonna happen." She laughs. "Here," I say as I hand her one of the glasses of shiraz, and she takes a sip, then sets the glass down. "Don't like it?"

"No, it tastes great, I'm not sure if I'm over my alcohol binge. It turns my stomach."

Good. But I don't say that out loud. I get chills every time I think about what I might've come home to if I hadn't come home when I did. She was working herself into some serious alcohol poisoning. The day after, she spent a good part of the day in the bathroom as her drunk haze seemed to finally wear off and her hangover really set in.

"Are you ready?" I ask, and she nods, heading toward the stairs.

******
Cami
******

When Tristan and I step out of the condo, there is a sleek black limo waiting for us. I look at him and he shrugs, but I can see his goofy, I-have-no-idea-what-you're-talking-about grin on his face, and I smile.

This is really the first time we've been out since returning from Tarah. Things have been pretty much business since the night he came home. Which has been good for me: It is keeping my mind off of the fact that we're going to Montana and that we will be a short distance away from the ranch, where Bobby has been living for the last year. While I want to go see him, I'm not sure I can do it without completely losing it and going postal on him.

Though combing through all those videos and all that documentation I sort of understand, there is more to it than what he is showing and I'm not sure I want to find out more about his reasons. So many decisions to make.

We take the limo to pick everyone up — Ty and Jo, Beau and Mick, then finally Travis and Naomi — then we are headed downtown to Excelsior, an exclusive restaurant and bar plus nightclub that is frequented by local and visiting celebrities. I did my due diligence to try and talk Tristan out of this place for tonight, mainly because, as we pull up, there is a red carpet leading to the door, and lining either side of that carpet are photographers waiting to see who is showing up.

"Oh, for hell," Beau says as we pull up.

Ty and Tristan both laugh. "We can take you around back?" Ty says to her, and she scowls at him. "Or not."

Everyone starts laughing, but I know that, deep down, Beau is actually enjoying this. I take her and Mick in. Mick looks nervous as hell, which is probably how he should be. It's a big night for him. I give him a reassuring smile as Beau is looking around outside, waiting for our driver to come and open the door. No wonder Tyson insisted on sandwiching me between him and Tristan.

"Tristan and Cami, you guys come out last. Maybe we can throw off the photogs if everyone else climbs out first."

"That might work if you weren't getting out first." Tristan chuckles. He knows that Tyson's face is as well known as Tristan's, given that he is in all of Tristan's candid paparazzi shots.

"Good point, but oh well. You know how this goes." The door suddenly opens and the flashbulbs erupt. Jolene is followed by Mick and Beau climbing out first, and the flashes stop.

"Hmph," Beau huffs, and I start laughing. Naomi is next, but then the cameras start up again. This group knows who she is, no doubt because she is caught with Travis constantly.

The flashes pick up in double time as soon as Travis unfolds himself from the car.

"Here we go, ready?" Tristan asks me.

"No." But he rolls his eyes. I say the same thing every time. I laugh.

He climbs out and I am immediately blinded by the mountain of flashes that begin firing off, and I am still in the limo. Tristan stands and presents his hand inside the limo, waiting for me to take it and climb out.

I do, and once again the cameras are going nuts. I know what is coming next. As soon as I am standing, Tristan pulls me close, and with his other hand he lifts my chin and kisses me in front of all of them. I ruin our kiss by laughing. I can't help it; he is so determined to keep the story straight and I love him a little bit more for that.

The questions start flying as we walk toward the entrance, but Tristan doesn't comment.

Once inside, it takes a minute for my eyes to adjust to the dimmer light inside. "Does that ever get easier?" I mumble.

"No," Travis, Tyson and Tristan all say at once, and all of us girls bust out laughing.

"Good evening, Mr. Michaels." The female voice is a little too sweet, and I look at her and watch her as she eye fucks my boyfriend. I lean a little closer into him and watch as her face scowls. "Your table is ready," she says, turning on her heels and heading into the restaurant.

"What was that all about?" Tristan whispers as we follow our group to the table, and I am instantly relieved that he didn't notice.

"She was eye fucking you, so I thought I would show her who you belong to."

He busts out laughing, then kisses my forehead. "I didn't even notice. Not that I would care. But I like this green-eyed version of you."

"Tristan Michaels, I am not jealous," I say a little too sharply.

He laughs again.

Okay, maybe a little, but I'm pretty sure he is coming home with me tonight.

We all take our seats, and within a matter of moments, two bottles of Cristal appear and our glasses are being filled. I squeeze Tristan's leg. Tonight is on him, and he is already eight hundred dollars down on two bottles. Once all of our glasses are filled, the bottles are placed in the center of the tables.

Tristan raises his glass. "A toast," he says, and everyone, including myself, raises their glasses. "To old friends." I watch as he looks from Tyson to Travis, who are sitting opposite each other. "And to new." He looks to everyone else. "May this be the start of lifelong friendships."

"Hear, hear," everyone says in unison, raising their glasses a little higher.

Tristan clinks his glass against mine and leans in to whisper, "And to the woman who's captured my heart."

"I'll drink to that."

About halfway through dinner someone approaches our table, and it takes me a minute to recognize who it is, but Beau doesn't hesitate. She knows him all to easily, and I feel a small hint of embarrassment at her eagerness.

"I hope you're all enjoying your dinner."

"Absolutely," I say.

"It's wonderful," Tristan adds as he stands up to take the gentleman's hand.

"Tristan, it is a pleasure to meet you."

"Likewise. Thank you for accommodating our short notice reservations."

"Anytime." The man takes out his card and gives it to Tristan. "If you need anything, just call. I'll be happy to make it happen."

"Thank you, sir."

"Oh, no, don't call me sir. Call me Mr. Aklund or Damon."

"Certainly, Damon. Thank you again."

"Absolutely, enjoy." He nods and leaves the table. Tristan returns to his seat.

"Was that who I think it was?" Naomi gets a little excited. Tristan and I both nod. "He's hard to recognize without his stage makeup. I had no idea he owned this place."

"I did, but never expected to actually see him here," I said, and though I recognized him, the name threw me off. He's better known as Nikki Cliff, an eighties rocker that has a strong presence in Phoenix.

The rest of dinner is a blast. We're all having fun and joking around, much the way we were in Tarah, and the alcohol keeps flowing, though after the initial drop of Cristal, we all switch over to our signature drinks. While alcohol turns my stomach, I decide that it is probably better to drink my way out of my aversion to it, and Tristan doesn't object.

Once our dinner plates are cleared away, we all order dessert. Though most of us are pretty full, I insist. Tristan looks out of the corner of his eye at me, probably because I'm very casually spending his money. But I have my reasons.

Desserts arrive, along with a dessert wine, and we are all treated to fresh glasses of alcohol.

We're all chattering on when I hear the clink of silverware against glass, and my heart goes about a thousand beats per minute. I look immediately down the table to Mick, who is shaking like a leaf.

"I'd like to propose a toast," he says, and we all raise our glasses. "To the most beautiful woman I know. The woman who keeps me sane and keeps me on my toes. The woman who has my heart in every way possible."

"Hear, hear." We all raise once again and take a drink.

We all set our glasses down as Mick continues. "I'm so glad we could all get together tonight, despite the fact that we are all going back to our work and our lives over the next few days. These last few weeks have been a lot of fun. But before you go, there is something I want all of you to see." Mick stands up, sliding out from between his chair and the table. He stands next to Beau at the head of the table. Then he drops to one knee. "I can't imagine spending the rest of my life without you in it. You mean more to me than anything I could've ever thought possible, and I need you in my life." He produces a small black box from his pocket. "Beauty Allison Robinson, will you marry me?"

I watch as Beau's face goes beet red — she knows no one at this table knows her as anything other than Beau — but she also starts crying. But she doesn't answer. I know she's toying with Mick, and he begins to grown uncomfortable. "Yes," she responds, and we all clap as Mick places the ring on her finger and they kiss. Many of the other restaurant patrons join in our applause.

Tristan leans over and kisses me, then whispers into my ear, "You knew about this?" I nod. "Why didn't you tell me?"

"Shh, it was a secret."

He kisses me.

I pull back and stand, walking around the table to give Beau a hug.

"You bitch, you knew."

I give her my best innocent face. "I have no idea what you're—"

"Liar." We laugh and hug.

I whisper in her ear, "Congratulations. I'm so happy for you."

"I love you, girl," she says, and we both squeeze a little tighter and then let go.

I go around her to Mick and hug him too. "Well done," I whisper in his ear.

"Thanks for keeping the secret."

I can't help the breathy laugh that escapes. "You deserve to be happy and I am honored that she's the one that makes you that way."

"Love ya, Cams," he says, and we pull away from each other.

I look down the table at all of our friends — Tyson, Travis, Jolene, Naomi and of course Tristan — and for the first time in twenty-five years I finally feel the love that has been hiding there all along. It's something I never knew I was capable of until I met Tristan, and right now I feel as though my heart could explode with all the overwhelming gratitude I'm starting to embrace toward each and every one of them.

Tristan smiles at me and I smile back. Those eyes are the eyes I know I can never live without, and I love him even more for that.

"Let's party, shall we?" I say, and everyone stands. Tristan handles the bill and we all head into the nightclub part of Excelsior and kick off what turns out to be a wonderful night of laughing, drinking, fun and lots of dancing.

TEN

We finally return back to the condo after dropping everyone off at their places. I'm exhausted but extremely excited about whatever Cami has planned. I behaved. Sort of. It's kind of hard when we're dancing and she keeps grinding her ass into my crotch. But I didn't do anything that would embarrass her.

She kicks off her heels as soon as we make it inside, even before climbing the stairs. Dammit, I wanted her to wear those.

She takes ahold of my hand and she leads me all the way to the top. We should've just taken the elevator, but when I tried to drag her that direction she kept climbing the stairs.

We come into the sitting area of her bedroom and she pushes me into the oversized chair. "Wait there," she says, and I obey like a lost little puppy wanting to be pet.

A few minutes go by and I start to wonder if she's passed out on me, but before I can stand to go looking for her, she's standing before me in a silk robe, and coming through the speakers is the first song she ever danced to for me. Porn Star Dancing by My Darkest Days.

Her hips begin to sway to the music as it warms up. My dick stirs in my pants, and I wish I'd shed my jeans. As soon as the singing starts, the shoulders on her robe fall, exposing the thin black strap of what I'm guessing is her bra, and I have to remind myself to breathe.

She struts her way toward me and then dips down, almost touching her ass to the floor, which it might have done, but now I notice the black peep toe pumps she has on. She slowly climbs back up, sticking her ass out as she does. Then suddenly her robe falls away and she catches it in her elbows, covering herself, though I can see just about every inch of her body underneath. The robe continues to fall away and she is left in nothing but her bra, garter belt, panties and thigh highs. Once she is free of the robe, she turns around, throwing her ass in my direction, and I have to remind myself to keep breathing. She steals my breath every time she gets naked. She's absolutely beautiful.

She backs up until she is straddling my legs and she begins to grind against my now-raging erection. I reach up to touch her, help her remove her bra, but she stops my hands. "You know the rules, no touching the dancer."

I groan my disapproval. I can't stand not touching her, but she takes my cue and begins to unclasp her bra in a very slow, agonizing fashion. Once it is undone, she holds it against herself, removing it from one arm and then the other until they're both free, but her arm still holds the bra against her breasts as she turns around.

The song ends and I expect it to start again, but it doesn't. I feel the familiar beat of "Closer" pumping through the bass of the stereo system and her bra falls away, exposing her perfect breasts and beautifully pierced nipples, and I see now why it took her so long. She is no longer wearing her barbells, and a rushed breath escapes my lips as I take in her elongated nipples, made longer by the type of nipple rings she is wearing, which leave only the tips exposed.

"Jesus," I moan, and she smiles, coming toward me just as the music picks up and the singing starts. She climbs into the chair, placing her knees on either side of me, and she grabs onto my hair, pulling my head back, causing my mouth to go slack, and I feel the coolness of the metal running through her nipple against my lips.

"Lick," she commands, and I do and she moans, grinding hard against my erection. "Suck," she says, and I pull her nipple and the contraption into my mouth and she shudders just as Trent Reznor sings, "I wanna fuck you like an animal."

She pulls back and her nipple pops free of my mouth and she climbs off of me, sliding down to the floor. Taking the button of my jeans in between her fingers, she unbuttons and then slides the zipper down. She hooks her hands in the waistband of my jeans and boxer briefs, tugging, so I lift my hips and my erection springs free, falling forward then flinging back, slapping against my stomach. She removes my shoes, then my jeans. She stands and I notice that she's somehow managed to remove the clips from her thigh highs, and she starts working her barely-there thong down her legs.

"I want you, right here. Right now," she says as she climbs on top of me.

She will get no argument from me. She reaches behind herself and lines up the head of my cock with the warm wetness of her sex and she slides down onto me. I feel like I am going to explode as soon as I'm deep inside of her, but I don't, and she begins to tremble as she slides up and down.

It's around nine the next morning when I wake up. Cami is already out of bed and I can't stop the pout that forms on my lips. I hate it when she does this, mainly because I love our morning cuddles and, even more than that, I love our morning sex, and I am left with a hard-on and no Cami.

Our flight for Montana leaves late this afternoon, and knowing her, she's around here packing, but when I look around the room, she is nowhere in sight and there are four suitcases standing between her bedroom and the sitting room.

I crawl out of bed, take care of business, throw on some clothes and head downstairs. She's not in the living room area, so I go down one more floor and find her in her office.

"Hi, beautiful," I say as I lean into the doorjamb.

"Hi beautiful yourself," she says, but she doesn't look up from her computer. What on earth could she be working on that has her undivided attention?

"Whatcha working on?"

"Rumor squashing."

"Oh, what are they saying this time?"

"Have you heard from Layla?" she asks, extremely deadpan and without meeting my eyes. Something in her body language tells me that her defenses are up and her jealousy is flaming again. I kind of like it, but it is unnecessary.

"No, not since we left Tarah that night. Why?" I step into the room, walk around her desk and lean in over her shoulder.

"Rumor squashing, remember?" she says, more as a warning than anything, and I understand immediately that she is warning me so that I don't fly off the handle when I see what it is that she has to show me.

There is a picture of Layla, and the caption reads:

Layla Brooks, released from rehab, sporting a baby bump. Who's the father? Tristan Michaels or the product of an elicit affair that allegedly broke the pair up? Reps close to Ms. Brooks speculated that it was in fact Tristan's child, but would not confirm.

All I can do is close my eyes and shake my head.

"Rumor squashing. This is what I get paid for."

"It's still bullshit," I say, finally opening my eyes to look at Cami. Her eyes are soft, but there is a hint of pity in them. "I don't need pity, but what I do want is for her to be put in her place, along with the reporters. I won't have this popping up again, month after month, when she shows up somewhere."

"Tristan, do you think I wouldn't stop this nonsense?"

"Of course not. I know you will. Forgive me for thinking otherwise." I kiss the top of her forehead. "Are you all packed?"

"Nearly, just need my electronics. What about you?"

I laugh. "You mean those four suitcases upstairs are all yours?" She laughs at the mock horror in my voice. "Nearly, but you know me, I live out of a suitcase. Packing will take me five minutes." I turn her chair toward me and fall to my knees in front of her. "I can think of other things to occupy our time."

"Yeah, rumor squashing."

I shake my head. "I woke up with a raging hard-on and you were nowhere in sight," I say as pathetically as I can manage.

"Oh, you poor—" She kisses my forehead. "—poor—" Now my nose. "—poor baby. Whatever shall we do about it?"

"Oh, I can think of a few things." I stand up, bringing her with me. She throws her arms around me and I brace myself to take on all her weight because I know she will wrap her legs around me. "You know, we haven't christened your desk yet."

She playfully smacks my shoulder. "Tristan Michaels," she says, and my name on her lips sends a shiver through my body. I pull her lips to mine as I lay her across her desk, pressing the sleep button on her keyboard.

ELEVEN

Desk sex with Tristan is most definitely something that needs to be repeated. Often. He's left me to finish up in here so that he can go take a shower. I want nothing more than to join him, but I need to finish this press release before we leave and get it off to Trinity to send out.

Something about the calendar and today's date catches my attention. Hoping to see what it is that's bugging me, I open the calendar icon on my Mac, but nothing sticks out, at least not for the next couple of weeks.

I remind myself to check my phone calendar, just in case something hasn't synced over to this, and finish up my press release.

Tristan, Tyson, Jolene and I are all in the back of a limo that's taking us to the airport. I received a text about an hour ago that Bold's plane had arrived at Glendale

Airport, which was our cue to get moving. We could've just flown commercial, but once Jolene's luggage joins mine and Tristan's, it is very obvious as to why I've chosen to use my plane. I'm still not used to that, but then again, just as soon as I thought I was getting used to the idea, I find out that Bobby is still alive.

I feel my nervousness regarding that whole situation creep over me and Tristan notices my change in mood almost instantly. How does he do that?

He takes my hand and squeezes it, silently telling me that whatever it is that is bothering me is all right. I only wish I knew how to talk to him about this, but I just can't find the words. And because of that, I feel like I'm pulling away from him, and sometimes I get the impression that he feels it too. I hate it, but I haven't got a clue how to fix it.

We arrive at Glendale Airport, and immediately the limo driver and the pilots begin loading the plane with our luggage. Before we take off, I grab a smoke. Flying isn't an issue for me except when it comes to these small planes like this. They creep me out. Smoking has become more of a nervous habit than anything anymore, which really bothers me, and I am thankful that Tristan hasn't once mentioned the fact that there were two empty packs of cigarettes and a full ashtray on the coffee table the night he found me.

Tristan takes a smoke from me and lights up. I scowl at him. "What are you nervous about?"

"Not a damn thing. I just want to stand with you." I roll my eyes and he smirks at me.

After a couple of minutes the luggage is loaded onto the plane and the pilots are ready. Tristan and I both climb on board and head to the seats that face Tyson and Jolene. Jolene is pale as a ghost.

"Oh shit, Jo." She looks at me. "God, I completely forgot." I unbuckle my seatbelt and go to the stewardesses cabin for the Valium that's stored there. "Here," I say as I come back with a bottle of water and the pill. "Remind me next time." She gives me a half smile.

I walk to the cockpit. "We need about twenty minutes before we can take off."

"We're cleared to take off now," the co-pilot says.

"I understand, but I am not in the mood to clean up vomit, so give her a minute, would you?"

"Yes, ma'am," the pilot says, then turns back and starts talking through his headset, delaying our departure.

I go back and take my seat across from Jolene. "Better yet?" She shakes her head at me. "Remind me next time." I give her a half smile.

Tristan and Ty are in their own conversation and I don't pay them much attention.

After a couple of minutes, Jolene's color starts to return and her eyelids begin to get heavy. "You good, girl?"

She nods slowly and I stand, walking back toward the cockpit. I knock on the now-closed door. It opens. "We're good to go as soon as we're clear."

"Yes, ma'am."

When I return to my seat, Jolene is sleeping and breathing softly. Tyson snuggles up to her and kisses her forehead.

Tristan does the same and whispers, "She doesn't like flying?"

"Not *like*. Loathe is probably a better term for it. It freaks her out."

"I didn't notice when we left Tarah, but she did sleep all the way back to Phoenix."

"Exactly."

"Oh."

It is around seven when we land in Billings. I've arranged for a car and driver to take us to the house I've rented for all of us for the next month. It is plenty big for the four of us plus the others, when and if they decide to come up. However, at the house are two rental cars — one for Tristan to use back and forth from the set, and one for Jolene and I to use wherever we want to go.

"Should we stop for dinner?" Jolene asks as we all climb into the car.

"Sure. The house should be stocked, but by the time we get there and make food, it will be really late."

Tyson turns to our driver and lets him know we want to stop somewhere good to eat and asks if he has any recommendations, and we're off.

"Am I going to have to worry about the fans tonight?" Tristan asks Tyson, who shrugs. "Thanks, that's reassuring."

Tyson laughs. "Well it is no secret that you're scheduled to start filming the day after tomorrow, and it is no secret that it is happening here in Billings, so I wouldn't be surprised. But given that this place looks like a hole in the wall, I don't think it will be too bad here tonight."

"Well, we will deal with it if it becomes an issue," I say to Tristan. "Don't worry about it until we have to."

He gives me a half smile. "You know I always worry about it." I smile and nod. Yes, I know.

"How are you feeling, Jo?"

"Ohmygod, so much better now that we're here. I slept like the dead," she says a little enthusiastically.

We all laugh. "Good. I'm glad." I can tell that something is a bit off with Jo — something about the way she looks at me — and I get the impression that she is dying for some girl time.

"Tristan, what time do you have to go by the set tomorrow?" I ask, trying to help Jolene see that I get her message.

"I have to be there by ten but should only be there for a couple of hours. Why?"

"No reason, was thinking that Jo and I could come back into Billings for some girl time. Was wondering how long we'd have."

"Oh, couple hours, but take as long as you like. I need to run some lines and focus a little bit tomorrow," he says, but I can tell he is reading what I'm really asking him. More than a couple hours.

"Great. How's that sound, Jo? Shopping tomorrow?"

She nods at me enthusiastically, and Tyson smiles at our plans.

TWELVE

Tristan Michaels in Billings, MT with alleged girlfriend and owner of Bold International, Cami Enders, daughter of the late Robert Enders, seen outside a family diner Wednesday night.

Tristan is in town for the filming of a new movie, Catalyst, which started filming earlier this week.

It is unknown whether Cami's presence is for personal or business reasons, though they were spotted sitting pretty close together inside the restaurant, source says.

I stop reading. Somehow I always knew they would end up together, whether personally or professionally. I'd wanted them to meet, but it just never happened.

"So you've come to Montana." My heart starts racing. Does she know that I'm here?

I pick up my burner phone and turn on the power, wait a moment, and the voicemail indicator pops up. I press and hold *1* until the call connects to voicemail. Entering *0616* I listen as the voicemail begins to play.

"She knows, she's in Montana, but I don't know what her intentions are at this point. Will let you know if I hear any more." *Click*, ending the voicemail, and I delete it.

No names, no identifying information. But I don't need it. It's Vincent.

She's been in town for two days. Tristan should've started filming today, but judging from the picture in the paper, they are not alone: Tyson I recognize, of course, and another gal, a redhead. I wonder who she is?

I leave my desk and head to the kitchen for a fresh cup of coffee, pondering how this will go when and if she does show up here.

A small part of me doesn't want her to. I don't deserve to be forgiven, at least not for the fact that I faked my own death, but I would like to hope she could forgive me for the other things in her life.

Evelyn was such a bitch. I did what I had to do in order to keep my children in my life. Well, for what they were in my life. I refused to let her win, and I refused to let her take them away from me. She hated them so much. I could never understand how. They'd done nothing wrong to her.

When we got together I already had Mark, but things with her toward Mark were fine. Things were good between us, and somewhere between then and Cameron being born, something changed in her and I hated every single second of it. She threatened me with divorce, and I was only too happy to oblige her until she wanted more than seventy-five percent of what I was worth and the children. The money she could have, but the children, no way in hell.

In all honesty, reflecting back on it now, my reaction to what I saw and the danger I saw myself in was no doubt over the top and unnecessary. I'm sure that there could've been a way to work it out. I mean, technically all I saw was a man and a lot of drugs. Not that I'd never seen drugs before.

But there was some seriously heavy weight on my shoulders between the company, the company's financial problems, and the fact that the supplier I'd hired to supply my clientele with drugs was likely responsible for the accidental overdose of one of my clients. Though she wasn't a big name, her death weighed heavily on me, but I rationalized it as being Tick's fault for changing suppliers and not telling her that she was working with the purest of the pure drugs out there.

Of course there was my own anger at Tick, knowing full well that he switched suppliers so that he could con my clients out of more money than necessary, therefore making himself more money. I heard about six months ago that he got his own payback when someone turned on him and shot him.

Also, by making myself disappear, Cameron and the others in the company had plausible deniability when it came to the drugs. That operation was between Tick and myself. Though Vincent knew of him, he didn't know details.

The whole operation was a way to control where my clients went for their drugs, to try to protect them from crap street drugs, shit that could kill them. Was I enabling them? Sure, but in my mind it was a way of controlling the source, considering I couldn't control the addiction.

I bring myself back to the present, out of the thoughts that led me to this point in my life.

Despite what I put them through, I was still at every major event in their lives, especially Cameron's. I hope she saw that part of all those discs I sent her. She hates me so; I couldn't even begin to tell her that I was there, and she never gave me the chance.

I just hope she will...some day.

THIRTEEN

"All right, man, no more games. What is going on between you and Cami?" Tyson asks. We've just returned to my trailer on set for our lunch break, despite the two o'clock hour.

"What the hell kind of question is that?"

He gives me that look, the one like, *Are you stupid?* "You know what I'm talking about."

"Dammit, Ty, this is not the place for this."

"Like hell it's not. You guys have been boiling hot, now you're lucky if you're lukewarm. And I'd be lying if I didn't tell you that it is affecting everything you do. Including this crap." He waves his arm around the trailer. "Thank God you haven't gotten to your love scenes because, ouch."

"Maybe that's what's bothering me."

"Bullshit."

I know what Tyson is getting at and I haven't told him anything about what I found out with Cami that night.

He'd have already hauled off and killed Bobby by now just to make Cami happy and take the damn man out of the equation. It is becoming clearer and clearer that the longer we're here in Billings, the more withdrawn she becomes and I hate it. It is eating at her.

"If I tell you, damn it, Tyson, this stays between us. You can't go telling Jolene or anyone. You get me?"

"I get you, but you know better than that."

He's right, I do. Everything between Tyson and me stays between him and me. "This is fucking huge, Ty, promise me."

"Damn, yeah, I promise."

I take a deep breath; I might as well dive right into it. "Someone Cami thought to be dead...isn't."

"Whoa. Who?" I give him a 'Think about it, stupid' look. "What the fuck? You can't be serious."

"As a heart attack." Fuck, wrong choice of words.

"How the hell..." He doesn't finish his question and he doesn't have to. It's something I've been wondering about for weeks now. "When did you find out?"

"Do you remember the night I came home from L.A., back in July?" He nods. "When I got into the living room, she was completely shitfaced. And I mean falling-down drunk. She was still wearing the same clothes she'd taken me to the airport in."

"Fuck, man."

"That's how she cut her foot. She shattered a wine glass when I scared the hell out of her. She was too drunk to remember about it breaking, and before I could stop her, she stepped on the glass. Anyway, the night that I left, Mick and Beau gave her a package that contained a shit ton of crap from Bobby. Which wasn't that big of a deal until she discovered his video apology."

"So how does she know he's alive?"

"The video. The date and time stamp on the video said it was June second, twenty twelve. A week before I met her, and two weeks before her twenty-fifth birthday."

"That could've been a mistake, those things are never accurate."

"That was my argument too, but then she continued the video, and he showed her where to find him. It was a long shot, and I'm not even sure she knew then where it was, but ever since we got here to Montana, she's slowly been pulling away from me. Closing in on herself. So I know now that she knows he is here and doesn't know how to handle it."

"How do you know he's here?"

"Mick told me. It's the house that Bobby bought and supposedly sold about three months before his 'death.' I'm afraid that we're going to go home one night and she'll be gone. Either to him or that she'll run away from Montana. But she needs to figure it out, she won't talk to me about it." I take a deep breath. It kills me to have to come to work, some days for hours upon hours, not knowing what is going on with her back at the house.

So far she's been there every night, but each day it eats at her a little more and it's killing me. I don't know what to do or how to help her.

We finally wrap with filming around eight at night and Tyson and I head back to the house. I hold my breath until we come around the corner and I can see the car in the front. I let out a rushed breath, and finally Tyson understands my own mood and how I've been different when I leave and when we come home.

The weather here in Montana has grown chillier; it is creeping into September and Labor Day weekend, which I will be working, unfortunately.

Tyson and I step into the house, and dinner smells great. We both head to the kitchen, only it is Jolene and not Cami standing over the stove. "Where's Cams?"

She smiles at me. "In your bedroom."

"Thanks." I step out of the room as Tyson embraces Jolene. It's sickly sweet the way he treats her, but then again, I do the same thing to Cami.

I walk down the hall to the double doors to the master bedroom, our bedroom. I can see the light coming from under the door, but I don't hear anything as I approach. My heart starts to pound a little harder and I'm instantly freaked out. I reach for the doorknob, and it's locked. I knock loudly. "Cams, open up." No response. Damn it. "Cami." I pound harder.

"What going on?" Tyson says behind me.

"It's locked." I turn and pound on it again. "Cami, come on, open the door."

Tyson is at my side and we're both trying to get her attention, and nothing. "Jo, how long has she been in there?" Tyson shouts.

"Maybe an hour, I don't know. She said she wasn't feeling good and was gonna go lay down."

"Fuck!" I throw my shoulder into the door; it ricochets back at me and doesn't budge. I go at it again, and finally on the third try it gives way and I storm into the room.

Cami is lying across the bed. She looks like she is sound asleep, except for one thing: She's holding a bottle of Crown in her hands.

"I got this, Ty," I say, and he understands and leaves the room.

"Holler if you need anything."

"Will do."

I close the door behind him; luckily it is a French door, so I didn't actually break anything, but it rubs a little when I close it back up. Probably knocked a hinge loose. I take a deep breath, go to the bed and sit down.

"Cami," I say, but she doesn't move.

I reach over and use my knuckles on her breast plate, and she jumps awake. "Ouch, what the hell was that for?"

"Welcome back." I take the bottle out of her hands.

"Hey, give that back," she protests.

"Not a chance in hell. What the hell is going on with you?" My voice is harsher than I mean it to be.

"What the fuck do you care?"

That's it. I stand up and walk around to the foot of the bed so that I am in her direct line of sight. "If this is your way of pushing me away, it's fucking working, Cameron. We promised to talk about everything and you're shutting me out, just like you've shut everyone else out of your life. Stop it."

"The son of a bitch is alive. He's put me through hell my entire life, then he goes and dies on me just when we're finally getting somewhere. I can't love anyone because I don't know how. So yes, Tristan, pushing you away is all I know how to do."

I'm going to let the 'I can't love anyone' comment go. She's drunk and I don't believe her. "If you have so much resentment toward your father, go, talk to him, tell him, yell at him. Do not take his choices out on me. Damn it, Cami, I am *not* him." I take a deep breath, trying to control the anger I am feeling toward her. "I am your boyfriend, your friend and your lover. I am not your father. Go, talk to him, find the answers you need to find in order to get back to the woman I fell in love with."

"Oh, great, now you don't love me either."

"For fuck's sake, Cami. Of course I love you, but this..." I wave my hand in her direction. "This is not you or who you are. This is your mind and body being controlled by something that scares you half to death. You can't even begin to imagine how to handle it. Except for with a bottle and, goddammit all to hell, I will *not* let you drink yourself into the ground. You are so much better than this, and you are so much better than Bobby. Get it off of your chest. Go, dammit, go talk to him. Or I will."

She looks up at me, tears streaming down her cheeks. "I can't. I can't face that kind of pain ever again."

"What do you call this? You're tearing yourself up inside because you think you can't face it. You're doing this to yourself because you haven't even tried. You once told me, on the beach, that you would give anything for one more chance to talk to him, one more chance to find out all the answers to all your questions. This is it, this is your chance, and you're wasting it in yet another bottle of Crown." I lean down so that I can get in her face. "I love you, Cameron, from the bottom of my feet to the top of my head and then some. I will not sit here while you destroy yourself, and you can easily fix your problem. Go, talk to him." She lets out a harsh breath straight into my face, and all I can smell is the Crown Royal she's been drinking. "Tomorrow."

After that I tuck her into bed to let her sleep it off. She needs to be able to clear her mind and, if need be, we can have this conversation tomorrow. I don't have to be in the makeup chair until ten tomorrow morning because we're shooting mostly afternoon and evening shots tomorrow. Once she is settled in, I take a large glass of water and two Tylenol from the cabinet in the bathroom to her. "Here." She takes them from me and drinks them down. I might not be able to help with the vomiting in the morning, but I can certainly try to ward off the headache that she is certain to have.

I leave her to sleep it off and I go back out into the dining room. Tyson and Jo are there, finishing up dinner. "Want some?" Jo asks.

"Nah, I'm not hungry." I go to the fridge, grab myself a Sam Adams and step out onto the porch, staring up at the stars. The ache in my chest is back, and I rub it, hoping like hell that something, anything, will help set us back on the right track.

FOURTEEN

After I down the first beer, I go back in for another. Tyson is sitting at the table, messing around with his phone.

"Wanna talk about it?" he asks me.

"Not particularly," I say, and walk back out the door. I sit up on the railing, where I was before I downed my beer, and I hear the door swing closed again.

"Tough shit. What's going on?"

"I told her she had to figure her shit out. Go get the answers she so desperately needs. Though I might have pushed her too far because I told her that I wanted to have the woman I fell in love with back."

"Ouch, man, is she really being that bad?"

I look at him and nod. "She has no sense of the spiral she is falling down. I can't even begin to imagine the spiral I would fall down if I found out my mom was still alive. But our situations are so different from one another. Bobby essentially threw Cami to the wolves and never even bothered to try, at least while he was alive. At some point their relationship started to get better, but before it could develop into anything, he 'died.'" I can't even begin to imagine, and to some extent, I understand why she is falling down this spiral. "I love her more than anything, Ty. I need her to come back to me."

"Give her some time. Maybe she will go see her father, get to the bottom of this. But don't expect her to be cured when she comes home. You need to remember why this is so hard for her. Her father was a douche to her in life, then faked his own death just for her to find out that he's alive, right when she is starting to really accept his death. I would not want to be in her shoes."

"I don't want her shoes, they hurt."

He laughs a little. "You know what I mean."

"I do know what you mean, and I can't help her unless she wants my help...or unless she starts talking to me."

"Understood."

Tyson and I sit on the porch for some time, not really talking about anything, just sitting in silence, drinking beer. Okay, I'm the only one drinking beer. Tyson is having apple juice.

After my fourth beer, I realize that it is after midnight and head to bed. When I climb in, Cami is snoring softly and I try my hardest to climb into bed without waking her up. She needs to sleep off her alcohol.

I'm not in bed for two minutes before she rolls over and snuggles into me, wrapping her arm around me and nestling into the crook of my shoulder. I can't help but pull her close to me. I love her so much it hurts. I kiss her forehead.

"I love you, I'm sorry," she whispers, and I think she's awake, but the soft snoring continues.

"I love you."

I fall asleep quickly after that.

******
Cami
******

I have got to stop doing this. My head is pounding, my stomach is swirling, and I am draped all over Tristan. I wasn't that drunk last night, and I remember everything he said to me. Every single word of it was true. Truer than I really wanted to hear, but he proved something to me last night. No matter what, he will always push me to do the right things.

He's right; I can't keep doing this to myself. This isn't who I am anymore, and I'm being a complete and total bitch to someone who doesn't deserve it. He's done nothing but support me and stand by my side since we met in Tarah.

What I wouldn't give to be back there again. Back to when things were carefree between us. Back to when things were sweeter, simpler and filled with rooftop swimming pools and room service.

I finally open my eyes, and as soon as I do, Tristan begins stoking my hair. "I know you're awake," he whispers.

I smile despite the major headache beating my brain to death. "How'd you know?"

I feel his small chuckle. "You started tracing my abs with your finger."

"Oh," I say and sit up, looking at his beautiful blue eyes. Eyes that I adore. They're vulnerable this morning, and I can truly understand why. He's waiting to see if I am going to snap at him. "I'm sorry," I whisper.

He gives me a beautiful, crooked smile. "So am I."

I cock my head at him and I can tell he is thinking that I don't remember last night, but I do. "Everything you said was the truth, you have nothing to be sorry about."

"You give me more credit than I deserve. Though I stand by what I said — you either need to talk this out or put an end to it. I'm always willing to listen, but I'm pretty sure I'm not the person you need to be talking to."

"You're right."

"I will go with you, all you have to do is ask."

I shake my head. "No, you've seen me at my worst without being around Robert. You do not need to see that, and he is someone I need to deal with on my own."

"I respect that, Cami. But know that when you're done, I will be here, ready and willing to talk about this. Without the alcohol." He kisses the top of my head.

I move to bring my lips to his and he turns away. "Nope, go brush your teeth. Crown in the morning is the worst breath ever." He laughs, and I leap up out of bed, stripping off my clothes as I go.

I'm standing there at the mirror, looking at my hair and brushing my teeth, when Tristan comes up behind me and grabs my ass. Then, in my stunned immobility, he takes my toothbrush from my mouth and puts it in his. "Hey, I wasn't done with that." I spit the toothpaste out and grab the mouthwash, rinsing. I watch as he brushes his teeth. He's watching me in the mirror.

We don't make it out of the bathroom. First he takes me on the counter, then again in the shower, and I know the moment he slides home inside me I am forgiven for my inexcusable outburst last night. But I know that if I keep this shit up, eventually he won't forgive me.

"I'm off tomorrow," he says as he pulls his t-shirt over his head. "If you change your mind and want me to go with you, I can go tomorrow."

"No, I think I need to go and get this over with, and I know that I need to go alone." I climb into my black pumps and straighten the pencil skirt I'm wearing, then tuck in the button-up, sleeveless silver blouse. I pull on the matching black jacket and watch Tristan's eyes rake over me. "Enjoying the view?"

"Absolutely, but more than that I'm trying to decide why you'd wear something so formal to meet your father."

"It's my way of feeling powerful. I know I will catch him off guard, and I will be dressed like this. It gives me confidence. Though I am going sans makeup. No one wants to see that." He shivers at the memory of seeing me that night. I have no idea what I looked like then, but the next morning was disastrous enough.

He walks over to me and wraps his arms around me. "Will you text me when you get there? Then again when you leave? If I can, I will text or call you back. But I have a busy day ahead of me and am scheduled to be on set until at least eight."

I groan. "Eight? Really?" I pout.

He smiles. "Yes, eight. But if there is an emergency and you need me, call Tyson and he can pull me off set and I will come home. No matter what."

"Tristan, you could lose your job."

"Fuck them, you're more important."

I can't help but smile at him. I know that he'd give up this life if I wanted him to...or if the right opportunity came around to walk away from it. "That won't be necessary, but I can't promise you will come home to a sober me. You might come home to a drunk mess."

He doesn't smile. "I'd prefer sober, but know that I do understand. I don't have to work tomorrow, so please, stay sober so we can talk when I get home."

"All right. I promise to try."

"Alcohol is never the answer, Cami, and you know that."

I nod and he kisses me again. "You better go, you're gonna be late."

"No, I am going to get there and sit around for three hours while they cover me in makeup. I might as well go back to sleep."

"Oh, the life of a beautiful actor."

"Oh, the life, indeed." He kisses me again and goes to the door. He looks back at me one last time, and I see it: fear. He's afraid of what he is going to come home to, and I'm not sure I can blame him.

FIFTEEN

The house from the picture is off in the distance, and I take a deep breath, trying desperately to control my heart rate, but it is nearly impossible. "Now or never," I say to myself and put the car in drive, but I can't seem to pull my foot off of the brake.

I grab my cell, pull up Tristan's name, and text him.

I can't do this

There is an almost instant typing bubble that follows. Then the text comes through.

Yes you can, be strong, remember Layla, remember I love you.

Layla. The foyer in Tarah. Bitch mode. Turn it on. Deep breath.

I love you

I call Beau.

"Please, for the love of God, talk me out of this."

"Cams, what am I talking you out of?"

"Seeing Bobby."

"Oh, for hell. Damn, Cams. No, I will not talk you out of this, you need to do this. You need to get it off of your chest. You're strong, you're beautiful and I love the living shit out of you."

"Thanks for the pep talk."

"I'm coming up there."

"No. Dang, girl, stay in Phoenix with Mick, he needs you more than I do."

"Bullshit, Cameron. I am coming. I'll see you tonight." And just like that she's gone.

"Thanks so much."

My phone chimes.

Love you Beautiful

I put my phone down and slowly pull my foot off of the brake, though I can't quite move it over to the gas pedal, and I am thankful that I am far enough away from the house that I am hidden behind a hill and whoever is inside can't see me sitting here like a damn idiot.

"Fuck it. Let's do this." I pump myself up, press the gas pedal and pull around in front of the house.

I take a deep breath and throw the keys on the front seat of the car. The likelihood that anyone would steal my car out here is nil. I climb awkwardly out of the car and walk the twenty steps to the door, taking a deep breath before pressing the doorbell.

A few moments later the door opens and I hold my breath.

"Good afternoon, ma'am, how may I help you?"

"I am looking for Bobby."

"I'm sorry, ma'am, no one here by that name."

I breathe finally. "I'm sorry, I must've made a mistake."

"Let her in, Alfred," a man says, though I'm not sure if it's actually Bobby.

Alfred? What, is he Bruce fucking Wayne?

The older gentleman steps aside to let me in.

The interior of the house is beautiful — log cabin style — and the walls are made from same logs you can see from the outside. It has a wide-open floor plan, and nearly every room can be seen from the doorway, but I don't see the man behind the voice.

My eyes follow the line of the railing that leads to the second floor, and standing there at the top of the stairs is none other than Robert Enders, my father.

The visual steals my breath away, and I fall back against the door that Alfred just closed. My vision is blurry, but I can see him coming down the stairs.

"Alfred, get her some water, please."

He comes to a rest at the bottom of the stairs just as I straighten myself out. But all I can see is red. I take the three steps to close the distance between us and I slap him hard across the face, then the tears come, hard and fast.

"You son of bitch! You know what bothers me about this most? Not only did I have to bury you once but, goddammit, I will have to do it again. I will have to go through that again!" I'm yelling, but he doesn't move, he doesn't flinch. He stands there and takes my words. "Just when I was starting to accept who I am, what I am, and where I belong in this fucking world, your goddamn package shows up and completely destroys everything!"

I expect him to interrupt me, to stop me, to want to talk to me, but he doesn't say a word.

"You throw me under the bus with your fucking business. Leave me no choice but to do your job. You force me to have to deal with my brother, who is an even bigger dick than you are. You've forced me to hate you with every fiber of my being because of the things you've done to me. Then, goddammit, I have to learn about it all over a fucking video. You couldn't do it yourself. You couldn't fucking explain it to me yourself. You selfish fucking bastard."

I turn to reach for the doorknob and open the door to leave, but he is behind me, holding the door closed.

"Fuck you, Robert! Fuck you and all your goddamn high horses. I hate you! I hate you! I hate—" The tears overcome me and I fall to the floor; all the fight is gone and I can't fight with him anymore. "I have to get out of here," I say, but my words are weak, just as weak as I am.

"I am an asshole, I'm selfish, and I deserve to be hated with every ounce of who you are, Cami. Believe me, I regret everything I've ever put you through in your life. I regret that I couldn't make things right with you, and more than anything, I regret that you never felt an ounce of the love that I have for you. But Cameron, that is my burden to bear, that is my mistake to live with for the rest of my life." I hear him take a deep breath. "I faked my death because I had no choice. Either I fake my death and disappear or be dead for real. I needed a way to free my life up in the best way that would protect you. I couldn't just walk away from my life and go into hiding. I had to make sure that no one knew about you, and that no one suspected otherwise. I needed to give up everything just so that I could have you in my life. I had no choice, but now I need the chance to prove it to you."

He helps me to stand up. I follow his lead and he leads me to a couch in the living room, but he doesn't leave my side as I take a seat.

"I was trying, I was trying so unbelievably hard to pull back my Bold responsibilities. I wanted to try and be a father to you. I was a father to you for years, I was the only thing that was there for you. She gave me no choice. I would've rather had you on the other side of the world than stuck in a life with her. You deserved so much better, and I failed at giving it to you."

The tears are starting to hurt, starting to burn as they stream down my cheeks.

"Did it ever occur to you that this pain is caused because you're capable of the love you thought you never felt? Of the love I am sure you feel for Tristan."

Tristan's name coming from his lips pulls me from my trance. "How—"

"Cami, I'm not blind. I do own a computer, a TV, and other means of finding things out, and I'm not going to lie, it makes me happy to see you two together." His voice is soft, comforting, and more than anything reassuring.

I just stare at him. He's the same as he was the last time I saw him, except his hair is a little lighter and his skin a little more rugged, and I realize that this year plus of isolation has been hell on him. "Why didn't you just quit?" I have so many questions and that's the first one that comes out.

"You know better what that answer is now than what it would have meant a year ago. Bold was in trouble. If I'd walked away, abandoned ship in its time of need, the company would have crumbled. I would have rather died than see the company that took everything away from me, that I worked so hard for, fold. I knew that if I died, the company would right itself with the business insurance, that you would take over the company and breathe new life into it." There is a deep sadness in his eyes. "I never wanted to see you tied to Bold the way that I was, and I knew you never would be. I knew, deep down, that your age and hatred of me would slow down your taking over the company and that you would blame me or think I was punishing you."

"Jesus Christ."

"So I wasn't wrong?"

I shake my head.

"Cami, I can't make right my wrongs, but I can try and make right your future and mine. No matter what the cost. If you tell me to stay away, I will. If you tell me to go to hell, well, I've already been there, but I will gladly go back there again." He takes a deep breath before continuing. "That choice is yours."

"What about Mark?" I ask; I am not the only child he owes an apology to.

"Mark is more complicated than I ever thought he would be. I knew as soon as he put every dollar of his inheritance into a charity there was no coming back from that. I won't try with him. I can't, he won't listen. He would rather kill me himself than see me again."

"I'm not so sure I don't want to do that."

He laughs a little.

I can't help but laugh, but at the same time I want to cry. "I still hate you."

He sobers. "If you didn't still hate me, I wouldn't believe you were sincere. You have every right to hate me, and I know full well that this cannot be fixed in one conversation, but it is a damn good place to start, don't you think?"

"You said you had no choice?"

He takes a deep breath and stands, leaving me on the couch alone. But he doesn't leave the room; he begins to pace. In a few moments, Alfred arrives with two large glasses of ice water, sets them down on the table, and then leaves the room. I take a glass and take a sip, then watch as Bobby walks from one side of the room to the other, deep in thought. "I wasn't given a choice. Well, I was, but this was the only one that would make any sense. A few days before my 'death'" —air quotes included— "I stumbled into something that put my life in danger. Only I didn't realize exactly what it was until I went to the police." He stops to look at me. "You're so beautiful," he says, and I watch his eyes light up, but I give him a look that tells him to continue. So he does. "While I was under interrogation, I was left alone until an FBI agent came into the room. He wanted more details about what I'd seen, where I'd seen it, and how on earth I managed to come across it." I am so confused. "It was a drug ring. A major U.S. and Mexico drug trafficking ring. After I finished explaining to the agent what I knew, he disappeared, only to come back into the room with a woman several minutes later. The woman was from witness protection."

I gasp and put my hand over my mouth.

"They wanted to pull me away, with twenty-four hours' notice, pull me away from Bold, away from Los Angeles and, more importantly, away from you. I was so scared, but it wasn't me I was worried about." He turns to look at me. "It was you. I was afraid that if I just disappeared from view, they'd go after you. They'd find you and kill you because they knew that I'd gone into hiding. That they would use you to draw me out and then they would kill me, or you." He's whispering by the end of his speech.

Though I never stopped crying, I start crying harder.

"I knew too that if I just disappeared, Bold would crumble into nothing. Thousands of people would be out of a job, not to mention the fact that there would be legal ramifications for doing so. Which is why my will was written the way it was. I didn't give you any choice but to take over the company." He stops and looks at me again. "You remember?"

"If I didn't take over, the company would be sold off and yada, yada. Yeah, I remember, and I remember why I stepped up — to save the jobs of the those already in place. I couldn't have that on my conscience."

"Exactly. I also knew that if I faked my own death, your inheritance would be paid and the business insurance I carried would right Bold. Get them out of the financial trouble they were in. Not to mention the fact that a new, fresh, unknown daughter steps up to take over. It was exactly what the company needed to get back on track."

"Weren't you worried about me once the news got out that you had a daughter?" I ask.

"No, because the timing of events and the media helped with that. My estranged, unknown daughter takes over the business. That, and the twenty-four hour window that they gave me, gave them enough time to get people in place to both keep tabs on you and keep tabs on those they were going after."

"So why come out to me now?"

"Because I couldn't stand it anymore. The latest news I had was the drug cartel has bigger fish to worry about now. So therefore my time in witness protection may or may not come to an end. But I don't and won't know that until it happens or I testify."

"What will you do if it does?"

"Retire. I can't go back to work, and more importantly, even if the feds take down this guy and this cartel, there is no knowing whether or not there will still be some of them around to make my life a living hell. They can still put two and two together that I was the one who tipped off the feds and come after me. So ultimately my life from here on out is exactly this. Living in hiding."

SIXTEEN

My phone chimes with a text.

"Tristan," Bobby says.

"Probably." I pull the phone from my jacket pocket.

Stay strong. I love you. We're wrapped for the day. Explain later. Heading your direction.

"Give him the address, have him come."

"I think that's a bad idea, he punches a lot harder than I do."

"You slapped me, you didn't punch me." I can still feel the sting of my slap across his face, but I won't apologize.

"I was afraid I'd break my hand. I already spent a week on crutches because of you." A puzzled look crosses his features and the image is similar to that of my own, but I owe him an explanation. "The night Mick gave me your package, I started watching the videos." I take a deep breath. "I spent two days in the same clothes, drinking myself into oblivion. Tristan came back from Los Angles sooner than I thought and he scared me, causing me to drop my glass and shatter it. Apparently when no one would get me a new glass I stood up, barefoot, before the glass was picked up."

"That was not the type of reaction I was expecting you to have. Though I'm not surprised."

"What's that supposed to mean?" The words come out pretty harsh.

"You're my daughter, I would've done the same thing. In fact I did. I went through four bottles of brandy over a week before I was finally able to make that final video."

I'm not sure that I really want to hear how much I am like Bobby. I barely spent any time with the man growing up; it's hard to take, and I flinch slightly.

I decide to text Tristan with the address, telling him that I'm all right and that the choice is up to him if he wants to come in when he gets here.

After a while, Bobby and I move into the kitchen. He offers me a bite to eat and I decline. Eating is the last thing I want to do right now. Seeing him move around this kitchen is so surreal. He's been dead to me for the last year plus, and it's a lot to take in. "Have anything stronger than water?" I finally ask. He doesn't answer, but I watch him pull some glasses and pour some amber liquid into them. He stops after about two fingers full. "More," I say, and he obliges me.

He turns and hands me the glass. I take it from him and take a huge swig, gulping it back, and it burns even worse than Crown does. But rather than let it bother me, I soak it up. Feeling that burn lets me know that I'm alive.

The doorbell rings, and my heart skips a beat. "I'll get it, Alfred."

"Bruce Wayne," I mumble under my breath, and I hear Bobby chuckle as he leaves the room.

I can hear the squeak of the door. "Hello, Tristan."

"Son of a bitch." I hear a loud thud.

"Ouch, dammit."

I come around the wall and see Bobby holding his nose and Tristan shaking his hand back and forth, flexing his fingers. I lean against the wall, watching as Bobby gains his composure.

"Feel better?" I say to Tristan, but I can't help the smile that spreads across my face at the satisfaction I feel for the fact that he probably broke Bobby's nose.

"A bit," He responds back to me. "All right?"

"All right."

"Tristan," Bobby says through his hands that are trying to hold his nose and probably hold back the blood. "Would you like to come in?"

"Oh, for God's sake. I slap him and you punch him. Please tell me that Tyson isn't here. I'm afraid of what he might do too."

"Well, might as well get it over with," Bobby says as he comes into the kitchen, going for the towel on the counter. He goes into the freezer, grabs a few cubes of ice and holds it to his nose. "Tristan, would you like some ice for your hand?" he asks, and the whole scene is fucking comical and I bust out laughing. Every ounce of tension I've been feeling for the last month an half washes out of my body and I crumple to the floor, laughing hysterically.

******

Tristan
******

I can't decide whether Cami is laughing at me, Bobby, or the whole fucked-up situation we're all standing in. I won't apologize to the idiot; he deserved what he got and so much more. I really wanted to shoot him, but Tyson wasn't stupid enough to give me his gun. Though it would be the perfect murder; everyone thinks he's dead already.

I don't go near Cami — she needs to let this mess work its way out of her system — but Bobby hands me a dishtowel full of ice for my hand, then hands me a beer.

"Well, I have to admit, I'd rather see her in hysterics laughing than the mess you've put her into these last few weeks."

"Believe me, Tristan, I wanted it to be over far sooner than it was, and I am sure I should've told her sooner than I did, but I needed to make sure we were in the clear."

"That doesn't excuse you from what you've done. You've damn near destroyed her." I breathe.

"I know, and I can't take it back, I can only try and change it going forward."

"I'm not sure how I feel about it," I say to him; I'm not sure how I want to go about letting this jackass back into her life. "I've seen her at her lowest and I won't have her back there again. Do you understand?"

"Believe me, Tristan, I want nothing more than to see her happy. If it means I never see her again after today, then that's her choice. But when she leaves here, she will have all the tools she needs to get in touch with me safely, if she needs or wants to."

"Don't hold your breath just yet, Robert." Cami finally comes to life and out of her hysteria.

I suddenly feel the need to defend Bobby from Cami's words, but he holds up his free hand. "I'm not. Just want you to know I'm here."

"Duly noted."

"Have you said everything you wanted to say to him?" I ask her, hoping like hell we can get out of here; it's awkward and extremely uncomfortable, and I'm not sure I can stay here anymore, but I won't leave without Cami.

"For now. I need a little time to cool off. Who else knows you're alive?" she asks Bobby.

"I'm afraid to tell you."

"Well I can tell you that the two of us are not the only ones. Tyson, for obvious reasons, Mick, and Beau know as well."

"For fuck's sake, Cami, who the hell else knows?"

"Don't you dare take that tone with me, asshole. Tyson knows because Tristan told him, because Tristan didn't know how to handle me anymore. Beau knows because she is my best goddamn friend, who has been there for me through everything. Unlike someone else in this room. Mick knows because he is my financial advisor and my contact when it comes to your fucking estate because I refused to deal with it and you forced him to deliver your dirty work. Mick and Beau are my two best friends, so yeah, they fucking know you're alive. Who else, Robert?" I can see Cami's face turning red with anger as she says all of this to Bobby, and so help me God, I understand why and I am more than willing to punch him again.

"Vincent."

"Son of a bitch! For how long, Robert?"

"Since the beginning. He helped me set it up."

Cami takes the glass she has in her hand and throws it up against the cupboard behind Bobby's head. "You son of a bitch. You get pissed off at me because the people closest to me know you're alive, but yet Vincent helped you orchestrate this whole fucking disaster?" I suddenly understand why Cami did not want me here; she's angry, beyond angry, and it's not something I've ever seen before when it comes to her. "I'm done." I watch as Cami takes off through the living room and toward the door. She throws the door back and steps onto the porch. "Dammit! Tristan, where's my car."

I set my bottle down on the counter and follow Cami out. Tyson's taken her car home, leaving us with this one. She is standing next to it, and I click the button so she can get in. Bobby is hot on my heels. I turn around, and this time he dodges my swing. "It's bad enough she doesn't trust you, but now, one of the two people she's confided in and turned to in the last year in regards to your business has been in cahoots with you this whole time. Un-fucking-believable, Robert."

"I did what I had to do."

"For what? For yourself?"

"No, I did it for her." The car horn blares from behind me. "I did it to protect her. To give my daughter what she so rightfully deserves — a loving father, not a dead one." I can see it in his eyes: the pain that he is enduring seeing this, seeing his daughter so angry with him. "She deserved so much better than what I gave her, Tristan. She deserved a loving family to grow up in and I couldn't give that to her. I wanted out. I needed out, and it was the only way I could without seeing everything I worked for and everything I gave up fall to pieces. I gave up her life to build a business that destroyed mine and hers."

"It's still selfish. No matter how you slice—" The car horn blares again and I hear the car door slam shut.

"Tristan, dammit, let's go. Or I'm walking."

"Here, take this." He hands me an envelope. "When she's ready, give it to her." I tuck it into the inside pocket of my jacket, turn around, and head toward the car. Cami jumps back into the car. "Take care of her. She deserves the best."

"I have every intention of doing just that." I try not to let the anger filter through my mouth, and I don't let the one thing I want to say to him slip past my lips.

I climb into the car. Cami is bouncing with rage and I can see the tears and frustration etched into her features. I don't say anything to her because I know that's not what she wants. She needs a chance to calm down and gain her own composure. I put the car in reverse and back up so that I can turn around. Once we're off of the property and out of sight of the house, I can see her visibly relax, but she is mulling something over pretty hard and I'm scared about what that might be.

After about five minutes in the car, heading back toward our rented house, she finally breaks the silence. "How's your hand?"

Oh, for Pete's sake. She's the one who's hurting here and she's worried about my hand. "It's a little tender, but I'll be fine." I sneak a glance at her, debating, weighing the consequences of asking or not asking, and decide that asking is probably my better option. "How are you?"

"Fine."

So this is how we're gonna be. "Please do not make me get angry with you."

"What the fuck is that supposed to mean?"

"Jesus Christ, Cami, I told you last night, stop hiding this shit from me. I can't take it when you hide shit from me. I know damn well you're not fine, so stop with the bullshit."

She just looks at me, but I can't look at her for more than a few brief seconds. I have the disadvantage because I'm driving; thank God because she'd have us in Phoenix by now.

"Tristan, I don't know how in the hell to process all of this shit. Put yourself in my shoes, what would you do if it were your mother?"

My heart aches. "You can't ask me that. Our situations are completely different, Cami. I spent the whole first year after her death begging for one more chance to talk to my mother for no other reason than to tell her goodbye and that I loved her insanely. I didn't get that chance, and the last time we talked, I was too busy with school and we talked for all of thirty seconds. Then she was gone." My heart hurts, not only for Cami but now at the thoughts of my mother. Not a day goes by that I don't think about her at least once, but this is harsh.

"How can you possibly understand what I'm going through then? So what's the point in talking about it?"

"Jesus, Cams. Whether it is me or a shrink, you have got to talk to someone. I'm sure I'm more equipped to be your sounding board than a shrink would be, if for no other reason than I've seen it firsthand. I am begging you, do not shut me out of this."

She doesn't say anything the rest of the drive back to the house. I breathe a deep sigh of relief when I realize that Tyson has taken my advice, come back for Jo and taken off. The car is nowhere in sight, and Cami and I have the entire house to ourselves.

"He had no choice. Tristan, he is under witness protection. The death was his way of protecting me, of protecting his own ass, his employees and his business."

The car swerves slightly as I take in what she's told me. I can't even begin to really process it at this point, but dammit. "What the fuck?"

"It's a long damn story, Tristan. I barely had time to get through it when you texted me. Bobby changed the subject and told me to invite you over. I guess he figured the broken bones should all be managed in one visit." I look at her, and the look in her eyes is dancing with humor. "Thank you for punching him." I snort. "Is it broken?"

"No, I'm all right."

"Where's Ty and Jo?" I can tell in her voice that there is disappointment and maybe even a little frustration. I think she was hoping to use them as a buffer, and I take a little pleasure in the fact that it is just she and I.

"They went into town."

"Damn it," she spouts as I put the car in park.

"Guess you're stuck with me, sweetheart."

The look she gives me tells me she's pissed, and I don't care. She climbs out of the car, slams the door and heads straight for the house. I'm hot on her heels because I don't want her to lock me out.

She gets through the door first and slams the door in my face, but it's not locked. Opening the door I can hear the click of her heels across the hardwood floor, but she isn't in the kitchen; she's headed straight for the bedroom. "Oh, shit." Fear races through me that she's going to pack her shit and leave. I go running down the hall after her.

SEVENTEEN

"Leave me alone!"

"Why, so you can pack all your shit and run away? Fuck that, sweetheart. I will not let you run away from me." She stops dead in her tracks and turns to look at me. Something is there in her eyes, but I can't even begin to make it out. "You see, Cameron, there is one HUGE—" I throw my arms wide. "—difference between me and your father, and I'm going to explain it to you right now, and I am only going to do it once. Are you listening to me?" She nods tentatively. "I love you with every fiber of who I am. Everything I do is for you. I am here, ready and willing to take whatever you want to throw at me. Yell at me, scream at me, cry, or fuck me stupid, it DOES NOT matter, Cameron Celeste Enders - I am NOT going ANYWHERE, and I will chase you to the end of the earth and back to bring you back to me. I love you for you and who you are, the woman you've become because of all the fucked-up shit your father has done to you. I love you because you're beautiful, you're strong, you're compassionate and you are downright fucking crazy when you want something."

"Keep going," she breathes.

I take a deep breath because I know that I am getting through to her. "I love to be around you. You make me happier than I have ever been in my entire life. We know each other better than we know ourselves, and there is nothing that will stop me from ever finding out more and more about you." I take a couple of tentative steps in her direction. Staring into her beautiful blue eyes is hypnotic and I'm dazed by her. The fight in me is gone, washing away like a hot shower. "I love the way you dress, the way you walk, the way you curl your hair around your finger when you're nervous." I watch as she realizes she is doing just that, but she doesn't stop. "I love the way your barbell clicks against your teeth when you're deep in thought." Another step toward her. "I love the way you get angry because, for the briefest of moments, you're vulnerable, and then you open your heart and lay it all out there." Another step in her direction. "I wear my heart on my sleeve, which makes me an open book, but I love the look in your eyes when you realize I've done something completely unexpected." Another step. Getting closer. "You are like a firework. Simple yet capable of the extraordinary. When you're lit, you explode into the most beautiful colors that light up the night's sky." I'm standing in front of her. I can see the tears in her eyes. I reach up to cup her cheek in my hand. "I will never, ever let you walk away from me. I'm yours, always. Be mine forever. Don't shut me out. Keep me close."

My words are interrupted abruptly by her lips on mine in a fierce, ferocious kiss that takes my breath away. Our bodies mesh together and I hold her to me, tighter than I've ever held her before. Her hands are in my hair, holding me to her. Our tongues begin to dance and my head begins to swim at the desire in her touch, and I feel dizzy, drunk on her.

My hands go to her waist and I find the zipper on the back of her skirt, unhooking the small clasp and slowly sliding the zipper down. Her skirt falls straight to the floor. Next comes her jacket. I slide it off of her shoulders and it joins her skirt in a crumpled heap on the floor. Her hands begin to move like mine. They are between us as she works on my jeans, getting the button and the zipper down. I feel her thumbs hook into the waistband and she pushes down, her lips becoming stronger and more demanding on mine.

Once my jeans are down to my thighs and my erection meets the air, it twitches, and then her hands are on me, lightly stroking, tugging, begging me. I start on the buttons on her blouse and decide that it is too much to handle right now, and the next thing I know the buttons from her shirt are flying against my chest and her hands are pulling my shirt up. Our kiss breaks and my shirt is off and over my head before I know it. Her hands slide greedily over my shoulders and down my chest and stomach, and then she is on her knees and my cock is in her hand.

She looks up at me through her lashes and I watch as her tongue runs from base to tip, and I shiver. Her mouth makes that perfect O and then I'm inside her mouth. "Shit." My mind goes blank as she sucks me in, inch by inch, until I feel the head of my cock reach the back of her throat, and just when I think she is going to slide back up, I feel the muscles in the back of her throat contract and I go a little deeper. "Damn it," I growl; she's taking me in just a little further until she slowly slides back up. Her hand follows her mouth along my shaft and I feel like I could explode. But she doesn't stop, and I'm coming closer. "Cami, stop." She sucks me in again. "Cami, stop, I don't want to come in your mouth." But she won't stop, and it is one more stroke and I come undone, spurting hot down the back of her throat. My eyes close and my knees tremble. I have to grab onto her head for support and she continues to flick her tongue across the underside of my cock, right on my piercing, and I tremble again.

I take a fistful of her hair and pull back at the same time I pull my dick from her mouth, and she lets it go with an audible pop. I look down at her; there is sadness in her eyes and I can't understand what's going on. I lower myself to my knees in front of her. "I'm sorry," she says, and the tears start.

"Sorry for what?" I embrace her, bringing her close to me.

"You said stop and I didn't."

"That's not why you're upset. Talk to me, sweets." My heart aches as I realize that is the first time since we left Tarah that I've used that nickname on her, and I vow here and now to use it more often.

"You're going to think this is really stupid."

"Nothing you ever say is stupid. Tell me."

She hesitates long enough for me to start wondering what it is that she's thinking. But I can tell she is fighting her own inner demons to tell me whatever it is that she has to say. I don't push her; I want her to tell me, but I want her to do so on her own time.

I hear her take a few deep breaths and I brace myself for whatever she has to say. "I'm sorry I didn't stop." That's it, that's what's bothering her.

"That's not it, Cami, and I know it. The only reason I wanted you to stop was because it didn't exactly seem fair to me."

She lowers her head into her hands. "I didn't stop because I thought that if I got you off, it would clear your mind and you'd see that—"

I stand up, taking a few steps back. "You thought that if I didn't have a raging hard-on my feelings for you would change?" I can't stop the anger from dripping into my voice. "You think that all I want from you is sex? That I have to say all those things to you to get laid?"

Though she doesn't open her eyes, she turns away from me and I can see her body visibly shaking with the tears that are wracking her entire body. "You think that all I want you for is your body, to be my receptacle whenever I feel like using it? What in the Sam fucking hell makes you think that? I am so unbelievably angry that you would ever consider yourself to be anything less than the woman I love. I am not him, Cameron. I am not your father and I am not Reed and, goddammit, I am NOT any of those other men you've had in your life."

I walk over to her and I sit down behind her, putting my legs on either side of her. I wrap my arms around her, trying desperately to pry my way in between her belly and her legs. I want to hold her. I need to hold her.

She relaxes her legs and allows me to grab ahold of her and pull her back into me. She turns slightly, tears streaking down her cheeks. Her lips meet mine once, twice. She twists around, looking me in the eyes, her hands in my hair. "Show me." She kisses me again and I'm at a loss as to what to do. Show her? How? "Show me how much you love me."

She pushes me down onto the carpet and then crawls up my body, licking and sucking her way to my nipples, where she flicks her tongue across one, then across the other. She comes up to kiss me and I seize my chance to straighten her leg and roll her over so that she is under me. "I'm supposed to be showing you." I kiss her once, twice, and finally a long, slow, passionate kiss filled with all my love and every ounce of anger that I feel, just so that I can feel the anger to make way for the flood of emotion I know she needs to feel and to understand. All while my free hand roams along her body.

I cup her breast in my hand, then hook my finger into the cup of her bra and pull it down, exposing that soft, supple swell of her breast and nipple in all its beauty. I pull back from her lips and kiss along her jaw, along her neck, down to her exposed breast, and I take her nipple into my mouth and suck, hard. Her back bows to my touch and her eyes flutter closed.

My hand finds its way under her panties and into the dripping wet slit of her sex. It's on fire with her own need. I find her clit and flick once; her whole body convulses with an urgent need for more. I flick again and again, feeling her clit swell beneath my finger, and I know it is only moments before she explodes. I pull back from her clit and plunge two fingers inside, hard and fast, just to pull them out soft and slow. I repeat the process again and again until the muscles of her sex clamp down hard on my fingers, and I watch as her whole body goes stiff and that soft red blush spreads across her entire body.

I pull my hand back to begin massaging her clit once again, but she is hypersensitive and I love watching as her nipples harden and her back bows as she quivers with each flick. I pull a nipple into my mouth and suckle and lick, then move across her chest to the other one. Then I slowly kiss my way down her stomach, pushing her panties down with my hand as I bring my lips closer to the spot my hand has occupied. It's my tongue's turn to devour her.

I ignore the fact that my balls are tight and my cock is throbbing until I've given her two more orgasms with my tongue. I then pick her up off of the floor and carry her over to the bed, laying her out and fanning her hair on the pillow over her head.

"I need you," she breathes. "I love you," she whispers as I slide myself in between her legs. My erection is pressed between us, but I don't move. I want to hear more. I feel her hips rock against my cock and I know she is probing and pushing, hoping to line me up just right so I will slide into her, but I don't.

"Tell me more," I whisper.

"I'm sorry I ever thought you were using me. I know now you're not and I knew before you weren't."

"So why say it, Cams. Why tell me that?"

"Because—" I watch her close her eyes tight. "Because we never talk about tomorrow."

"Tomorrow?"

"Or the day after that, or next week, or next month, or next year. We've never once talked about our future and where we will go from here."

It all makes perfect sense now. She's afraid that this is all we'll ever be together. "Look at me, sweets." I watch a tear escape her eye at my nickname for her. "Cams, look at me."

I give her a minute to compose herself and she does; she opens her eyes and she looks right at me. Her eyes are full of love and doubt and fear. "So let's talk about our future." I kiss away the tear lines streaking down into her hair. "Let's talk about tomorrow, after I'm done loving you." I kiss her on the lips and her hips flick once more against my erection and I get that we are both back on the same page, both fighting for proof. I lift my hips at the same time she lifts hers. This time she holds herself up and I feel the head of my cock sliding into her. We both shiver as the realization of our overwhelming love for each other washes over us.

EIGHTEEN

"The only reason I've never brought up a future with us is because I was afraid I would scare you," he says soft as a whisper. His fingers are lightly playing with my hair and turning circles on my arm with his thumb. We're curled up in bed after what I can only describe as the most intimate and passionate experience of my life. Tristan and I have had strong passionate sex before, but this was so much more.

"It scares me that we don't talk about it."

"I can see that now, but this is why I keep telling you that you need to talk this stuff out with me. Cami, as much as I'd like to, I can't read your mind."

"It's hard. Especially when it comes to things like Bobby. Did you know that Beau and I were roommates for over a year before she found out that I had a trust fund?"

I feel him shift to look at me. I lift my head so that I can look at him. "Why?"

"Because I knew almost immediately upon meeting her that money was a sticky subject with her. I didn't want to flaunt the fact that I had more money than I knew what to do with at that time. I eventually told her, and it was hard. I honestly thought I was going to lose her as my best friend over it. When Bobby's funeral came around, I didn't want her to come. I knew it was going to be ugly and I didn't want her to see it. But she insisted and she came, and it turned out that I was glad she did. She was, too. That was when she met Mick for the first time." I smile tentatively at him, hoping to hide the fact that, like Jolene, I feel a little jealous about Beau's engagement. But I'm not fooling him.

"Is that where some of this is coming from? Mick's proposal?" I know I blush beet red and I try to hide my face by putting my head back down. His hand is there, on my chin, pulling me back to look at him. "It is, isn't it?"

"No," I say too sharply.

"Uh huh. You should know better than that by now, I know when you're lying to me." He smiles. "Tell me."

I decide that it is not worth the fight anymore. "It's part of it. It is part the fact that Beau has found that man she wants to spend the rest of her life with and he sees that in her too. The other part of that is the fact that they will be getting married and they will eventually be starting a family, and I'm deathly afraid of where that will leave me in Beau's mind."

"I love it when you're jealous."

I playfully smack his chest. "I am not jealous."

He laughs. "Yes you are." He kisses my forehead, and there is that shiver of goose bumps that flies across my skin. That is something I know I never want to get used to when it comes to him. "Cami, every single minute of the future I see is filled with images of you and me, and maybe even little ones running around. I'd propose to you right now if I knew you'd say yes, but I am also enjoying us just the way we are. We start talking about marriage and then other things factor in."

I pull my hand up to rest on his chest and I place my chin on top. "Other things like what?"

He takes a deep breath. "Things like you starting your career at Bold, me getting my post-*Love Is Burning* career moving forward. Hell, Cams, I don't even have a place to live. When I'm not with you, I'm in hotels. I feel so unstable and I've felt that way for a long time. When I'm with you, I'm finally starting to feel some sense of normalcy and stability, but I'm not quite there yet." He pauses momentarily. "Sure, I have loads of money — because I don't spend it."

I can't help the chuckle that escapes my lips. "Don't spend it? My ass. Do you not remember your Tarah bill?"

He laughs a little at that. "Oh I remember it, it's hard to forget over two hundred thousand dollars."

"I told you that I'd pay for half of that."

"Shh, we're done talking about that. I told you no before, and I am saying it again. No." I roll my eyes at him and he smirks at me. "Seriously, though, my career could be over tomorrow. I could get cut from *Catalyst* or whatever the hell the next one in New York is the minute they find someone better or decide to give up. I could not find another script I like, then I end up settling just so I can do movies. Cams, my career is a nightmare and there are no guarantees."

"There was one point you were ready to give it all up."

He adjusts himself underneath me and puts his head back onto the pillow. "I'm still not sure that might not happen."

"Is that what you want?"

He sighs. "I don't know. It's not as fun as it was before."

"That's my fault."

His head comes off of his pillow and he looks at me. "Explain, please?"

"Well look at the last six weeks. Things were great, you go to L.A., then you come home to find me in the mess I was in, then we come to Montana and I've been miserable and a bitch. Look at everything around you, Tristan, don't you think that factors into why you're not enjoying yourself?" As soon as the words leave my lips I'm not sure that's really how I wanted to say that, but I do my best to brace myself for whatever he has to say back.

"These last six weeks have downright sucked. I won't lie, Cami. I was so afraid to leave you, scared shitless about what I was going to come home to. I thought maybe if we got away and came up here, out of your condo, things would be better, but they only got worse because he's thirty minutes away, and after today, I don't know what to expect from you anymore and it scares me."

His voices falls off to a whisper toward the end.

"I see it now. What he said to me today, about how he was trying. It started the day I left for college. He could have been long gone from the house, but he wasn't. He stayed and waited for me. He told me to be careful, and even then I wanted to forgive him, run back to him, hug him, tell him things should and would be different. But I didn't. I couldn't make my legs do it because I wanted more, I wanted more than a morning at home. I wanted explanations that I thought I deserved or was entitled to, and I'd never gotten them and had finally gotten to the point that I'd accepted the fact that I was never going to get them when that package showed up." I lift my head and start to draw circles along his chest around the outline of his dragon head. "Now I have them, now I know, and I haven't the first damn clue what the hell to do with them."

He takes my head in his hands and he kisses me. "No one said you have to decide today...or even tomorrow. This is not something that is going to heal in a matter of minutes, Cami. It took you a year to accept that he was gone and those answers were never coming to you. Now that you have them, you need time to process them, no matter what, and you have all the time you need." He kisses me again.

NINETEEN

"Will you come with me?" I ask Tristan as we're both getting dressed.

We spent last night heavy on each other and light on the conversation until we fell asleep. "Where are we going?"

"You'll see."

"Of course."

Tristan has the day off from filming today. He'd expected to lose the day off after yesterday's incident with the set and them calling it before anything was filmed. But when he called to check in, they told him he wasn't on the call sheet today. So he shrugged and hung up the phone.

We climb into the car and I'm driving. I start heading north and west. It doesn't take long for him to figure out where we're going. "My hand still hurts, Cams, I really don't want to have to punch him again," he says, completely serious, but there is a hint of a smile in his voice.

"You won't need to. We're not staying, but there is something I need to do."

"Oh?"

"You'll see when we get there."

******
Tristan
******

Half an hour later we're pulling into the driveway of the ranch where Bobby is living, and before Cami or I can get out of the car, the front door opens and Bobby steps out onto the patio. I can tell even from here that his nose is jacked up. I feel a little guilty about it, but it doesn't seem to be bothering him any. His eyes grow wide in shock as he takes in the scene before him.

Cami climbs out of the car and I'm a little slower to follow her; she's not moving fast, by any means, but I'm not sure what her plan is. Today she is in skinny jeans, a cute butterfly t-shirt and a pink hoodie, topped off with pink Chucks. She looks so much like a teenager, but it's cute and refreshing to see.

She climbs up the six steps to the porch, where he stands looking very much like a rancher and not a CEO.

She stops at the top of the steps and waits for me to reach the bottom. "You can thank Tristan for this later," she says; her voice is soft and not angry. Then, before Bobby or I can even register what she's doing, it's already started.

"Whoa. Where's this coming from?" he says as he wraps his arms around his daughter, who's wrapped him up in her own arms. He has one hand on the back of her head and the other along her back. He begins to play with her hair as she squeezes him. He kisses the top of her head. I can see the tears forming in his eyes as he looks over to me and mouths, *Thank you.*

"Don't thank him just yet." I can't stop the laugh that escapes. "This doesn't mean I forgive you or that I'm over what you've done."

"I'd expect nothing less." Bobby's voice is heavy with emotion.

"It is simply a start. It is the hug I should've given you seven years ago." She looks up at him, and even I can read the puzzled look on his face. "The day I left for college. I know now what I was too blind to see then."

"What's that?"

"You were trying and I didn't see it. But you have to understand that you never gave me any indication that you were."

"I was, but you never saw it. Do you guys want to come in?" he asks both of us. I don't answer; I let Cami decide.

"Not today. But what do you mean, I never saw it?"

"Cami, I mean I was there, at your graduation, both of them."

"Why didn't you tell me?" she asks, but her voice is hesitant.

Bobby gives her a half smile that looks just like the one that she gives me. "Because I knew you'd be mad and I didn't want you to have to explain to your friends, and more importantly, I didn't want to ruin the most important days of your life by being there. I knew how much you hated me, I didn't want your hate for me overshadowing your biggest days."

"But I hated you even more for not being there."

"But I was there, and you have all you need in that package to prove it. So maybe we can start with you not hating me for not being there?"

"I will try," she says. The emotions are still heavy in her voice. She hugs him again and I see him smile.

"Thank you, Cameron," he says and kisses her head once more.

Cami climbs into the passenger seat of the car when we leave, a few minutes after their last hug. "I have to go to the airport."

"Where are you going?" Panic seeps through me.

"Los Angeles."

"What for?" I say, turning to look at her.

"I need to deal with Vincent and my anger about him knowing and never telling me."

"Are you sure you want to do all of this?"

"Tristan, I have to."

"Why?"

"Because our talks yesterday made me see that I can't ever move on to being truly happy unless I take care of everything I can, and I have to do it quickly or it will only grow and fester."

"You're afraid it will come between us." I look at her, but she looks out the passenger window.

"It already has, and I don't want it to happen again."

In that moment, Cami grew up just a little bit more, right in front of my eyes. She's not running away from it; she is running headfirst into it, and I have nothing but respect for her.

"Today is my only day off. After this, I am filming for the next thirteen days, and honestly I really would rather you wait. Calm down a bit?"

She smiles at me. "Depends, what did you have in mind?"

"Oh, I don't know. A little of this, a little of that.... A whole lot of something else."

"Tristan Michaels, you're a pervert."

I snort. "Look who's talking."

She busts out laughing. "It's all your fault, I can't get enough of you."

And just like that, all of our fighting washes away and we're right back to the Tristan and Cami we were before this whole mess started.

TWENTY

Two weeks later...
******
Cami
******

With a few days left to go in Montana, Beau and Naomi show up to hang out with me and Jo. Tristan told me that the last few days of filming are always the worst because they will try to cram in everything that's left to film, plus reshooting and redoing scenes that need changes done. He told me last night that this is the easier part of filming this movie because all the stunt work is done; they just have to film the in-between stuff.

The girls and I spend our days shopping, sitting around the house and even horseback riding. We're now several days into September, and Tristan's birthday is coming up. "Tristan's birthday is the twenty-first."

"What?" Naomi says to me as we're heading back to the house.

"Yup, next week. We need to plan an epic party for him. Something he won't expect."

"Take him back to Tarah," Jolene says from the back seat.

"I thought about it. Might not be a half-bad idea, actually. But you guys have to come too. Naomi, can you take the time off of work?"

"Work? Oh hell, Cams, I've barely worked since I met Trav, I'm not sure I have a job anymore."

"What?" I turn to look at her. "Why didn't you tell me?"

"What? Why would I do that?" she says back to me.

Beau cuts in. "Oh, I don't know, Cami only owns a company more than capable of taking you on her payroll."

"Thanks, Beau."

"No problem. At least since you moved me over to Mick's payroll, it frees you up to replace me."

I shoot her a look over my shoulder since she is sitting behind Naomi. "Yeah, because I need three assistants."

"Well, Cami, you know Trav's agent contract ends at the end of November. Maybe you can get him over to Bold and he can hire me to be his assistant," Naomi says rather calmly.

"What? You didn't tell me that," I say to her.

I reach for my phone and realize that in order to make this happen I need to call Vincent, and it turns my stomach. So I call Trinity instead.

The phone rings twice and she answers. "Hi, Cami."

"Trin, are you aware that Travis Jackson's agent contract is up at the end of November?"

"No, but shouldn't you talk to Vinnie about this?"

"Probably, but he didn't pick up." No need to tell her that he and I are not talking at the moment. "Get him on it. We need that contract."

"This doesn't have anything to do with the fact that he's Tristan's best friend, does it?"

"No, it has everything to do with the fact that we need that contract. It's a good, consistent one to have. I don't care what it costs, but get him away from that jackhole of an agent he has now and bring him to us."

"All right, Cami, I'll get Vinnie on it. Is this really going to be a fight to get him here?"

"I doubt it. I'll get Tristan to talk to him, or at least find out what I can about Travis's standing agent, then we can go from there."

"Good, call Vinnie next time." I roll my eyes at Trinity.

"Thanks, Trin."

We both hang up.

"There, problem solved." I also make a mental note to discuss Naomi's financial situation with her later, in private.

"You're fanatical when you want something, you know that?" Jolene says and laughs.

"Yeah, I guess I am." The rest of us join in.

"All right, so Tarah it is then?"

"Huh?" Beau says.

"Tristan's birthday?"

"Oh, yeah, of course." I look at her again and she's pre-occupied with her phone.

"Woman, put that crap away."

"Bitch, please. You should watch yourself when you're not driving. You're the same way." Beau is referring to the fact that I always seem to have my phone in my face, which really isn't true, but I am not going to argue.

After we get back to the house, I call the hotel in Tarah, only to find out that our penthouse suite is booked for two weeks starting next Wednesday. I try quickly to think of something else to talk about with the girls before the guys come home and I draw a blank.

I head out to the kitchen, where the girls are waiting on me. I hope that maybe with their help we can come up with something new.

"Tarah is out."

"What? Why?" Beau says, but I see a smirk on Jolene's face.

"The penthouse is booked starting next Wednesday for two weeks."

"So why can't we just get rooms and still hang out for the weekend?" Beau says back.

She's trying to convince me. "The penthouse is easiest for Travis and Tristan. We can all hang out, have a good time and not have to worry about him being seen."

"But sweetie, he's not hiding this time. He's not trying to get away from everyone who might recognize him," Naomi says. "It just means that we'd all have to hang out in Blu or on the beach, nothing wrong with that."

"I hadn't thought about that," I say to them.

"See, there you go. So what if he's seen in Tarah? You know the hotel will keep out the riffraff, and you don't have to make the reservations in either one of your names. You can do it under your aliases. Or use our names." Beau gives me a reassuring smile. "Or we could just go back to Bora Bora."

"All right, I'll call them back tomorrow." The girls clap, but something about Jolene's smirk bugs me.

"Why don't I take care of the reservations and the flights? This way you don't have to worry about it."

The alarm on the door chimes. "Hello," Tristan calls out.

"Shh," I hush the girls. "In the kitchen." But all the girls bust into a fit of giggles and Tristan is quick to hear us. He comes around the corner.

"What is going on here?" None of the girls can stop laughing.

"Nothing, just being girls."

"Uh huh," he says as he stalks toward me with a shit-eating grin on his face.

"What?" I shrug my shoulder and produce the goofiest smile I can manage, at least until his arms wrap around me and he gives me a big kiss.

"Get a room," Beau says, and I flip her off. She laughs.

"We have one, thanks," Tristan says as he pulls away from me. I look over, and Tyson and Jolene are in a similar embrace and I suddenly feel awful that Mick and Travis are absent from this equation.

"I should be done on set day after tomorrow. But I will have to wait until they release me before we can leave Montana."

"Good, that's a day or two ahead of schedule."

"Thank God. This movie hasn't been one of my favorites," he says as he strips out of his jeans and t-shirt.

"Why is that?"

"Not used to it. All the pyro crap, it's annoying and I'd just rather be done with it all. I probably could've been done by now had it not been for all the damn retakes." He smiles at me.

"So, I need your help," I tell Tristan as we're getting ready to climb into bed.

"Oh, with what?"

"Well, it has come to my attention — two things, actually, that I need some help with." I smile.

"What would those two things be?"

"First of all, I found out today that Naomi is on the verge of losing her job because of all the traveling we keep putting on her, plus Travis too."

"So she needs a job so she can be around us whenever she wants. Give her one."

"I thought about it. As it is, I have Jolene and Rayne in the office for assistants. I'm not sure I can afford another one, at least not without raising some eyebrows at the office. Giving all my girlfriends jobs."

"Well you have Beau, too."

"No, she is on my personal payroll. I do not pay her through Bold. I pay her through the money I make from Bold. The same thing I do with Mick. They are both disassociated with Bold in that respect."

"Okay, so I'll hire her as my assistant."

I smirk at him. "You really think that will fly with me?"

He snorts. "Why not? It's not like I'd be working her to death."

I laugh. "This is true, but I usually handle most of your stuff, and anything I don't do, you do yourself. Are you really sure you can relinquish that to someone else?"

He ponders the idea for a moment and then he shakes his head. "No, probably not."

"So that leads me into the second part of what I need your help with." He cocks an eyebrow at me. "I've learned from a rather reliable source that one of our good friends has an agent contract expiring in November."

"You mean Travis?" I give him a quizzical look. "If you want my help in convincing him to switch to Bold, forget it. You don't need it."

"What do you mean?"

"Cams, seriously? You can't figure it out for yourself? Travis has been very impatiently waiting for his contract to expire for the last two years. He hates his agent, and he blames his agent for the crap movies he keeps getting stuck into."

"*Rebound* wasn't that bad."

"Please, Cams, that movie was bad. At least for what Trav is capable of. He needs a better agent, capable of getting him the roles he wants to play verses the roles he has to play to stay in the business. Would you happen to know of any one like that?" His eyes grow wide, mocking me.

"I already talked to Trinity about it."

He climbs up on the bed, crawling across it to get to me. "What did she say?"

"She told me to call Vincent."

"Oh."

"But I managed to fill her in on it. She said she'd tell Vincent and get him working on it. I just wanted you to talk Trav into it, but I doubt that is something that needs to be done at this point." He shakes his head at me then pulls me closer to him and I climb on the bed, knees to knees. He takes my head in his hands.

"No, not really, but I will let him know to be on the lookout for Vinnie's call, or someone's from within the Bold organization. I'm not sure Vinnie will take him on personally, but—" He kisses me. "I'm sure it can be arranged."

"Good, then he can hire Naomi as his assistant, she has a job and can go where he goes." I kiss him.

"Then it's settled."

I laugh and he kisses me, twisting so that I'm laid out on the bed beneath him, and his hands go to work ridding me of the shirt I just put on and our conversation is over. Nothing else matters but he and I.

TWENTY-ONE

"I've got the reservations," Beau says the next morning as soon as the boys leave the house.

"Oh good, when do we leave?"

"Tuesday. I figured we'd be in Tarah by Wednesday. Then—" She points around the room. "—we're leaving on Tuesday morning."

"When you say 'we're,' what are you implying?"

"I mean we — us girls and the guys. You and Tristan will stay until the following Tuesday. We'll all be there for his birthday, then you and he can have a few days alone."

I roll my eyes. "That's not necessary."

"Shut up, it's settled. This way you guys can have some alone time. A week after you'll get back, he's due in New York for that romantic comedy he's filming. Don't ask me the name because that's your job." She smirks. "Not mine."

"Yes, ma'am," I say. I notice Naomi sitting out on the porch with a cup of tea in her hands. "Can you guys excuse me a minute?"

"Of course."

I grab a cup of coffee and go out on the porch to talk to Naomi.

"Hey, girl."

"Hey."

"What's up?" I ask her.

"Nothing, it's gorgeous out here. I miss these kinds of days in Phoenix." I sit down next to her and take in the view of the mountains.

"Me too. Hey, I wanted to talk to you without the other girls."

"If this is about my job, don't worry about it."

"But I am worried about it, Naomi. It's my job to worry about it. We drag you around to all of these places and I guess I never stopped to think about how this would effect you," I tell her.

"It's not so much you, or this, it's more Travis. He always wants to go places and I feel like a killjoy because I'm tied to a job."

"Has he offered you any help? I know it's none of my business, but I like having you around with us, but I won't if it means you're going to lose your job."

She lets out a deep sigh. "The truth is, I lost my job a few weeks ago. But not because of you or Trav. They did some major cutbacks and I was one of them."

"Jesus, Naomi, why didn't you tell me?"

She shrugs. "Because I'm all right." She looks back out toward the mountain.

"I'm calling bullshit on that one. Does Trav know?"

"No. I couldn't bear to tell him. He'd be really upset. Plus—" She stops, takes a sip of her tea, and doesn't continue.

"Plus..." I prompt her.

"Plus, I don't know where Travis and I are headed. We never talk about the future, but yet he never seems to get enough of me. The only reason he's not here is because he's shooting in San Diego. But I don't know where we're going as a couple."

I want to tell her to give it some time, but I'd sound like a hypocrite. I did the same thing to Tristan two weeks ago. "Well, what do you want to see happening between the two of you?"

"You and Tristan, or Mick and Beau, maybe even Tyson and Jo. I want to be with him. I've never been happier than when I'm around him, and when he has to leave it fucking sucks." She smiles a little. "I'm sure you can understand that."

I smile and nod. "Yes, I can. So here is what we're going to do. The only reason I can't bring you on board as my assistant is because I have two, Jo and Rayne, in the office. I don't want to raise any questions with anyone in the office about why, as a not-so-active CEO, I need three. But I will transfer twenty-five grand to your account."

"Cami, no. I can't let you do—"

"Stop, you can and you will. I want you to take care of your affairs, pay off some bills, do whatever you need to do so that when we all decide to do things, like go to Tarah, you're not stressing about money. Obviously Tarah — the airfare and the hotel — is on me, they will always be on me when I ask you to come along. But I want you to be able to go a little less stressed out and then Travis doesn't have to know. If I'd known you were having troubles like this, I would've given you Jolene's job first."

I look at her; she's crying. "I don't know how to thank you," she says.

"Just be yourself, have a good time, and don't stress about it. If you need anything — anything at all — you come to me. If not me, go to Mick. I'll make sure he has instructions to help you, no matter what, and he doesn't have to involve me."

"You're too much."

"Not really. It's the least I can do. I don't want you to be uncomfortable."

She reaches over and hugs me. "Thank you, Cami."

I hug her back. "Of course, it's what friends are for."

She laughs.

"Hey, guys," Jolene says as she comes out of the house, followed by Beau. "Okay out here?"

"Absolutely," I say as Naomi wipes her eyes before turning toward them.

"Cami, remember that bar we used to go to all the time?" Jolene asks.

"Yeah, Stomp or whatever it was called, the one over off Grand?"

"Yup, that's the one. JD has put the building up for sale."

"No way. I thought he was going to pull it back together?"

She shrugs. "That's what I thought, but I'm guessing something happened. The band has been playing gigs around town. I was gonna try and catch him this weekend, try and talk to him about it."

I immediately start spinning around a couple of different ideas. "What if we bought it?"

"We? As in who?" Beau says.

"We, us girls. What if we bought it?" Beau looks at me like I've lost my mind.

"Yeah, because we have that kind of money."

"All right, fine, what if I bought it. Bring it back to life." I turn to Jolene. "Would JD run it?"

She shrugs. "I don't know, not sure if he is backing out because he can't do it, or if he lost any funding he may have had. Either way, that spot is a damn landmark in the city. I'd hate to see it go to some stupid idiot that tears it down."

"Well, we can't let that happen, can we." I pull out my phone.

"Who are you calling?" Beau asks.

"Your fiancé."

"Oh."

TWENTY-TWO

******
Tristan
******

"You have no idea how glad I am to be going back to Phoenix," I say as we all climb on board Bold's plane in Billings.

"I second that one," Beau says as she takes her seat. I watch as she gives Cami a look, then nods. It's an encouraging nod.

I look at Cami, expectant.

"So, do you want to know what I've been doing these last two days?"

"Of course, I always want to know," I say, curious as to where she is going with this.

"Well, I've been doing two things, actually. One, planning your birthday party."

Oh no. "You're kidding, right? I don't need a party."

"Too late." All four of the girls say all at once.

"So what are we doing for my birthday?" I say a little dramatically, and I wonder idly how bummed she'll be that I've already made plans for my birthday party.

She's bouncing up and down in her seat. "We leave Tuesday for Tarah."

I knew that already. "Who told you that?" I watch as confusion washes over her face and it dawns on me: She still doesn't know about my plans to take her to Tarah.

"You're the one who has the penthouse reserved, don't you?" she says, looking over at Jolene. "That's why you couldn't keep a straight face when I was— Well dammit." Beau busts out laughing. "You bitch," Cami says, then laughs. "You knew?"

Beau puts her hands up in mock defense. "Not until Jo came to me that night, told me that there were already plans in play for you and Tristan to go. I guess we're just tagging along." Well there goes my romantic weekend with Cami. "That's also why we're leaving so early. We didn't want to intrude on Tristan's plans completely." She looks at me. "We'll stay for your birthday because, well, you don't have a choice." She smirks at me. "And then we will leave you two in peace." She looks back to Cami. "We did, however, make separate room reservations, so you and Tristan can have the penthouse all to yourselves." She winks at me before the smirk of satisfaction spreads across her face.

"So, great, I get to spend my birthday with a bunch of women." I laugh playfully.

"No, the guys will be there too," Cami tells me, and I wink at her. I'm not mad; in fact I like the idea of having our friends there.

"You said you were doing two things. That would be one, what would the second one be?"

"Well, I um..." She smiles and looks to Jolene, who's obviously already taken a pill to help with the flying, then she looks to Beau and Naomi, who are both super excited. "I bought a bar."

Whoa. "You did what?" I can't help the surprise in my voice.

"When we were in college we all used to hang out at a bar in Phoenix. It used to be a country bar, we'd go line dancing and we'd have a blast. A few years ago, it closed down. The owner at the time was hoping to get some investors involved and rejuvenate the bar. But that never happened, and he needs to get out from underneath of it. So he put it up for sale. So I bought it."

I can't help but smile at her enthusiasm. "So what now? You own a bar."

She laughs and the plane finally starts moving. "Well, we're going to remodel it. Beau is going to design it, and then the four of us are going to run it."

"I—" I don't know what to say. Though I want to talk through this with her, away from everyone else, I'm excited for her. "I'm speechless. I don't know what to say."

She's so excited; I can see it in her eyes. "Well, we have a lot of work to do on it before it will be inspection-ready. The place has been empty for a few years. Plus all the licenses we're going to need and everything else, it will be at least a year before we can think about opening it. But I think it's great, and it gives us all something to do besides be your traveling companions."

"I think it's a great idea," Tyson chimes in. I look at him, and I can tell he's a bit skeptical about it. But Cami is a smart woman; I have no doubt that she has this all planned out and figured out.

We spend the rest of the flight talking about the bar and the upcoming trip to Tarah, but I won't lie: I'm super excited to be back in Phoenix...and to be alone with Cami.

"Hey, sweets?"

"Yeah," she says as she plops down on the bed.

"What brought on all this bar talk?"

"Huh?" she says as she sits up.

"I was just wondering where it all came from."

She smiles, but I can tell she expected this conversation. "It was two things, really. One, I can afford it and it gives me something that is my own. See, Bold was given to me. I didn't earn it, which is why I have such a hard time with it more often than not. Despite the reasons I now know behind it, I never expected to own it. So this gives me something of my own."

"How do you plan to run Bold and a bar?"

She shrugs. "I don't know, but that's why I have Beau, Jolene and Naomi. They will be the primary operators of it. I will just be in the background, with the money, more or less."

"What if the bar folds?"

"Then it folds. At this point I'm not out anything, Tristan. I paid way less than asking price, and the main reason I managed that is because JD still wants to be a part of it in some fashion. He doesn't care what. So by giving him that chance, I reduced the price to three million." She slides to the end of the bed. "If I have to sell the bar because it's not doing anything, by then, even with the money I put into it, I can sell it for a higher price because it won't be the shell that it is right now. So I have very little to lose. Not to mention the fact that, since I signed the paperwork yesterday, I am just over a day away from making that much money through my job at Bold and I've done nothing to earn it. So why not give it back?"

I can't help but see the excitement she feels about doing this, and it warms my heart to see it. "You said there were two reasons. What's the other?" I take a seat in the chair near the bathroom and kick off my shoes.

"The morning after we talked about Travis and his agent status?"

"Yeah."

"Well, I talked to Naomi privately." I nod. "She lost her job, Tristan."

"What? Oh, man."

"She says that it wasn't because of the traveling and Travis, that she was let go, but I have a feeling that's not the case. I feel a little guilty about it and feel that it is partly my fault because we dragged her to Tarah back in June, she met Trav, and then it's been kind of downhill from there for her. So I gave her twenty-five grand to get her affairs in order and so that she wouldn't have to tell Trav. So I thought that if I bought the bar, it would give her something to do, something to work on, and something to focus on besides sitting at home with no job to go to while Travis is off doing his Hollywood thing."

"Wow. I had no idea."

"Please don't tell Trav. Let her do it on her own. She's confused about Trav, she doesn't know what he wants or if this is a long-term thing. She's not oblivious to the fact that he goes out when he's away from her, and she certainly isn't blind to the tabloids."

"Ah, babe, I didn't know. Trav has been like that for as long as I've known him. I thought Naomi had changed that." I don't know what else to tell her. I don't know what he's been up to, but I'm sure there is some truth to it.

"It's not your fault, and to be honest, we both know how they like to stir up shit. So until Trav decides where they're going, she's in limbo and probably more emotionally invested in their relationship than he is." She shrugs. "So at least the bar will give her something to work on, keep her busy, and if things really do go south with Trav, she has something else to do."

I lean forward and put my head in my hands. "I can talk to him."

"No, don't, this is their battle, per se, let them handle it." She comes to stand in front of me and I look up at her. "Are you mad that I bought the bar?"

"No, I'm not. I'm a little worried that it was a rash decision without much thought, but I can see now that was probably not the case and I'm even a little proud of you." I put my hands on her thighs.

"Besides, it gives me something fun to do."

"That's my girl." She bends down and kisses me. I kiss her back and, before I realize it, she's gone from in front of me. "Hey," I pout.

I hear her laughing from the bathroom and then the door clicks closed. I'm excited for her, at least about the bar. I'm not sure it was the best decision on such a short time frame, but she seems to have it under control, at least for now. I don't think she understands what is going to happen in regards to Bold. Though, I know she won't move to L.A., so maybe this is a step in the right direction. Getting her to divide her time a little more. Who knows, and only time will tell.

She comes out of the bathroom in her lacy black bra and matching panties, and I can tell that the conversation regarding the bar is over for now. I resolve to let her do her thing. It is what she needs to do right now, if not for herself then for her friends, and I'm perfectly okay with that.

She smiles seductively at me and beckons me to follow her to the bed. Half a second into our kiss, all thoughts of bars and Tarah cease to exist.

TWENTY-THREE

It's Monday afternoon and Cami and I have spent a good part of the weekend just being us and not worrying about a lot of things. She went to Trinity with the information I gave her about Travis, and then yesterday Travis called me and said that he was in negotiations with Bold to take over his contract and he was very excited about that. When I told Cami, she was over the moon.

"Cams, where are you?"

"Bedroom," she shouts back.

I'm coming back from running to the store. I needed to pick up a few things before we leave in the morning. While Tarah has nearly everything we need, I decide this time it would be better to go prepared. I climb the stairs to find Cami sitting in the oversized chair in her sitting room, her laptop on her knees.

"Hi, beautiful."

"Hi beautiful yourself."

I laugh. "You know that comment doesn't make any sense."

She laughs. "I know, but it's kind of our thing. Besides, you're absolutely gorgeous."

I know I turn beet red. I hate it when she says that, but at the same time, I like hearing her say it. "What are you working on?"

"Nothing really." She closes her laptop and looks up at me.

"I don't believe you."

"Well it is none of your damn business." She laughs. "You're the birthday boy, some things are meant to be a secret."

I roll my eyes. "You know, I'm not a big fan of my birthday."

"Is anyone?" She smiles. "But I'd like to help you change your mind about that."

I snort. "Good luck with that. I turn twenty-nine, not exactly something to be overly excited about."

She laughs. "Well you don't look twenty-nine, love."

"That's because I'm not. I'm twenty-eight." I can't stop the smirk that spreads across my face, and she busts out laughing.

The rest of our day goes on with the same kind of mood, lightening the overall mood of the condo. Cami refuses to talk about anything to do with her father, and right now, I'm okay with that. The couple of times I've brought it up, she shut it down, but the initial irritation she had when she shut it down didn't linger. The next thing that comes out of her mouth is usually something different and carefree. I really am liking this new Cami, though I feel like I'm balancing on a tightrope, waiting for it to snap.

TWENTY-FOUR

We're met outside by a limo that holds not only our luggage but our friends too. "Good thing someone got the Hummer." Cami laughs as she climbs inside.

Inside, the limo is tricked out for a great nighttime party, with rope lights lining the top, the sunroof and the bar. Everyone is here — Travis and Naomi, Beau and Mick, Tyson and Jolene. Cami and I are the last inside, and we're off to the airport and off to a weekend in paradise. This time will be so much different. I won't need to hide from sight and we can all indulge in some of the amazing amenities the hotel has to offer.

When Cami asked me what I wanted to do for my birthday, I told her that being in Tarah was enough, and she wasn't buying that. "Keep it simple," I told her. Birthdays are really hard for me since my mom passed away, and this is honestly the first time it's been celebrated since she passed. But I don't want to ruin her fun. She said it's payback for Bora Bora and her birthday, but if I know Cami, the extravagance will be to a minimum.

TWENTY-FIVE

"Mmm." I try to stretch until I realize what woke me in the first place.

I look down the length of my body, and pitching a tent beneath the sheets is a raging erection. Then I feel what woke me up — a warm, wet tongue and lips kissing along my inner thigh — and I see her head under the covers. I try not to move. I don't want to spoil her fun, but dammit she's driving me insane. She kisses, then licks, then sucks slowly along my inner thigh, painfully slowly, but gradually the sensations begin climbing higher and higher up my leg until I feel the tickle of her hair against my balls.

Oh, for hell. "I wish it was my birthday every day if it means I get woken up like this," I whisper, and she still doesn't stop. I lift the sheets up so I can look down at what she's doing. I love watching Cami suck on and play with my cock. It is a beautiful sight to see.

She doesn't disappoint. I make eye contact with her just as her tongue makes contact at the base of my shaft, and my eyes flutter. It is, like, the sweetest torture a man could ask for, waiting impatiently for the prize moment when a woman takes you into her mouth.

Cami slowly licks and kisses her way up my shaft. I can hear and feel the clink of her tongue ring on each of my piercings as she passes them, and each passing kiss is more and more excruciating than the last.

Finally she reaches the head and I wait in anticipation of what she will do next, but she does nothing; she just stares at me, love and affection in her eyes, and I can tell she is waiting for me to say something or squirm or do anything that tells her I want her to continue. But two can play at this game. She opens her mouth and blows hotly, and I moan. Dammit, she wins and I squirm, begging her to touch me again.

Her tongue slides past her lips and my heart rate increases with the anticipation I feel, wanting and needing her tongue on me. She licks once; he twitches. Twice, he twitches again and the raging fire of orgasm consumes my veins. She hasn't touched me and there is absolutely nothing I can do to stop it. I groan as the orgasm explodes and her mouth covers the head of my cock, trying desperately to catch as much as she can. My eyes close as her tongue finishes me off and my orgasm subsides. "Fuck me," I breathe, "how the hell did you do that?" I ask her.

She giggles a little bit. "I've been down there a while." Well, don't I feel stupid. "But it was on purpose. I was trying to drive you crazy so that you'd explode, I just—" She laughs. "I didn't expect it to happen like that."

I smile at her. "Come here," I say, and she crawls up my body, straddling me, and I take her head in my hands, kissing her like nobody's business, and she moans into my mouth. Her tongue tastes of sweet Cami and me, and it never ceases to amaze me how wonderful it tastes.

My hands slide down her neck, over her shoulders, and it takes me all of two seconds to realize that she is naked. My erection is hot and hard once again, and I take her breasts in my hand and squeeze. She doesn't flinch, but the moan she lets out tells me that something is off. I pull my head back and look at her. "Did I hurt you?" She shakes her head. "Then?"

"They're just tender."

"Oh, too much playing with them?" I cock an eyebrow at her.

She smiles. "It's never too much, but they are very sensitive." I use my fingers to lightly graze the peaks of her nipples, and they harden instantly and she moans.

"Mmm, I could get used to this." I sit up slightly and, very gently, take one into my mouth, gently sucking and licking. Her hand goes into my hair and her hips start to rock back and forth across my erection. I reach between us, pulling him free and lining him up. She slides back onto him slowly. I release her nipple and lick and kiss my way to the other. As soon as I take it into my mouth she slides down my cock hard and fast. I hiss and try to control my sucking. I don't want to hurt her; I want this to feel good.

She doesn't stop her motions, sliding up and down my cock. I can feel her hot wetness sliding down onto my balls, and I know she is beyond turned on. Her pace increases from want to need, and I release her nipple and slide my way back to the other. Gently rubbing the one I just left with my thumb, I feel her nipples harden further, and the faint red blush washes over her skin. The muscles in her pussy clamp down hard and her body stiffens. "Tristan. Oh God," she moans as her orgasm takes her.

In her post-orgasmic weakness I roll her over. Now she is underneath me and I start to move in and out slowly, allowing the tight muscles from her release to relax and fade away to my slow assault.

She moans and I move faster, desperate to get her off one more time so that I can join her in her release. She doesn't disappoint me, and when I am near explosion she begins to arch her back and all her muscles tighten. "God, I love you," I breathe as my orgasm takes me — and her — beyond the moon.

TWENTY-SIX

Have Tristan and I really been having too much sex? Is that even possible? The tenderness I feel in my breasts and even down below tells me that yes, I really can have too much sex. But the moment anything starts between us, all tenderness is gone and replaced by my overwhelming need for him.

It is after noon when we finally emerge, showered and ready for the adventures of today. It is his birthday, and I want to give him two of his presents. The last one will have to wait until tonight.

We're in the sitting room and this morning, before I started my torture, I came out here to set up the first two, and he sees them sitting on the coffee table in the sitting room. "I told you not to get me anything." He laughs.

"Yeah, we know how well I listen. Open them."

He smiles and hops onto the couch, almost like a kid at Christmas. It is sweet to see. Despite all of his 'No birthday party or presents' arguments, I can tell this really does mean something to him and I'm happy to see it. He goes for the big one, which is fine. I like the idea of him being excited for the bigger and better.

He tears into the paper to find a long tube, and I suddenly start panicking, not sure how this is going to go over, but I can't help but be excited about it too.

He gives me a quizzical look, but I encourage him to open it and he does.

Inside the tube is a thick stack of papers. Well, they are large pieces of paper rolled up. He pulls the papers free of the tube and looks at me, trying hard to figure out what it is. I smile, and he unrolls the papers, moving the other present and laying them down on the coffee table.

Clipped to the top page is a cream-colored piece of paper. He leans forward to look at it closer.

Across the top, in fancy script, it says, *Deed*.

"Cameron Celeste Enders, what have you done?" he says, but I can tell he's not mad.

"Turn the first page," I say and smile.

He looks back to the documents, reaches for the first large page, and turns it over.

"Oh my God," he breathes.

I look over the piece of paper, and drawn out in black and white is a large drawing of the front of a large, two-story colonial. There is a rounded rotunda for an entrance, with pillars from the ground to second floor. The house has several peaks in the roof, and it is very much a beautiful house.

"What have you done?" he asks, almost sounding angry. I look at him, shocked, but he's not angry.

"Do you like it?" I ask, hesitant of his answer.

"It looks gorgeous."

"Keep looking." I encourage him to turn the page.

The next page is an overhead layout of the interior design. From the rotunda entrance, to the left is a library, and straight ahead is a stairway that leads to the second floor. Running next to the stairs is a hallway that leads to the master suite, the two-story living room, the dining room, the kitchen and a family room. The house wraps around to the right, where it extends into a three-car garage. Across the back of the house is large deck area, suitable for sitting space, along with a built-in grill and bar. Beyond the plans is a pool.

"Jesus, Cami. Before I go any further, what is this all about?"

"Nope, keep looking." He gives me a look of *You can't be serious; I need an explanation here.* But I shake my head and make a show of zipping my lips.

He turns the page; it is the second story.

Upstairs there is a railing opening to the two-story living room, along with three additional bathrooms, storage and walk-in closets. If you follow the plans to where the garage is on the first floor, it says, *Studio.*

His eyes look from the plans to me and back again. I knew this was going to capture his attention, so I tell him, "Turn the page."

He does exactly that, and it is all laid out. I watch as he reads the descriptions of the layout and then looks to the computer-drawn images of what the studio will look like. He looks up to me again.

"I remember you once told me that acting wasn't necessarily your passion. Producing and directing, however, are another story." I can't help the tears that creep into my eyes as I take in his awed expression. "So, for your birthday, I am not only giving you your own studio, but I am giving us a house. Built from the ground up. In Los Angeles." He abandons the plans in front of him and he crawls over to me on his knees. I can't quite tell what he's thinking, and I'm a little scared.

"What about the condo?"

I shake my head. "Nothing has changed with the condo. I will keep it because I would really like to still live in Phoenix. But I understand that your career, as well as mine, is really in California, and we will need to be there a lot more than we are now. So rather than live out of hotels while we're there, I thought that a place that is ours—" I put emphasis on *ours*. "—is what we needed."

"Cami, I don't even know what to say." His eyes are filled with fear, and it worries me.

"Do you not like it? They're just plans, we can change it."

"Stop right there. I absolutely love it." He kisses me. "I love it just as I love you. It's just a lot to take in."

"I know. But the condo is mine. Designed for me, not for us, and while I absolutely love having you there, I feel as though you don't feel at home sometimes and I wanted to give you a place that really was your home."

"Cami, I feel at home wherever you are, whether it is in the middle of Montana, or in your condo in Phoenix, or even here in Tarah." The fear in his eyes is replaced by the look of love that I've come to adore about him. A look that is just for me.

"There's more. To the house."

"I don't care." He smiles.

I giggle a little bit. "But really, it's kind of cool. Please look."

He kisses me then pulls back, but he takes my hand, bringing me with him, and we both kneel over the coffee table. He turns the page. The next page is the entire layout of the property. He uses his finger to go from the house to the deck to where the pool is. Then, surrounding the pool and some distance away, at least enough to give us some privacy, are three smaller houses.

He looks at me.

"The designs aren't done because it is up to them how they want them to look. They're our best friends'. Travis and Mick are handling their own builds, paying for their own houses to be built. Tyson and I have worked out an arrangement."

"No, I will pay for Tyson's house. It is the least I can do for all he's done for me."

I smile and kiss him. "I had a feeling you'd say that."

"The entire lot is about sixty acres and is on the outskirts of L.A. I needed an escape from the city, but...turn the page."

He turns the page and he quickly realizes what he's looking at. "Cameron Celeste, are you kidding me?"

I laugh. "No. I love the ocean and the beach too much."

He kisses me again. The front side of the house faces west, and about fifty yards away is a beach and the ocean. "I know this is a gift, Cams, but how much is this going to cost?" I knew that was coming — I'm not dumb — but I'm not sure if he is going to like my answer.

"The property or the build?" I stall.

"Let's start with the property. Sixty acres of oceanfront property in California is — wow, Cams, that's huge."

"Well, it is technically two lots. The lot that our house is on, ending about here—" I point on the map to the middle of the pool. "—is the only 'ocean front' part of the property. That property set me back—" I pause and scrunch up my nose. I don't want to tell him. "—about eighteen million."

"Jesus. And the other lot?"

"Six."

"Million?" I nod. "And the build?"

"That depends. Estimates right now — for the build only, no equipment or furniture or anything — stand at about fourteen." I flinch, hoping that he doesn't freak out on me, considering that the price tag, right now, stands at forty million.

I can see the shock on his face. "You cannot afford this."

I stand. Money is not something that Tristan and I have talked about and I'm not sure he truly understands my wealth. But I guess now is the time to really explain it to him.

"Tristan, take a seat." He looks at me. "Up on the couch." I grab a cigarette off of the mantel across from him and light it. I take a deep drag and hold it, just for a second, composing myself. "We've never talked about this, mainly because, as far as you're concerned, I don't feel it is my business to know your financial situation. But I do know that if you can afford Magic Mick to do your financials you're not poor, and even if you were, it wouldn't matter to me." I look at him, hoping to get the message to him that I love him for him, not for his career and certainly not for his money. I think he understands, so I continue. "When Bobby died, for the lack of a shorter explanation, I was left with what I thought was half of his net worth. At least now I know it was probably only about a third, given his current living situation. Anyway—" I take another drag; I'm getting off track. "—the money I've spent so far, and will spend to build this house, does not even begin to eat up the money I inherited from him. It barely makes a dent, and I am more or less using interest that I've earned on that money to build this house." I look at him and his eyes widen a bit.

"How much are you talking about?"

"Are you sure you want the answer to that question?" His hesitant nod says more than his words do. "Two hundred million dollars."

"Jesus," he blurts.

"Mick has invested the majority of it, and the money I spent on my condo in Phoenix and that I spend on a daily basis comes primarily from my trust money, which is far more than I ever needed in a lifetime to begin with. Couple that with my own shares in Bold, complements of Bobby's disappearing act, and I make on average about fifty grand an hour and I do nothing to earn it. So to answer your question, yes, without a doubt I can afford this house, and a whole lot more."

He doesn't say anything for some time, and I do not blame him for that at all. I finish my cigarette and light another one. He is watching me, wondering what I'm thinking, no doubt, and right now, I am concerned that I've freaked him out.

I let him sit there until I'm done with my second cigarette and then I can take the silence no more. "Say something," I blurt.

He doesn't say anything for a few more seconds, and they feel like hours. "I had no idea."

"You had no idea because flaunting my money is not something I do, Tristan. It is what it is, and there is nothing I can do about it. Short of give it all away to charity or something like that. But it is a part of who I am, and it will always be such." I watch him carefully.

"Well your money has nothing to do with why I love you, if that's something you're concerned about."

I shake my head. "No, it's more that I'm concerned that I've freaked you out. That you—that...I don't know."

"That I feel inadequate?"

"That's a good word for it."

"No, I don't feel inadequate about your wealth, though my own wealth is like pocket change, compared to yours. And it washes away all the worries I had in regards to the bar."

"You were worried I couldn't afford the bar? Is that why you haven't been that excited about it?" I ask, and he nods. "Well, I've already made that amount of money plus, just from Bold, since I told you about it. So no, the bar is not at all a loss in my book. While I'd love to hand my friends money left and right, I don't believe that they would like it very much, and the subject of money always comes between friends and I don't like it. Beau knows, of course, because of Mick. Jolene has an idea and I'm sure Naomi does too. Look, it's not a big deal, and more than anything it doesn't drive who I am. Sure, I like nice clothes and expensive shoes. I carry expensive purses and I indulge when it comes to things like spending some time in Tarah with you. But at the end of the day, Tristan, I am still me, and I've worked very hard to keep that because I don't want to throw my money around and I don't want people to take advantage of me or my generosity."

He leans forward on the couch, putting his elbows on his knees, and I can tell that he's lost in thought. He doesn't stay that way for long. "The amount of money you have doesn't change a thing about how I feel about you." He looks up at me standing on the other side of the table, and my heart grows a little bigger for him in that moment and I realize that I love him even more than I thought was ever going to be possible.

TWENTY-SEVEN

******
Tristan
******

"You have another present to open," she tells me, and it brings me out of my haze after learning what I've just learned about Cami. I had no idea she had that much money. I knew she was wealthy, that much was obvious, but not *that* wealthy.

"I haven't finished looking at the plans yet," I say and smirk at her.

"They're kind of boring, really. Just overall layout designs of the kitchen and the patio, which includes a built-in grill and bar." She smiles at me. "We can look at them later. Or discuss them with the designer."

"Who might that be?" I ask her with an all-knowing grin on my face.

"Take a wild guess." She laughs.

"Beau."

"Who else? She's bloody brilliant at what she does." And just like that her British accent rings true to form. It's

182

been a while since I've heard it...or I've just really gotten used to it.

"That she is." I grab for the smaller package. "This isn't keys to some sports car, is it?"

She laughs. "No, but if you want one..."

"I'll buy it myself," I say with a big grin and a chuckle.

I tear into the package, and the box inside says Rolex. She got me a watch? I smile and open the box. Inside is a silver-faced, black-banded watch. It's good sized, too, but what catches my attention the most is that the face isn't a typical watch face, but it is a holographic image of Cami. It's the picture that is on the background of my phone and computer. But the image is such that you have to be looking straight at it in order to actually see it. "Cami, it's beautiful."

"You like it?"

"I love it." I stand up from the couch and walk around the table, embracing her and kissing her like there's no tomorrow. She laughs, ending my attempt to try and take her back to bed. "It's perfect. Thank you." I kiss her again and then reach for the box, pulling the watch free of its padded cushioning and unbuckling it. "Help me," I say, though I don't actually need her help with it. She does and she buckles it onto my wrist. I look at it, checking the time. It's just after one, but I can't stop staring at her face on the watch.

"I didn't know how you'd feel about walking around with me around your wrist. So when I was talking to the designer about it, he suggested this concept. It's one of a kind, not only because of my picture, but it is the first one they've ever come up with." She smiles and I can hear the pride in her voice.

"It's perfect. Thank you so much." I kiss her again.

Just then I hear the door chime and I know that our time alone has come to a close.

"The girls do not know about the house."

"What?"

"The boys agreed to unveil it to them after you'd seen it. So leave the plans. They've all already received theirs as well."

"Okay," I say as I go to the door and open it. Beyond it is the entire gang, and they all serenade me with an awful rendition of "Happy Birthday" as they file into the penthouse.

It doesn't take long before everyone realizes that Cami has already given me my birthday present, and we spend the afternoon hanging around the pool, having a good time and talking about the house plans.

Cami is very animated with her friends, and it strikes me that something might actually be bothering her. But I don't want to spoil the fun everyone is having by pulling her away to talk about it.

Shortly before sunset, we all leave the penthouse and go out to the entrance of the hotel. Sitting there, waiting for us, are two Jeeps. "Where are we going?" I ask.

Cami wraps her arms around me. "It's a surprise."

We all climb in and we're off. I half expected the docks and a boat, but we actually go to the south side of the island, rather than the north where the boats are.

When we arrive on the beach there is a bonfire going, surround by logs, and off to the right is a table set out for dinner. I smile when I see Jessie manning the bar, waiting for us.

Everyone climbs out of the cars, and I pull Cami toward me. She starts before I can. "You said you wanted something small, and after I talked to Trav and Ty about your birthday, I discovered that neither one of them knew when it was." She gives me a look that tells me she understands. "So, I thought tonight we'd spend it having dinner on the beach and hanging around the bonfire. Just the eight of us."

I kiss her. "It's perfect. Thank you."

She smiles and leads me toward the table, where we all gather around. I look at the group of people before me — everyone laughing and having an amazing time. I can't understand it completely, but I am filled with an overwhelming amount of love and support that I never thought existed...or even realized I was missing in my life. Then suddenly Cami's house plans all make sense. We're a family. All of us. Whether we have our own families someplace else, we, right here, are one big huge family, and I want nothing more than to have every one of them around me for the rest of my life.

TWENTY-EIGHT

Before we know it, our friends have already left, our two weeks in Tarah have come to a close, and Cami and I are back in Phoenix with only a few days to spare before I head off to New York. Cami is staying here — well, on this side of the country, at least — for a couple of days. We both agreed on the plans for the house, so she is going to California to get that started and also to deal with the pressing issues of Bold and Vincent. But I managed to convince her to stay in Phoenix at least until I leave. I don't want to miss any time I can spend with her.

Our two weeks in Tarah were refreshing on the levels of needing to be able to reconnect with one another, to forgo life for a while, and we're very good about doing that in Tarah. After the two weeks we spent together and all the talking we've done, I am starting to feel closer than ever to her, and I am starting to feel truly happy about wanting all the things she has lined up for us: the house in California and the bar here in Phoenix. Though her confidence regarding the bar is wavering slightly, I think our pep talks about it have helped; at least that is my hope.

"I hate that you're leaving again."

"You can always come with me."

"I know, but I can't put this off any longer, I need to deal with Vincent, and then, to top that off, I need to get things started on the house. When I'm done with that, I'll come to New York and spend the rest of your filming days with you."

"Sounds good to me." I kiss her and grab my bags. "Ready?"

"No. I hate this, you know that."

I smile at her. "I know, but it's a few days, then we have until March before I'm scheduled on another set. But by then you're going to be busy with Bold and I'll be the one waiting for you."

"Don't hold your breath," she says as we climb into the car. "Oh, I forgot to tell you."

"What's that?"

"Mick and Beau have set a date."

"Oh, and it is what?"

She laughs. "Valentine's Day."

I laugh with her. "That doesn't surprise me, though I expected something like eleven, twelve, thirteen or something like that."

"Hey, just be glad I convinced them to skip the Justice of the Peace. Plus, if we push it, the bar might be ready by then and they can get married there."

I laugh. "Why the bar?"

"You know them, they don't want anything over the top, they want to just get married and be done with it. If the house were going to be done by then, I'm sure they'd do it there. But at this point we'll be lucky if we have it by May."

I shrug. "I'm in no hurry."

She smiles at me. "At least I know where I want to get married."

This surprises me and I look at her in mock shock. "Oh really, Madam Enders, where might that be?"

She gives me a one-word answer: "Tarah."

"Penthouse or beach."

"Beach, sunset."

"I see you've already planned this out." I can't help the overwhelming warmth I feel at her talk of getting married. Especially considering everything she's said so far is only consistent with me. It means she's never thought about this until now.

"All except the date."

"Shouldn't you get engaged first? You know, before you start planning your dream wedding?" She punches me in the thigh. "Ouch." She busts out laughing. "Subtle hint received." I hold up my hands in defense and she laughs.

Our routine at the airport this time is no different than the last time, only this time she's crying a little harder. I can't help but wonder what that's all about. But I don't question it, and faster than I realize, Tyson and I are in first class, one way to New York City. I don't think I could get further away from Cami if I tried, and with each passing minute, the ache in my heart grows and I miss her already.

TWENTY-NINE

******
Cami
******

"Ugh," I say as I scramble out of bed and head straight for the toilet, where I unload the contents of my nearly empty stomach. I try and think about what would've caused this except for the fact that Beau and I went out to dinner at a new restaurant last night. But once I'm done, I feel a little bit better. I crawl back into bed and lie down. Before I know it, I'm sound asleep.

I call Beau around eleven, after I've woken up again. Though I don't throw up, I don't feel much better. "Hey, girl," I say when she answers.

"Hey, wench."

I roll my eyes. "Are you feeling okay?"

"Yeah, I'm fine, why?" she says. I can hear her concern.

"I think whatever I ate last night doesn't agree with me. I feel like crap."

"Do you have anything to do today?"

"Not really, other than pack for tomorrow, but it can wait until tomorrow."

"Then I'd just take it easy today, see how you feel tomorrow."

"All right. Need me, call me," I say.

"Will do." And she's gone.

I lie back down in bed and continue to doze off and on throughout the day. Finally around three I start to feel better, and I get up and go downstairs. I make myself some toast and grab a seat on the couch. I start flipping through channels and end up watching — against my better judgment - the first *Love is Burning* movie; though I've read the books, I've never seen the movie. Tristan will kill me if he knows I'm watching this. But I can't help it.

About an hour into the movie my phone rings. It's Tristan. "Hi, beautiful," I say before he can beat me to it.

"Hi beautiful yourself. How are you?"

"Tired and lazy."

"Oh, late night last night?"

I debate whether or not to tell him about my being sick this morning, but it's just what I ate, so I tell him.

"Babe, why didn't you call me?"

I roll my eyes. "You're in New York, what were you gonna do?"

"Good point."

"Don't worry about it. I think I just ate something last night. I went out to eat with Beau to some new place she's been wanting to try."

"Is she sick?"

"No, but we ate different things, so I'm not surprised."

"Did you drink?" he asks.

"Nope, just had water and tea." I haven't drunk anything since my last binge in Montana, which is probably a good thing. Tristan brought it up when we were in Tarah and I told him that I just didn't feel like drinking.

"Well, take it easy and get some rest. What time is your flight tomorrow?"

"Oh, I am. I'm watching a movie. My flight is at four."

"Okay, I should be able to call you before you leave. But please, call or text me if you're not feeling well. What movie?"

Oops. "Not much you can do from NYC, love." I avoid the movie question.

"I know, but I worry about you. What movie?"

Relentless bastard. "Calling you while I'm sick will only make that worse. But I will let you know how I'm feeling, how's that?"

"All right, what movie?"

"You're relentless and you don't want me to answer that."

"You better not be watching one of my movies."

"Maybe." I bust out laughing.

"Oh, I see how you are, laughing at my movies."

I sober. "No, Tristan, I'm laughing because you automatically assume it's one of yours."

"Then tell me what movie."

I laugh again. "It's actually a very good movie. Though I think I'm falling in love with the lead actor. He's quite sexy, and I happen to know that he knows very well how to use his sexiness, which makes it that much more sexy."

"Grrrr..."

"I love it when you growl."

"Grrrr..." He laughs. "I thought you said you never wanted to see my movies."

"Um, well, there wasn't anything else on."

"Oh, great, so now I'm second best." He is laughing on the other end of phone.

"No, you're the best, ever."

He laughs a little more. "All right, sweets, I have to go back on set. Call you later?"

"Please."

"All right, love you."

"Ditto," I say, and we hang up.

I wake up the same on Sunday morning, but because I'm leaving, I don't lie around in bed. I get up and start packing, but I quickly become exhausted. Before I can even begin to try and figure out what this is, Beau shows up to take me to the airport.

"You don't look good," she says when I climb into her car, putting my bag between my feet on the floor.

"Good to see you too."

"Are you sure you're okay?"

"Yeah, I'm just really tired. I don't sleep well when Tristan isn't here."

"That's not it. Cams, are you sure—"

"I'm fine, I'll be fine. I have got to go and take care of this crap, I can't keep letting it bug me. I'll take something when I get to California to help me sleep."

She looks at me out of the corner of her eye. She's watching me like she's afraid of something. I don't say any more about it, and it takes us but a few minutes to get to the airport from the condo. I hug her goodbye, and I'm through security and on the plane in a matter of thirty minutes.

But something Beau said is nagging at me. I pull out my MacBook and begin looking at the calendar. It's October seventh. There's very little on my calendar for October, at least outside of Tristan being in New York. I click back to September. Nothing. August is a little fuller with the trip to Montana and my documentation of what happened, but...

August 2nd, 2012 - 1:45 p.m. Dr. Shaw

My heart starts pounding and my palms start sweating as I realize what I missed. I start counting the months and days, at least until the flight attendant tells me to stow it for takeoff.

Getting my period or not getting it is nothing new: I've been on the shot since I was seventeen. I don't get periods unless I miss an appointment. The skipped appointment was supposed to be in November, to give myself a chance to...

I start to think, think about anything and everything that could've possibly—

No, there's no way.

Is it?

I land in L.A., but rather than take a cab to the hotel, I rent a car and stop at a Target along the way. I run in, hoping like hell that my jacket, glasses, rasta beanie and the less-than-elegant clothes I'm wearing stop me from being recognized. Though I'm a long way from Hollywood, this is California, and people snoop out celebs like nobody's business.

I'm wearing my skinny jeans, which, if I really think about it, were a little snug this morning. Not beyond wearing but— Damn it.

I go to the family planning section of Target and grab two boxes each of two different pregnancy tests, then go to the grocery section and pick up a couple of bottles of water and go to checkout.

After a few minutes I am back in the car. The white bag on the passenger seat taunts me on my drive from Target to the JW downtown.

Once I'm in my room, I start to panic a little more. Should I take it now or wait? I look at the box for instructions; I've never taken one before, but I've helped Beau before. Though I still have no clue about it.

The instructions say that I should use my first morning's urine. "Damn it." I really don't want to wait. "You have four of them." I talk myself into it. And I do; I open it and do the whole pee-on-a-stick thing. Then I sit there panicking. I finally manage to pull myself out of the bathroom and away from the ominous stick sitting on the counter.

When I go into the bedroom, where my stuff is, I remember that I never turned on my phone when I landed; I was too freaked out. I go to it and turn it on. After a few moments it chimes with two missed calls, two voicemails, and then finally three text messages.

Hope you made it to L.A. safe. Love you.
Cams, where are you?
Call me.

The last one was sent just a few moments ago, as my phone was loading.

"Hi," I say when he picks up the phone.

"Hi, beautiful. Did you make it?"

"Uh, yeah, I forgot to turn my phone on." That's all I can manage. I keep looking over at the bathroom, wanting to go in there.

"What's wrong?"

"What? Oh, nothing."

"You're distracted, what's the matter?"

"Nothing, just tired and reading through emails." That should do it.

"All right. I'm shooting late tonight, but can I call you when I'm done?"

"Of course." Hopefully by then I will be relieved because that test will be done and negative and I can relax.

"All right, sweets. I miss you."

Crap. "I miss you too."

"I love you." His voice is sweet, and something about it is reassuring me.

"I love you."

We hang up, and I stand there staring at the light coming out of the bathroom. It's like the light at the end of a big, long tunnel: I'm drawn to it, but I can't bring myself to walk toward it.

THIRTY

"Hey, Beau."

"Hi, Tristan. What's going on?"

"Did you take Cami to the airport today?" I ask her. I know she did, but I'm just trying to make sure.

"Um, yeah, why?"

"Was she okay when you saw her?"

She doesn't answer my question. "Why, what's wrong?"

I roll my eyes and hold my finger up to one of the stagehands. "Listen, I need to go, but when I called her a minute ago, she seemed frazzled and distracted."

"She didn't look that well when I picked her up. But she said it was nothing."

"She wasn't feeling good this morning?" I ask. "She didn't say anything to me."

"I'm not sure, she shut me down when I asked her. But I'm not surprised she didn't tell you, you're in New York, not much you can do."

She sounds just like Cami when she says that. "I know but I still worry about her."

"I know. I'll try calling her and I'll let you know what I find out."

"Thanks, but don't tell her I'm prying."

"All right, Tristan, I won't."

"Thanks."

We hang up. I walk back toward the set and hand Tyson my phone. "What's going on?" he asks.

"Later," I say and step on set, instantly turning off everything in order to do my job, just so I can get this over with and call her back.

"So what's up?" Tyson asks as we're walking back to my trailer.

"Cami seemed off when I talked to her."

"Dude, don't push on her too hard. What she's planning to do tomorrow can't be easy on her."

He has a good point, and I try and shake it off a little. I look at my phone: two text messages.

She seemed off when I talked to her too, but no info to share. Sorry, will talk to her tomorrow after her meeting.

I type a quick reply to Beau.

Thanks, let me know if you hear anything. Appreciate it.

I flip to the next text.

I'm fine. Promise. Just freaked about tmrw. I'm tired & gonna lay down, tlk 2mrw? Love you.

I take some comfort in her text. Though I'm sad she doesn't want a phone call, I can understand. Then I look at the time and realize it's nearly one in the morning here. That's ten in California. Still early for Cami to go to bed.

No problem. She'll be all right.
I knw. Thnks

Tyson and I get back to the hotel and make our way through the screaming girls on the sidewalk and up into my room. This is why I hate filming in New York: Everyone seems to know right where you are and where to find you when you're not someplace they expect you to be. No doubt the pictures from my coming home are spreading like wildfire across the web.

I wish Tyson goodnight, go into my bedroom and plop down on the bed. I'm worn out, and quickly fall sound asleep.

THIRTY-ONE

Freaking out, that's hardly the half of it. I hardly slept last night and I kept wanting to call Tristan. Then I received a news alert, and there was an article about Tristan returning to his hotel around one this morning, and after that I couldn't sleep. I knew when I talked to him he said he was working late, so I didn't dwell on it too much, and I hated the overly jealous streak that arose as I clicked through some of the pictures. But despite the pictures, I could see the worry in his features and no doubt that is because of me.

"You have good reason to worry, Tristan."

I'd managed to fall back to sleep around three, only to wake up around eight by a turning stomach, and I rush to the bathroom. "Get used to it," I tell myself. God, what am I going to do? Tristan — he is going to be so mad, I just know it. I was so stupid. How could I even begin to forget about my appointment? That's always been a huge priority to me and it slipped my mind and slipped my calendar. "Damn it."

After throwing up twice, I lie back down and start dozing off and on for a while until my phone chimes with a text from Tristan.

On set, long day ahead. Hope you're feeling better, good luck today. Love you.

I sigh. Feeling better? Absolutely not.

Skipping office today, meeting with builders around 1. Not sleeping well. Miss you. Love you.

It's true: I miss him like crazy, and I wish he were here, telling me it's all right, but...it's not. I know it's not. How could I be so stupid.

Wish you were here.

I give my phone a half smile, but I'm glad he's not calling me. I don't know how to talk to him right now. What am I going to do?

The meeting with the house builders goes great and they've assured me that I can expect an initial layout walkthrough around the middle of February, and they will be breaking ground on Thursday. I'm surprised by how quickly they're getting started, but I imagine this is a pretty big, expensive job and they're anxious to get started. Working with them and seeing the house and the layout again makes me think of everything I've learned in less than twenty-four hours, and it terrifies me to no end. I'm worn out and exhausted by the time I get back to the hotel. Before I can even manage to text Tristan, I fall asleep on the bed on top of the sheets.

When I wake up it is nearly midnight and I look at my phone. Thirty-seven missed calls. A combination of Tristan and Beau. Oh, for crying out loud. I need to get my shit together.

I try calling Tristan and he doesn't answer. I doubt he's sleeping — at least, if he is freaking out about me. I call Beau. She answers immediately.

"Where the hell have you been? I was about to get on a plane to L.A."

"Oh, for Pete's sake. Chill. I'm fine. I'm still not feeling good, and after I met with the builders I came back to the hotel and passed out on the bed. On top of the sheets, still in my clothes."

"Something is not right with you, Cameron. You need to go to the doctor." No, I don't; I know exactly what's wrong with me.

"No, I'll be fine."

"Damn it, Cameron. Are you pregnant?" Holy fuck. How the hell? I hesitate long enough in answering her question; I don't want to lie to her. "Oh my God, Cams. Seriously?" She doesn't sound pissed, at least not like I thought she would.

"I—"

"That would explain it."

"What do you mean?"

"The vomiting, your exhaustion. You're distracted. Cams, talk to me." I start balling on the phone with her; I can't help it. "Babe, oh, please don't cry."

"I can't help it," I manage to say between quite ugly crying.

"You missed an appointment, didn't you?"

"Yeah," I ball.

"Stop crying. Is this why you're avoiding Tristan?"

"I'm not avoiding him. I just...I'm freaking the fuck out, Beau."

"Want me to come out there?"

"No. I need some time to get my head wrapped around this. Figure out how I'm going to tell Tristan."

"Are you scared of the fact that you're pregnant, or what Tristan will think?"

"Both," I say as I wipe the tears from my cheeks.

"Cams, Tristan isn't that kind of guy. He's not going to leave you or hate you. Believe me."

"I'm trying, Beau, I'm just...I'm so confused."

"Take a deep breath. Your secret is perfectly safe with me. I won't tell him, but if you don't want him further freaking out on you, you need to pull yourself together and talk to him. Or placate him. Tell him you're going to the doctor in the morning because of how sick you feel. Something — just help him to understand that you're okay. He can't do anything from New York, so make him feel comfortable. All right?"

I take a deep breath. "All right, I'll figure something out." My phone beeps. "He's calling me."

"I'm sure he is, he's really worried about you."

"All right, I'll talk to you later."

"Kisses," she says, and she's gone. I click the swap button on my phone.

"Cams, are you all right?"

I take a deep breath and yawn. "Yes, I'm fine."

"Where have you been?"

"I didn't sleep for shit last night. And when I got back from meeting with the builders, I fell asleep on top of my covers."

"Why didn't my calls wake you up?"

Shit, I don't know. I look at my phone. "Because it is still on vibrate. Shit, Tristan, I'm sorry."

I hear him take a deep breath. "It's all right," he whispers, and I can hear him yawn.

"You need to get back to sleep. We can talk in the morning. Go get some sleep. I miss you and I love you."

"Ah hell, Cams, I love you too. Will you come tomorrow after you're done at the office?"

Crap. I need some more time. "Let me see what time I get done. If not tomorrow, I will come Wednesday. Okay?"

"Sooner, please. I need you. I miss you."

The tears start again. "I miss you too. I love you."

"Ditto."

"I need you to say it."

"I love you," he says, so soft and so sweet that the tears come a little harder. "Call when you wake up? Please?"

I nod, then realize he can't hear my head shake. "Yes. I will."

"Goodnight, sweets."

"Goodnight."

The conversation ends, and before I can have a complete crying fit, I go into the bathroom, then change into some more comfortable clothes. I stand in front of the mirror, trying to see if anything is any different, and it doesn't really look that way.

I climb back into bed and let the waterworks fall until I fall asleep again.

THIRTY-TWO

"Good morning, Rayne," I say to my assistant as I step into the waiting room of my office floor.

"Ms. Enders— I mean Cami. To what do we owe the pleasure."

"Surprise inspection."

Rayne laughs. "Yes, ma'am. Trinity is in her office."

"I need to talk to Vinnie, actually."

"I haven't seen him yet this morning, but that doesn't mean he's not here. Check his office first."

"That's where I'm headed."

I walk past her desk and head down the hallway. Trinity sees me walking past her office. "Cami," she shouts after me.

"Later, Trin." I take three steps past her office and then I stop in my tracks and take a few steps back. "Actually, come with me," I say, and she stands up and grabs her jacket. "Leave the coat. We're only going to Vinnie's office."

"Uh, I haven't seen him this morning."

"He's here. Come on." She scurries out of her office and down the hall with me to Vincent's door. I pause momentarily, taking a deep breath, hoping to keep myself in check during this encounter.

We reach Vincent's door and I knock twice. "Come in, Cami."

"See," I say to Trinity as I open the door. I step inside first; Trinity is hot on my heels, curious, no doubt, as to what has me so worked up. I get an eyeful of one man sitting on a couch inside the office, and I damn near turn around to push Trinity out the door, deciding that this might not be the best idea I've ever had, but fuck it. Sitting opposite my father is Vinnie.

Trinity gasps behind me, and I can hear the breath leave her lungs. Thankfully she falls against the door, and it's now closed.

"Well done, Cami," Bobby says from the couch. His irritation is obvious and I don't care.

I shake my head. "You're the one sitting in Vinnie's office, anyone could walk in here. How the hell did you get in here without being noticed?" I pause but don't give him time to answer. "Never mind, I don't want to know." I turn toward Trinity, who is as white as a ghost. "Breathe, Trin." She takes a sharp breath, then another. "Welcome to my life," I say, sarcasm dripping off of every word.

She looks at me with big eyes. "How did you know?"

"How did you?" I ask her back.

"I didn't. I—" She looks past me at Bobby. "It's like looking at a ghost."

"Pretty much. But how I know is not important, what is important is that I'd only known for a couple weeks that there was a possibility that this could really be true until a month ago, when I saw him in the flesh."

"I need to sit down," she says as she steps gingerly toward the couch that Vinnie is sitting on.

"So what now, Bobby, are you making a grand return to Bold?"

"Stop that right now." Bobby stands and stalks toward me, forcing me back into the corner Trinity was just standing in.

"I came here to deal with Vinnie on my own, and I walk in to find you."

"Which is exactly why I'm here. You can't fire him. I made him do it, and it has eaten him alive every single day since. Do not be angry with him. Be mad at me."

"I already am." He backs away, straightening himself out. "So what now? I finally feel I am actually ready for this job, in a loose interpretation of that, at least, and now you want back in?" I ask Bobby as he takes his seat on the couch.

"We can't do that. The board will have a shit fit, not to mention the fact that we would have to pay back the insurance money and Bold's reputation would go down the drain. Once that happened, it'd be all downhill from there. Sure, we've reestablished our client list and we've turned the largest profit in over ten years, but that doesn't mean we are anywhere near stable enough to consider bringing Bobby out of the woodwork." Vincent seems to have this all under control.

"You both realize that I could have gone the rest of my life without knowing he was alive, right? That I didn't need him pushing me silently from the mountains in Montana?"

"I won't be in Montana long. They've started rounding up what we talked about." He gives me a look of, 'Keep your mouth shut. "So I'm going further into hiding."

"Great, so what exactly was the point of making your presence known if you never had an intention of coming back?"

"That is a conversation for you and I to have. Alone and on a different day. Not here." I glare at Bobby.

Trinity just sits there, quietly staring at Bobby, who is now staring back at her. It clicks, and I know my eyes get wide when realization dawns. I want to scream. "Are you kidding me right now?" I put my hands in my hair and grab hold, bringing myself out of the rage I feel like flying into. "Un-fucking-believable."

"Wha—"

"Jesus, Vinnie, you're fucking dense, aren't you. Look at them. Oh my God. I am getting new furniture in my office, PRONTO!"

"We never did it in his office."

"Thank fuck for that."

"Watch your mouth."

I bust out laughing. "You're kidding me, right? How long, Bobby?"

"How long what?"

"What? How long were you fucking her?"

"Damn it, Cameron, calm down."

"Just when I thought you couldn't drop any more bombs on me. This is great. I feel like I'm stuck in the middle of a damn conspiracy theory here." I take a deep breath in desperation to calm myself down. Everything in my life up to this moment feels like a smokescreen. Rose-colored glasses being shattered into a million tiny little pieces. Robert is alive, and in hiding, verses actually being dead. Though now I don't know that I truly understand his reason for hiding in the first place. Yeah, okay, I get it: He was trying to protect me. But if he was going into hiding as though he were dead, why not just be dead and everyone's life could go on. "Your web of lies stops right here, right now," I nearly growl at Bobby. "I don't care what your reasons were for doing what you did, I don't care how or why. I'm exhausted, and all I want to do is turn all of this off...or wake up from this goddamn nightmare you've created for me." Watching the way Trinity is reacting to my yelling at Bobby makes me see what I was failing to see for all these months. "Oh my God!" I nearly shout when I realize that there is more between Trinity and Bobby, more than even Bobby is no doubt aware of. I am staring at Trinity now. Our eyes meet, and she pleads and begs me to not say it, to not say anything. She knows what conclusion I've come to. "He doesn't know?"

"Cami, don't, I'm begging you."

"Don't what?" Bobby chimes in to our private conversation.

"Do it, Trinity, or I will." More frustration and anger wash over me. On top of everything else, I can't handle this. My father had an affair with Trinity, and— *HOLY FUCK!* I shout in my head.

"No. I won't do it." Trinity is beyond adamant. Trying desperately to stand up, to come after me, to stop me.

"The depth of the depravity in this room is un-fucking-believable." I turn and open the door, head back the way I came and barge into Trinity's office. It is exactly where I expect it to be. I grab the little silver frame off of her desk and go back to Vincent's office.

Trinity sees what I have in my hands and she reaches for me and for the picture. "Dammit, Cami, don't do this. I don't even know—"

"You don't even know if it's his. Well let me enlighten you. It is!" I turn the picture frame over and I hear Bobby gasp. "From the moment I first saw his picture, I knew there was something familiar about it, but I was far too blind to see it. Or refused to see it. You never told him you were pregnant, did you?"

Trinity slinks onto the couch, tears streaking down her face. "I never found the courage to tell him. When I finally built it up enough, he was gone."

"He was gone and left you with nothing. No money, no anything besides your job, and right now I have half a mind to fire both of you. And you—" I look at Bobby. "Don't fuck him up the way you fucked me up."

I throw the picture frame onto the couch next to Bobby, and I barely see him pick it up before I am slamming the door and walking down the hallway. I fly past Rayne and hit the stairs — I'm not waiting for the elevator — and I am thankful that Bobby is trapped in that room, otherwise he'd be coming after me.

I pull my phone from my pocket. Please don't pick up, don't pick up. Dammit, don't pick up. "You know what to do." Thank God!

THIRTY-THREE

******
Tristan
******

"Do we know what time Cami is taking off?"

"Not sure. She said she was going to the airport when she was done." Tyson is reassuring me. The last time I checked my phone was this morning before we started filming, more than eight hours ago, and she was getting to the office.

"Tristan." I turn around and it is one of the student directors. "We need to do one more scene."

I roll my eyes. "All right, but then I'm done." It's already after ten and Cami should be in the air by now. I turn back toward the set and get ready to reshoot one of the scenes. Pyrotechnics are not my strong suit, and they've been the cause of so many of our retakes today.

Another hour and a half goes by and I'm finally back in my trailer. "Let me wash up and change and we'll get out of here."

"Sure thing," Tyson says as I head into the bedroom and close the door.

Once I'm showered, the makeup's gone, and the clothes changed, Tyson and I walk out of the trailer. We're about fifty feet away when I go searching for my phone. "Shit. I'll be right back." I turn around and run back into the trailer, grab my phone off of the bed and press the button, lighting up the screen.

1 Missed Call

I slide the button; it's Cami. From one this afternoon. I roll my eyes at not checking it sooner. She's left me a voicemail. I click the button and press play.

"Tristan, I'm sorry, I can't do this anymore. If you want to blame someone, blame Bobby. I'm sorry, I love you."

The call ends and I can tell that she's out of breath, like she's running.

I sink onto the bed and it is probably not three minutes before Tyson is pounding on the door. "Come on, man. I wanna see Jo." I feel the trailer shake as he climbs inside. "Shit, what's wrong with you?"

I don't say anything; I just replay the voicemail.

"Tristan, I'm sorry, I can't do this anymore. If you want to blame someone, blame Bobby. I'm sorry, I love you."

"She's gone."

"Dammit, get up. She ain't either." He grabs his phone, presses a button. "Jo, have you heard from Cami about her flight?" He listens. "Okay, we'll be back soon.... Oh, I'll let him know. Thanks, babe."

He clicks a couple buttons on his phone. "Hi, Scott, I need Cameron Enders's room, please." Pause. "What? When? Okay, thanks." He turns to me. "She checked out of the hotel around eleven this morning. Where's Bobby's information?"

"Wha—?"

"The information he gave you that day?"

"Back at the hotel, on my laptop. Why? What's going on?"

"Nothing yet. Give me a minute." I watch as he clicks a few more buttons on his phone.

"Mick, we need to put a tracer on Cami. Find out what flight to New York she was on." There is a pause as he listens to Mick. "All right, thanks, we'll be at the hotel shortly."

"Hotel?" I ask, trying to follow his thought process with who he's calling, but my world has stopped spinning.

"Beau and Mick showed up at the hotel a few hours ago, but Mick knows nothing of Cami buying a ticket. He's looking into it."

"Fuck! She's gone. I fucking know it. That son of bitch did or said something to her and it's freaked her out."

I stand up, and Tyson and I go running out of the trailer and to the car. I climb into the driver's seat and drive toward the hotel. Tyson doesn't say anything, which is a good thing because— Damn it all to hell. "I'll kill him."

"No you won't."

"Why not? He wouldn't be missed, he's already 'dead.'"

Tyson doesn't say anything the rest of the drive.

"What's my schedule look like?" I ask him when we're in the elevator.

"Um, you're on set tomorrow morning, then you're supposed to be off until Friday afternoon. What are you thinking?"

"I want to go to Montana. I want to kick his ass."

I try calling Cami, over and over again, and all I get is voicemail. We got stuck in traffic trying to get to the hotel. Fucking New York.

I call Mick. He answers on the first ring. "Tristan, I'm tracking her cell phone, it's at the house in Phoenix. I called Naomi and told her to go and check on the house. I'm waiting for her to call back."

"Will she stay in Phoenix?"

"I doubt it. I am trying her financials. Tristan, she pulled out a hundred grand in cash, cashier's and traveler's checks from her account. She's going off the grid completely. I don't have much hope that we will find her in the house in Phoe— ix."

"What was that?"

"Naomi, she's at the house."

"We'll be at the hotel in a few minutes." I hit end and try Cami's cell again. This time no voicemail. "Cami."

"Jeez, Tristan, no, it's Naomi. Her phone is here, and the house is trashed. She left in a big damn hurry." Damn it.

"Where would she go?"

"I don't know, Tristan, I'm looking for any sign of where she may have gone. The only thing I see is that her second passport is gone."

"Thanks, Naomi. Can you stay there, at the house, in case she comes back?"

"Trav is on his way here from San Diego now."

"Thanks."

I try to think my way through this. A second passport. I didn't— "That's it!"

I grab my phone and call Trinity. She answers on the second ring. "Tristan?"

"What's on her second passport?"

"Excuse me?"

"Cami's second passport, the one Bold made for her so she could travel anonymously. What's the name?"

"What's the opposite of yours, Tristan?"

"Dammit, I don't have time for games, Trinity." Then it hits me. "Velma Kelley."

"You got it," she says, and I hang up the phone.

We're pulling up in front of the hotel and I go running up the walk to the door and throw it wide. I bypass the elevator and take the stairs; Tyson is right behind me and we enter the room. "Search for passengers leaving Phoenix or L.A. under the name of Velma Kelley."

"What?" Mick and Beau say in unison.

"It's the name on her other passport. Velma Kelley. Just because she used cash to pay for her ticket doesn't mean she doesn't have to give them her name."

Mick turns to his laptop and punches in a few things on the keyboard.

I can hear the sound of an internet search. It's so cliché, and it feels like I am suddenly in a movie. Then after a minute, the laptop beeps. "Where?"

"New York. But she's already here, flight landed over an hour ago."

"Search New York, all airports. She won't stay here," I say, anxiety taking over. While the computer searches, Beau tries to calm me down.

"You don't know she won't stay. She may have changed her mind."

"She came into New York on cash and with her anonymous passport, Beau, she won't stay." I just want to break down, to scream, to cry, to...I don't know what, but dammit, I've got to find her.

The search of all the New York airports for all possible names yields nothing, and she doesn't show up at the hotel. Tyson convinces me that I have to go to work the next day. He calls in reinforcements to help keep an eye on me. The only reason I stay to finish filming is because I know that if I don't, it will end up costing me far more than I can afford. Complements of Mick's mad legal skills and knowledge of the business, they are making some adjustments to the filming schedule so that I can be done faster.

Mick is running airport searches on all nearby and surrounding airports, looking for flights out of Boston, Philadelphia, Baltimore, and Washington D.C., hoping that she will turn up flying out of one of those airports.

Beau has become the tabloid scanner. If Cami is in New York, she's been around me enough to be recognized and there is a chance that the paparazzi will catch her somewhere.

Days go by, and all hope seems to be slipping through our fingers. Mick continues to check through her bank account, looking for additional withdrawals, but even with what little we could tell she took from Phoenix, a hundred grand is a lot for her to live on for a long time. I didn't believe Mick about that — at least not until he explained some of Cami's financial history to me.

A week goes by, then ten days turns into two weeks, then three, then finally four and I'm done filming. As soon as I'm released from filming duty, Mick, Jo, and

Beau go back to Phoenix; I go to Billings, Montana. I have a score to settle with an asshole. All of my attempts to contact Bobby have yielded nothing. No return phone calls or emails. When I went to Billings the first time, he wasn't there.

I'm hoping we can find something, anything that will lead us to Cami. We've even gone so far as to put Tarah on speed dial. I'm hoping and praying that she will show up there again. But she hasn't, not yet.

THIRTY-FOUR

When Tyson and I pull up in front of Bobby's house, the lights are on inside, and before I even turn off the car I go running and start banging on the door. "Open the door, you son of a bitch." The door opens, and the old man from the other day is standing on the other side of the door. "Where's Bobby?"

"I'm right here," a voice calls from inside the house, and the old man steps out of the way, letting me and Tyson into the house.

"What the fuck did you do?" I say, charging into the room before I can take in the scene before me. Sitting on the couch is Bobby, and next to him is Trinity, and sitting on her lap is her son. "Jesus Christ, how much more damage are you going to cause along your path to come back from the dead?"

"Tristan, what's going on?" Trinity asks.

"What do you think? She's gone. No sign of her anywhere. She went back to Phoenix and never showed up in New York." I cock my head in Trinity's direction. "You knew he was alive too."

"No, I found out the day Cami came to the office. When Cami dragged me into Vinnie's office, Bobby was there, on the couch. After that I went on leave and came up here."

"What the fuck are you doing here now?" My brain doesn't operate as fast as Cami's does, but it is finally starting to register. I point to Bobby. "You—" Then Trinity. "—her and—" I charge toward Bobby, but Tyson is faster than I am, and he wraps his arms around me, holding me back.

"You can't find her if you're in jail, brother. Come on, let's go."

Bobby stands up. "I had no idea, Tristan, believe me. I tried to tell her, but she left before anyone could explain everything. I couldn't chase after her without exposing myself and ruining everything for her."

"You already have." I turn toward Tyson. "Let me go." He doesn't release his grip. "Fine, then carry me out of here. We need to get back to Phoenix." I turn back toward Bobby. "Stay away from her. Never contact her again. I will not put up with your shit on her plate any longer. She put herself out there when she came that day to try and start forgiving you. She took the steps she needed to take in order to try and move on from all that you've done to her, then this happens. She will never forgive you for this."

Tyson drags me out of the house and throws me into the passenger seat of the car. As he leaves he peels some rubber, kicking up gravel and dirt in his haste to pull away and get back to the airport.

It's been six weeks, countless trips to New York and endless hours of searching, trying to find her, trying to find Cami.

Mick and Beau don't come around much anymore, mainly because they don't have anything new to tell me other than that she will come back around when she's ready. But dammit, I miss her. I miss her like fucking crazy, and it's killing me.

I convinced Vinnie to get me out of my next movie contract. Guilted him might be a better word for it; I told him that he was partially to blame for her running off, and I didn't feel one bit of guilt about doing so.

I took over dealing with the builders on the house in L.A., hoping that she will be back before it's finished, but I am beginning to lose faith that she is ever going to return. I slowly start to pack my things, a little at a time. Everyone has asked that I at least stay through this weekend. Give it a few more days and don't give up yet. Those seem to be their lines lately, and I'd like to believe them, but it's getting harder every single day.

THIRTY-FIVE

"Under a lover's sky... Gonna be with you..." I stir. "And no one's gonna be..." My eyes shoot open; that's Cami's ring tone. That's Cami's phone. I scramble up off of the couch and grab the phone from the coffee table. I don't look at the number; I don't care who it is.

"Hello?"

Silence.

"Hello?"

Silence.

I pull the phone away from my head and it's cleared off. The call has gone dead. I pull up her recent call log. It's a six-two-three number, which is Phoenix.

Suddenly my phone starts to ring. The same number is popping up. I answer it immediately. "Cami."

"Mr. Michaels?"

"Yes, who is this?"

"Mr. Michaels, this is Doctor Tolleson from John C. Lincoln Hospital." Oh, God. "We have a patient here by the name of Cameron Ende—"

"What happened?"

"She is being admitted, but you're listed as her emergency contact. Can you please come down to the hospital?"

"I'm on my way." I hang up the phone.

"Shit!" I scream, and Tyson comes running down the stairs.

"What's up?"

"She's here, in Phoenix. She's in the hospital."

"What are we standing around here for, let's go," Tyson says as he grabs his keys off of the table.

I follow him down the stairs and out the front door. Luckily his brain is functioning because I don't even think about my keys or locking the door. I'm fumbling through my phone, trying to find Beau's number.

I climb into the car and Tyson is on the phone. "Hi, baby, we found her." He pauses to listen. "She's at the hospital." He pauses then looks over at me. "Which hospital?"

"John C. Lincoln."

"You get that? Okay, see you there."

I finally manage to dial Beau's number. It rings once, twice, three— "Hi, Tristan."

"She's here, in Phoenix."

"Holy shit, where?"

"John C. Lincoln."

"Fuck. We're on our way." And the phone goes dead.

******
Cami
******

Knock, knock...

"Hello, Ms. Enders, I'm Doctor Tolleson."

"Hello."

"How are you feeling?"

"Scared."

"Are you in any pain?" I shake my head; the pain stopped shortly after I got here. I hadn't been feeling good all day, and then I get here and I suddenly feel better and wish I hadn't come, but there was so much blood. "That's good. I have some good news for you."

"Everything is all right?"

"It is, for now. We were able to detect a strong heartbeat during the ultrasound, but we're going to keep you overnight for observation and at least one — if not two more — ultrasounds, just to be safe. You came in here alone, is there anyone we can call for you?"

Tristan. "No."

"Okay, the nurse will be along shortly to take you up to a room. Have you sought medical care for your pregnancy?"

I nod. "My second appointment is next week."

"Okay, good. You'll want to follow up with your doctor in less than a week. For now, I just want you to rest and we will keep an eye on you. If you have any pain at all—" He reaches over the bed. "—press that button there."

"Thank you, doctor."

He leaves the room and I put my head back. I should've called Tristan the minute I found out, but I couldn't bring myself to do it. I promised him that I wouldn't run away, but I did. Then again, I didn't. I never left Phoenix and have been staying in my old apartment. I'm surprised no one managed to look there. But I think everyone thought I'd gotten rid of it. I was going to, but it just kept slipping my mind with everything else that was going on at the time. Regardless, this whole thing has become a huge damn mess, and I highly doubt that there is much I can do about it now.

They move me upstairs. I freak out when I see the *Labor and Delivery* sign as we passed by it, but the nurse tells me that this is where all pregnant women go when they have complications. Once I'm in the room, she puts a microphone to my belly, and there is a strange whooshing sound that comes piping through the speaker in her hand. She seems satisfied with what she's hearing. "Sounds great. Try and get some rest and I'll be back in a little bit. Press the call button if you experience any pain."

"Thank you."

She smiles at me and leaves the room. I put my head in my hands.

What am I gonna tell Tristan? He is going to be so mad. We've never discussed kids; we've never even talked about anything beyond what we've been doing right now. I've been such a bitch to him. I can't imagine him forgiving me now. God, he will never forgive me for what I've done. I haven't slept for days, except little tiny cat naps here and there. Every time I close my eyes I start to panic. Panic about what I've done and the decision I've made. Sure, financially I can do this, but every single time I start thinking about being a mom, I see the look of disgust on Evelyn's face in those videos Bobby sent me — all the resentment she felt about Mark and me — and since I ran away from Tristan, that's what I'm afraid I'll do. I'll end up resenting this child because I pushed its father away.

I can't stop the tears from falling down my cheeks. I put the heels of my hands in my eyes, hoping like hell that I can turn off the waterworks. I've got to call him. I have to build up the courage to do it. Sooner, before it's too late.

It's already too late.

"Cams."

I sob harder when I hear his voice, and in a second he is next to me. He doesn't say anything, but his hand comes to rest on my belly, and I feel his forehead press against mine. I can tell he's crying because I can hear the short breaths that accompany his tears.

"What are you doing here?" I sob.

"They called me. When I filled out your paperwork for your foot, I had to put an emergency contact down. I put me."

"Tristan, I'm sorry. I'm so very sorry. I missed my appointment—" The words come out fast and almost inaudible. "I didn't mean to, I thought about it before we left for Montana, but thought I still had time. I—"

"Shh. Cams, it's all right. Are you okay?"

"Yes," I breathe.

"The baby?"

"Yes."

"Oh, thank God." The words are followed by a sob. "Thank God."

It takes me a minute to soak up what he's said. He's thanking God that... "Ohmygod, Tristan, I thought you were going to be so angry with me."

His head comes off of mine and his beautiful blue eyes meet mine. "About you running from me? I'm furious. But this — no, Cami, never this."

I sob again; this time my heart fills with happiness that seemed to have been forgotten these last few weeks.

"Shh, baby, please." He wraps his arms around me as best as he can. "Cami, I could never be mad at you for something like this. Not now, not ever. I think the timing is off, and far from the best, but that doesn't change the way I feel about having a baby." He sits back down. "I'm hurt, beyond words, that you ran away from me. That you left me with no idea where you were, where you were going, if you were all right." I can see the tears streaking down his cheeks. "I've been so scared that I would never see you again. I haven't been able to work or hardly function for the last six weeks."

"Jesus, Tristan, I'm sorry. I felt so betrayed, like everyone was against me. I didn't know who I could trust not to drop more bombs on me. The longer I stayed away, the more stupid I felt, then I didn't know how to come back. Or what I would find when I came back. I didn't want to know that you'd moved on, that you'd left. It broke my heart knowing that I hurt you."

"Shh. Please." His hand, resting on my stomach, fists. "I love you," he breathes, and I lose any hold I had on the fact that I thought I'd lost him forever. He's here, with me. He loves me, no matter what I put him through. He is still here.

"I...love...you," I say through my sobs, and he holds me to him. After a moment, he climbs awkwardly onto the bed to lie down next to me.

"Please, don't ever do this to me again. I can't take it again."

"What have I ever done to deserve you?"

He doesn't answer, and I don't need or want an answer. Having him here is all the answer I need.

THIRTY-SIX

******
Tristan
******

"Where have you been?" I ask her.

"Here, in Phoenix."

"What?" The word comes out harsher than I meant it to. "We tracked you to New York."

"No, you tracked a ticket to New York. I never boarded the plane. I couldn't leave. Despite my best attempt to do so, I couldn't do it. I've been staying at my old apartment."

I don't know whether to be happy or angry at the fact that she was here this whole time. But I decide that it doesn't matter. Seeing her here, safe and alive, is all the reassurance I need to know that she'll be okay. "How long have you known you were pregnant?" I don't want the answer because it will make me feel worse than I already do. But I need to know if she'd ever planned on telling me.

"I found out..." She pauses, not good. "The day I arrived in L.A."

"If you hadn't ended up here, and they hadn't called me, did you ever plan on telling me?"

"Yes, but I didn't know how." Deep breath. "I played our conversation that afternoon over and over in my head — about how you felt about our future — and it scared me to tell you. I didn't know how you'd react." She's crying again, and I don't want to make her cry; this is stressful on her enough as it is. "Then I kept playing what happened in Vincent's office that day, and how Bobby didn't know that Trinity was pregnant, and how he probably would've never faked his own death if he'd known, and I knew I had to tell you. I've been to the house about thirty times over the last month, but I didn't know how to come in, I didn't know how to tell you. I didn't know how to apologize to you." She is damn near hysterical by the time her speech ends. "I didn't know if you'd forgive me for screwing up so bad and, believe me, I never expected you to walk in that door."

"Shh, sweets, please. You need to calm down. Please, baby." I hold her in my arms as tight as I can. "We can work through this, work through us, but right now I need you to take a deep breath and relax. I'm not going anywhere. I promise."

She wraps her arms around me and holds me tightly against her; my own tears won't stop, but I have to find it in myself to be strong. For her.

We lie here for a little while. "I need to go tell everyone what's going on. Do you want to see anyone?"

"No, not tonight."

"Okay. I will be back soon."

"Promise?"

She wants promises from me? "I promise."

Just as I'm about to leave, a short, plump woman comes into the room. "How are you feeling, Ms. Enders?"

She nods but doesn't say anything. The nurse looks from her to me and back again. "We're fine," she says. "It's a long story, but we're fine." I hear her say the words, but I'm not sure she believes them herself.

"I just want to check your vitals, and the baby's, okay?" Cami nods.

The nurse produces a microphone-looking thing, and Cami lowers the blankets and lifts her gown. The sight before me is in slow motion as I take in what I'm looking at. If I didn't know better, I'd assume that Cami'd gained some weight — there is a small swell to her belly, but not noticeable — but I know her body so well, it is obvious to me, and my heart pounds a little faster.

The nurse places the microphone to her stomach, and within a few heartbeats there are whooshing sounds coming through the speaker. My eyes dart to Cami's and she nods. I sit down on the foot of her bed. My knees have gone weak. "Sounds good. Your vitals look good, but, Ms. Enders, I recommend that you relax and get some sleep."

"I will," she says, but again the conviction isn't in her voice.

"We can give you something to help you sleep."

"Let me try first."

"All right," the nurse says, putting her equipment away, and she leaves the room. Cami's stomach is still exposed; my eyes go to it and she quickly tries to cover it.

'Never, ever cover yourself from me," I say as I take her hands and move them from her gown. "Not now, not ever," I say as I lift her gown again. I lean forward and I kiss the small swell of her stomach. I can hear Cami start crying again. Her hand comes to rest on my cheek. My head turns and I kiss the palm of her hand, and she uses her fingers to tell me to come to her. I stand and walk toward her, leaning over her and the bed. She takes my face between her hands.

"I love this," she says as her fingers play with my stubble. "I love you." She pulls me down and kisses me. She kisses me like she's never kissed me before, and I can't help but kiss her back. All the love we have for each other pours between us: no walls, no barriers, just pure love.

I reluctantly pull myself away from her. I need to go and talk to everyone. They're all downstairs, waiting for news on Cami and what is going on. As soon as Beau sees me, they all come running toward me. "She's all right. Shattered, but she's all right."

"What's going on?" Beau asks, "what happened?"

I walk past them to the waiting room and take a seat. I feel like I've just run three marathons. "She's been here in Phoenix the entire time."

"What? Where?" It's Mick who asks.

"Her old apartment."

"Oh, for hell," Beau says.

"But what about her now? What happened?"

"She called an ambulance because she was weak and exhausted, she started bleeding and she thought something was wrong. She's pregnant."

There are joint gasps of shock. I am sure someone is doing the math in their head, but frankly I don't care. I know it's mine.

"Did she?" Jo asks.

I look up at her standing next to Tyson, who has his arm wrapped tightly around her. "No, she's fine. The baby's fine. They're keeping her overnight for observation."

There is a heavy weight that lifts from the room; the tension is gone in one big swoop and all I want to do is cry.

Beau kneels down in front of me, looking up into my eyes. "How are you doing?"

"I'm wrecked, Beau. I'm so unbelievably happy that she's alive, that she is well, and that she is here. But I am scared shitless that she will leave again. I'm scared shitless about the baby, I'm happy, I'm tired, I'm— I don't know. I'm just wrecked."

She puts her hand on my knee, a comforting gesture, and I put my hand over hers. "Thank you for putting up with me these last few weeks."

"She's my best friend, Tristan, and whether she believes it or not, she loves you insanely. We just need to do what we can to protect her from all this stupid bullshit, and after she has this baby, I'm kicking her ass." She smiles, but I know she's ready to just lay into Cami for what she's put me through.

"Later," I say with a half smile. "She doesn't want to see anyone tonight. I'm sure she feels awful about everything and what she's put you all through. So let's give her some time."

Everyone agrees, and they all head out, little by little. "You need to call Trav," Jo tells me as she hugs me goodbye. "He's worried about you."

"Thanks, Jo. For everything."

"Always. We'll see you later," she says as she takes Tyson's hand and they leave.

I pull out my phone and call Travis.

"Please tell me you have some good news for once."

"She's all right. The hospital called me."

"Shit, what happened?"

"She's pregnant, Trav."

"I don't know whether or not to congratulate you or tell you to run like hell."

"Congrats will do. It is going to be a long road, but we'll figure this out."

"You sure?" I know that voice. It's the same one he uses whenever he's concerned.

"Yeah, I'm sure. It won't be easy, but I'd rather work through us and this than not."

"All right, bro, we'll be in town in a couple of days. Kiss Cami for me."

"Tell Naomi I said hi."

"Sure thing. Later."

And just like that, he's gone. Travis and I understand each other in ways I never knew two men could understand anyone but their partners. Travis loves Cami to pieces and he wants to see me happy, and despite the rollercoaster ride of these last couple of months, she makes me happier than anything.

Before I can enter Cami's room again, my phone rings. Blocked. I roll my eyes and decide that I don't want to go into Cami's room hot because of her father. It's time for his nightly call, wondering if we've heard anything. He can wait until tomorrow.

That is the only thing that has stayed consistent since she disappeared: Bobby has called every night, wondering and waiting with me. Though I don't think he deserves it, Cami needs to know he's been trying. Another day.

I enter Cami's room and get past the curtain. She's sleeping, and it is a beautiful sight to see. Judging by the bags under her eyes, I imagine that she, like me, hasn't slept much. Maybe even less than I have.

I rub my chin, debating on whether or not to keep the scruff. Her comment makes me smile, and before long, regardless of how uncomfortable this chair is, I doze off.

I'm woken up several times throughout the night when the nurse comes in to check her vitals. I'm thankful that Cami manages to sleep through it all, but I never get tired of hearing that whooshing sound.

At some point I fall asleep with my head on the mattress and am woken up to the feeling of Cami's fingers stroking through my hair. "Hi, beautiful."

"Hi beautiful yourself." It is so great to hear her say that. "They're going to be in here in a few minutes to do an ultrasound. If everything looks good, I'll get to go home."

"Please tell me you're coming home to your condo."

"Is that where you want me to be?"

Did I not make it clear enough last night? "Absolutely. It is your home, Cams, not mine. Hell, I've been sleeping on the couch."

"Well, we don't need to both be miserable." She gives me a half smile.

"But you need to want to be there too. This isn't about me."

"I want to be there, and I want you to be there with me," she says. "If you'll stay."

"I can't think of any place I'd rather be."

THIRTY-SEVEN

******
Cami
******

He's here, and he's here to stay. I don't deserve him or his willingness to forgive me, but I can't even begin to imagine how I was going to go through this without him. I was so stupid to run away, especially considering all the answers to all of my problems were simple solutions.

A nurse and Dr. Tolleson come into the room; the nurse is pushing a cart with an ultrasound machine on it...or at least I'm assuming that's what all that equipment is.

"You look better this morning, Ms. Enders. Did you get some rest?" Dr. Tolleson asks.

"Yes, I did."

"Good. We're going to take a look, see how you're doing. Judging by your skin color, we've managed to rehydrate you some. That's a good thing." He busies himself with the machine, setting it up and getting ready to do his thing. I look at Tristan and there is an awed look in his eyes as he takes in what's about to happen. It probably mirrors my own look. When I came in last night, I was in really bad shape, and they were quick with the machine.

Once Dr. Tolleson is finished with the machine he looks at me, then at Tristan. "Mr. Michaels, I presume."

"Yes, sir."

"Seems as though I made the right call last night." I smirk a little bit at their exchange. "My daughter is a huge fan."

I watch as Tristan's shock registers; he looks like hell, and how in the hell could he know? "Thank you, sir."

Dr. Tolleson nods and then reaches for my blanket to pull it down. I can't help but look down my own body and realize just how much it's already changed and is going to change over the next few months. "Do you know how far along you are, Cameron?"

"Cami, please? And—" I'm ashamed to admit it. "—no, I don't."

"Well, let's see if we can find out, shall we?" Tristan and I both look at each other. His eyes light up.

"Absolutely," he says, and he smiles — a real, genuine smile of excitement.

Now that my stomach is exposed, Dr. Tolleson takes a tube off of the cart and squirts a warm liquid across my pelvic bone. "Ready?" I nod at him and he puts a transducer to my stomach. I can't see anything that he's looking at, but I can see Tristan trying to see too. "Let me take some measurements first, then I'll share. Would you like pictures to take home with you?"

"Please," I say, and he continues what he's doing.

A couple of minutes go by and he's ready to show us what he's looking at. He turns the stand and the monitor in our direction. It takes a moment for my eyes to adjust to what I'm seeing, but there is a lot of static surrounding a black hole. In the center of that black hole is what looks like a little baby. My eyes fill with tears and I can't really see what I'm looking at.

"This little one is about three inches long, about the size of a peach. Which puts you at about thirteen weeks pregnant. Have you been sick?" he asks me.

"In the beginning I was, but for about the last two weeks or so, not so much," I say as I try and clear my eyes.

"That's pretty normal for this stage of pregnancy. The blood tests we ran from last night confirm the ultrasound at about thirteen weeks. Do you know when your last period was?"

I shake my head. "I was on the shot. I was scheduled to have received it again on August second and I missed my appointment."

"Well, if your blood and the measurements are correct, you probably conceived around September fifth." Instantly my mind starts going a million miles a minute, trying to think about that day, but nothing comes to me. "Which would put your due date about May twenty-seventh."

"You're kidding," I say, slightly shocked.

"Nope. Is there a significance to that date?"

I shake my head; it is not my doctor's business. Tristan looks at me too, but I just shake my head.

"Well, you're well on your way. I would still follow up with your regular doctor within the next seven days, just so that they can check things out and make sure you're doing okay. Drink plenty of liquids and get some rest. I recommend bed rest, at least through the weekend, but there are no restrictions. I will have the nurse come in with your discharge papers and you're free to go."

"Thank you, Doctor Tolleson," I say, and Tristan says the same. We shake hands, and he's gone from the room; the nurse stays and removes the IV from my arm and tells me I can get dressed and she'll be back in a few minutes with my papers and a wheelchair.

As soon as she leaves, Tristan says to me, "May twenty-seventh?" he says with a smile, but I can see he's a bit wary about it and my reaction. I start to climb out of bed and stop with my feet hanging over the side of the bed.

"May twenty-seventh could quite possibly be our baby's birthday," I say, trying to steer him away from the date.

"That's not it. Come on, Cams, don't hold back on me now."

I look up into his bright blue eyes. I'm transfixed by them and I feel like I can tell him anything right now and he won't care what it is, at least not to the point of getting upset. "It's the day that Bobby 'died.'" Air quotes included.

I watch him as he throws his head back in an 'Oh, crap' manner. "There is something I should tell you about your father."

"If it's that he's really dead, I don't care," I say before I can stop myself.

"No, not that. He's been calling me. Every night since he found out you disappeared." I can see the worry and the fear in his eyes as he tells me this.

"It's about time he worried about someone other than himself." I climb off of the bed, looking for my clothes from— "Shit."

"What?"

"Can you go out to the nurses' station, see if they have some scrubs or something I can wear?"

"Why?"

"They cut off my clothes when I came in here last night." I'd hoped to keep how bad it really was from him, but he catches it right away and he knows instantly.

"You're never leaving my side again." I scowl at him, but he dutifully goes to the nurses' station and comes back with a pair of light blue scrubs for me to put on.

I go into the bathroom to change. Not that Tristan has never seen me naked before, but I'd rather save the rest of the shock for when we're at home. Not to mention the fact that the oversized hospital gown and the scrubs will cover up the fact that I'm not wearing a bra, and my breasts have grown pretty close to a size bigger and my nipples have changed color...only slightly, but given he noticed the bump, I have no doubt he will notice that too.

When I come out of the bathroom, Tristan is on the phone. "Thanks, we'll see you in a few."

"Who was that?"

"Beau. Tyson took the car home last night, we have no way home."

"Oh." The nurse comes in, hands Tristan a package that contains my discharge papers and some information on dehydration as well as some sample prenatal vitamins and some other junk, but I don't care. I want to go home.

THIRTY-EIGHT

******
Tristan
******

"Thanks, Beau."

"Of course." She scowls at Cami and I want to stand in between them to stop it.

"Yes, Beau, baby, I know. You can chastise me later."

"That's not why I'm scowling."

"Then what's the big deal?" Cami asks her.

"Do either of you two know what day it is?"

We both shrug. "No," we say in unison, and Beau smiles, enjoying the fact that we're back together or that we're absolutely clueless.

"It's Thanksgiving." She climbs back into the car and I help Cami into the front seat.

"What?" Cami says.

"You know — turkey, stuffing, cranberries and family. It's Thanksgiving."

"I'm sorry we pulled you away from your food fest," Cami says to her, but I can tell she's teasing Beau, and she laughs.

"We were at your condo anyway," Beau says.

Cami and I both say, "What? Why?" at the same time, and Beau bursts out laughing.

"I am so glad the two of you are back together. I missed both of you terribly." She pulls out of the hospital parking lot, and the streets are nearly empty. "Yes we're ALL at the condo. Waiting impatiently for your ass to be discharged...or to be told you were staying."

"You're too much, you know that?"

After a couple of minutes, we pull in front of the condo. Tyson's and Naomi's cars are here. I help Cami from the car. She rolls her eyes when I help her up the stairs to the doorway, but I can tell that she's still weak. We head for the elevator and go to the living room floor. Once the door opens we're assaulted by all the smells of Thanksgiving, and I can hear commotion coming from the kitchen. Cami and I both look at each other.

"I told you we were all here waiting for you to get discharged. If you were staying, we were bringing Thanksgiving dinner to you." She smiles and kisses Cami on the cheek. Then she embraces me in a hug. "Told you."

She had told me, several times, that Cami would be back, though I don't think either one of us expected it to be after finding Cami in the hospital. But still, she is here.

"I don't know if I have the energy for this."

"For eating? You always have energy for eating. We're cooking."

I help Cami into the kitchen and everyone smiles at her. It's nice to see. Travis, my best friend on this planet, comes over first. He bypasses me to hug my girl. "Welcome home," he says. "Missed you, small fry."

Cami laughs. "Same here."

One by one they all file over and give Cami a hug, kisses and huge welcome-homes. I get the usual pat on the back plus some attaboys when it comes to the fact that I managed to knock her up. Well, those were Travis's words.

I can't pull my eyes away from her; she is so beautiful. Though exhaustion is running hot in her veins, she still has this radiant glow about her. She catches me staring more than a few times and smiles at me. She is warm and carefree and I watch as every once in a while her hand comes to rest against her stomach. After the second time, I stop asking if she's okay. "Sometimes I still don't believe it. That's all." I can't help but smile at her. I can't believe it either, but I'm not sure I've ever been happier.

After we finish eating, our friends clean up and Cami goes upstairs to lie down. It is killing me; I want to be up there with her, but I don't want to be rude to our friends. I help them finish up.

"How are you doing?" Beau asks me, but quietly and away from prying ears.

"I'm good. I won't lie, I'm freaked out, and I worried about her, but I'm okay."

"Good." She leans in a little closer. "Go to her. We got this."

"Are you sure?"

"Absolutely. I've already told them, don't worry about it. We'll see you guys on Sunday. The game is on." She's such a football fan; I love it.

"All right, sounds like a plan. That will give her a couple of days to rest. Thanks. For everything."

"It's what friends are for. Just remember, she's just as torn up as you are. I know what she did was wrong, she knows it too, but she is also very hurt by what her father has done to her. No, she had no right to hold you responsible for that and make you suffer, but remember, she's spent her entire life alone." She kisses me on the cheek and then everyone else joins us.

"I can't thank you guys enough." They all smile at me. "For this and for everything else you've done these last few weeks." I manage to bite my tongue to stop myself from just completely breaking down. Everything is crashing down on me, and I finally realize the gravity of what these people standing here really mean to me.

"We're always here for you. Both of you," Naomi says. "But now that we're all stuffed to the gills, we're going home to pass out."

Everyone laughs. "I'm right there with you." I can't stop my eyes from darting to the ceiling as though I can see her through the two floors.

"We'll get out of here. Sunday for the game?" Tyson says.

"Absolutely."

Tyson comes over to me. "Don't go anywhere without me this weekend. The stores will be packed. If you need anything, call. We'll get it and bring it over. We stocked up the fridge and the kitchen a little bit, so you've got plenty of food, plus leftovers."

"Thanks, Ty."

After a couple more minutes of the pity eyes and 'Are you okay?' stares, they leave to go back to their houses and I look at the clock. It's four in the afternoon.

I climb the two flights of stairs to Cami's bedroom. When I come around the corner she is sitting up on the bed. She's crying. "Cams, what's wrong?" I can't hide the worry in my voice.

"I'm so tired, and I can't sleep."

I walk over to the bed. "So why are you crying?"

"I don't know," she says through sobs and I climb onto the bed with her.

"Want to take a bath?"

She nods.

"Okay, give me a minute."

I kiss her cheek and climb off of the bed. I head into the bathroom and turn the dimmer down low so that the room has a soft glow about it. It's relaxing; at least, that is the mood I'm going for. I want her to be able to relax enough so that she can fall asleep.

I start up the water and pour in some of her lavender bubble bath, and when I get up to go and get her she is standing in the doorway. My eyes land on her feet and I very lazily move them up her legs. She's shed her clothes along the way and she stands before me naked, and it steals my breath away.

Between her hips is a beautiful swell that reminds me that she's pregnant and I'm going to be a father. But my eyes continue their inspection of her beautiful body. Her bellybutton ring glistens in the light of the bathroom, and my eyes slide up to her breasts; they're bigger — not much, but slightly — and the beautiful points of her nipples are darker. I see her shoulder tattoos and then the line of her jaw and her face. She is staring at me.

Our eyes meet. "You're beautiful." Then, as if the weight of the world comes crashing down on me, I start crying.

I close my eyes, trying to stop the tears from escaping my eyes, but I fail and I can feel her standing in front of me. Her hand goes into my hair. "Please don't cry. I can't bear it. Everything I've put you through. Tristan, I am so sorry. Can you ever forgive me?"

Forgive her? "Of course, I can and I do. Cami." I look up to meet her tear-filled eyes. "Sweets, I love you." I stand up. "Nothing in this world will ever change that. But please, dear God, never run away from me again." I take her head in my hands. "I can't bear it." I lean down and our lips meet. I kiss her — softly, warmly, and lovingly. I feel her tears hit my hands. "We're both beyond exhausted. Let's get you in the bath, then we can go to bed."

She nods. "I like that idea." Then she reaches for my shirt. "Join me, please," she breathes, and I can't resist her. She slides my shirt over my head, then she finds my dragon and she kisses him, and my heart burns with the love I can no longer hold back from her. Her hand slides down along my stomach to the button of my pants, undoing them quickly and sliding them down my legs. I really wish that her beautiful nakedness hadn't woken up the monster in my pants, but he's missed her as much as I have.

I'm thankful when she ignores it. Now is not the time to get worked up.

I step into the tub and hold my hand out for her. She takes it and climbs in. I sit down, much like I did all those months ago after she cut her foot, and she slides down on my thighs. I kiss her shoulder and hold her close to me, savoring the touch of her skin against mine, and I'm content to just sit here. But I begin lathering up her sponge, and she pulls her hair off to the side, then leans forward, and I begin washing her shoulders and down her back. "No ribbon?" I ask when I notice that her corset is empty.

"No, I pulled it out because it was bugging me. I've just never restrung it."

"We'll have to fix that." I wash her back, and when I'm done she leans against me, her soapy back against my front, and I hold onto her for a little while before I begin working on washing her front.

I can hear her breathing change when I start at her chest and work my way down her body. I don't linger, but my hand rubs along her belly and I drop the sponge and place my hand there and kiss her shoulder. Her hand slides over mine and we just sit there.

"I never imagined being a father until you came into my life. I'm not sure I ever imagined getting married to a woman I loved more than anything. I've always been afraid that I would settle for someone because I thought they made me happy." She turns in my arms to face me. "But these last six weeks have proven that I love you more than life itself. Cameron, I never want to lose you; no matter what comes between us, we can and we will work through it, we always do. Say you'll marry me?" I look into her eyes, searching her soul, searching for everything I need to see, and it's all there: love, devotion, admiration, and lastly happiness.

"Yes," she breathes. She takes my head in her hands and her lips are on mine, hotter and more passionate. "I love you," she breathes and kisses me again.

"I love you," I breathe. She kisses me again and the whole world stops spinning. This woman is all that matters to me; nothing else matters, nothing else is more important than she is.

I pull back, and we finish our bath.

When we climb out, I throw a towel around my waist and take my time drying her off, gently, from head to toe. I can see the exhaustion washing over her and it is the reason I stopped our kissing. She needs to rest, and right now, I want nothing more than to have her in my arms and fall asleep.

We crawl into bed and do just that. She snuggles up to me, her back to my front, and I wrap my arms around her, holding her to me tighter than I probably should, but if it weren't for the pain I feel at the loss I've endured, I'd think I was dreaming.

THIRTY-NINE

When I stir in bed, it is still dark outside. Wait, it was light when I went to sleep. I can feel Tristan wrapped around me and his breath caressing my shoulder. I manage to bring my eyes to the clock. It's four thirty in the morning. I've slept for nearly twelve hours, but I feel as though I could fall right back to sleep. If it weren't for feeling Tristan at my back, I would've panicked when I woke up, but I realize this isn't a dream.

I've been walking around in this dream-like state for weeks — barely getting through life, barely breathing. But for the first time since all of the Bobby bullshit started, I finally feel like the weight of the world is gone from my shoulders.

Other things start to come to me, all the things I've neglected these last six weeks: the house, Bold, Tristan, us, and life.

When I discovered I was pregnant, I panicked about what Tristan would think, what he would say. I was so afraid he'd be angry with me, and I can tell that I was extremely stupid about that and it kills me knowing what I know now. His reaction to the way I look reiterates the fact that I was wrong; he's not disgusted or turned off by it. When we climbed into the bathtub, and even when we crawled out, he had an erection, and even when we crawled into bed, it hadn't gone away, but he made no move to do anything about it, putting my needs before his own. After everything I've put him through, I am so selfish.

I can't lie here anymore. But I can't move either. I wouldn't move if I didn't feel as though my bladder were going to explode. I move slowly, hoping and praying that he will stay asleep. I've managed to move his arm, and his breathing hasn't changed. Sliding off of the bed slowly and quietly, I race toward the bathroom.

Then I realize that this is the first morning I've woken up without the pressing need to throw up, and I smile a little bit. Maybe I'm finally moving past the morning sickness. Thank God, because I miss food — at least eating like a pig, anyway.

When I come out of the bathroom, Tristan is still asleep on the bed and I can see him in the light of the moon coming through the curtains. I stand there in the doorway, just looking, just watching him sleep. *What have I ever done to deserve you?* I ask myself, and it's something I can't answer. But I do know that I will spend the rest of my life making sure he knows how much I love him.

I stand there a couple more minutes before I return to bed, reversing the process I used to get out, hoping that he'll stay asleep. If he wakes, he doesn't move or indicate as much, and I curl back into my spot. I pick his arm up and wrap it around myself, and he pulls me into him, burying his face in my hair. I hear his deep inhale and he squeezes a little tighter. "I love you," he breathes.

"Ditto," I whisper, and his breathing changes when he smiles into my hair, but we don't say another word to each other as we both fall back to sleep.

The smell of eggs and bacon wakes me up sometime later, and Tristan sits down on the side of the bed. "Breakfast in bed," he says with a smile, and it warms my heart.

"After I um..." I scramble out of the bed and head for the bathroom. I shut the door behind me, and after a moment he knocks.

"You okay?"

I can hear the worry in his voice. "Yeah, I just had to pee."

I can hear him laugh, and the laugh fades as he walks away from the door. I finish up and wash my hands. When I open the door he is standing there, holding a tray, and I smile. "Hi, beautiful."

"Hi beautiful yourself," I say back, and I can't help the smile that spreads across my lips as I crawl into bed. I prop the pillows against the padded headboard and I pull the sheets up to my lap. Once I'm settled in, he puts the tray down in front of me and pulls back the dome from the plate.

"I wasn't sure if you were awake."

"Bacon woke me up." I laugh and grab for a piece.

"I can make more."

I smile at him. "Let me eat this first, then let's see." I haven't eaten many big meals the last few weeks and yesterday wiped me out. I've been eating — absolutely — but a lot of smaller meals.

He just sits there watching me eat. "What about you?" I ask him.

"I'm good. I nibbled a little while I was making it. You're missing a couple pieces of bacon." He gives me a cheesy grin and I laugh.

Before I know it, I've eaten everything on my plate and drunk both the orange juice and the glass of water he brought up. "Do you want more?" he asks, hopeful.

I shake my head. "Not right now. I'm full."

"Okay," he says, then he stands and takes the tray.

"I wouldn't mind some more orange juice, though."

"Okay, I'll run this downstairs and be back in a few minutes." He leans over and kisses me on the forehead and then heads down to the kitchen. I want to go with him, but based on the breakfast in bed and his willingness to wait on me, I'm guessing he isn't going to let me out of bed and, surprisingly, I'm okay with that. I look at the clock for the first time and it's nearly eleven in the morning. Well, I slept forever.

Surprisingly, I didn't hear Tristan come back upstairs; I doze off and wake up again just after twelve, and I see him sitting in my favorite chair. His back is to me, but he looks like he is reading over something. I pad quietly behind him and wrap my arms around his shoulders. "Jeez, babe," he says as he jumps. "You scared me." He turns to look at me.

"I'm sorry." I laugh a little and he smiles at me.

"How are you feeling?"

I do a quick assessment. Breakfast doesn't seem to want to make an appearance again, and I actually feel a little rested, but I could easily go back to sleep. "Pretty good I think. Whatcha reading?" I ask him.

"A script."

"Oh, any good?" I watch as he scrunches up his nose. I walk around and climb onto his lap. "Well, I guess we should work on that, shouldn't we?" He points to the coffee table. Sitting on top of it is a huge stack of scripts. "Or not," I say, leaning forward to grab the next one off of the pile. I look at the title and toss it onto the couch. He laughs.

"No good?"

I laugh. "I nearly fell asleep reading the title."

He laughs. "Well okay then."

We sit there for a couple of hours, going through the stack of scripts. The ones I like, he starts to read through a little bit. He settles on two of them. One he really likes and spends a good amount of time reading. "Good?" I ask.

"Really good. But I can't do it."

I scowl at him. "What? Why not?"

He hands me the script and I look at the filming dates.

May 15th, 2013 to June 23rd, 2013.

"What's wrong with that?" I ask, though I know his answer and he knows I know it, too.

"I won't miss it, Cams. Not for a movie, not for anything."

I climb off of the couch, stand on my knees between his legs and look up at him. "Did you see where it's filming?"

"No, once I looked at the dates, I stopped."

I reach for the script off of the couch where I left it and I show it to him. "I think you should sign this contract, Tristan. If you love the script as much as I can tell you do, nothing should stand in your way. Not me or the baby. Besides, I'll be there with you." He looks down at the script and sees the filming location.

"But the house won't be done."

I shrug. "So what? We can rent a house, like we did in Montana, and it will be fine. I'm certain that if I go into labor, we will be able to reach you and you will be there for it."

He takes my head in his hands and kisses me. "This is why I love you so much. What about doctors? We live here, it makes sense to have a doctor here."

I shake my head. "We can travel to California for appointments. Tristan, we can work this out. Please don't throw away a good script because you think it can't be done, because it can — without doubt — be done. We will make it work, no matter what. And..." I pause. "While I was struggling with myself about this—" I place my hand on my stomach. "—I decided that I need to make some choices — beyond me, beyond us, and beyond this little one. I think it's time I start running the company."

"Cami, you have more money than anyone I know. Your working is not a requirement to having a child."

"No, Tristan, it's not. But despite my father's awful flaws, he did one thing right. He built a business, and that business was handed to me. I'd like to hand it down to someone one day. But I also made a promise to myself that I would not be my father. That I would be there for my children, no matter what the cost." I take a deep breath. It feels good to finally say it out loud.

"I didn't know it was possible, but I think I just fell in love with you a little more."

I climb back up onto his lap and kiss him. "Show me," I breathe.

He stiffens and I can sense the hesitation. "Is it okay?" he breathes.

"Tristan, I'm pregnant, not made of glass." I smile at him, and the next thing I know, he's standing with me and we're walking toward the bed.

"I've missed you so much."

"Prove it," I say as he lays me out on the bed.

He smiles wider. "With pleasure."

FORTY

I crawl on the bed between Cami's legs; I know she's not wearing anything under my Ravens t-shirt, and just knowing that has me hard as a rock. I kiss her on the inside of her knee, then slowly, lovingly kiss up her thigh; at the same time, my hands begin slowly sliding up the shirt, up past her sex and her hips. My eyes follow the line of her body, and when she is lying flat, there is a definite swell to her stomach, and I love it almost as much as I love her.

I keep up with my kisses, but I skirt the area I know she wants touched and go to her right hip. I kiss it, then lick and kiss my way across her stomach, and she squirms beneath me; then she moans as I reach the center and then kiss and lick my way to the other hip and down. Her skin is soft and smooth as I kiss down her thigh, turning in toward her clit, but I pull back and go down her other leg.

"You're killing me," she groans, and I smile, nibbling a little as I climb my way back up her body, sliding the t-shirt higher and kissing up her belly to her ribs, just below the swell of her breasts. She tries to sit up, so I let her, slightly confused, but then she sheds my t-shirt, tossing it aside and lying back down. I continue my kisses across her breasts, sucking a little harder but avoiding her nipples, which are hard, tight buds against her barbells. Her breathing has increased and she's anxious, but I stay slow and steady as I kiss my way to her shoulder, then her neck and her jaw, until finally my lips meet hers and she moans into my mouth, wrapping her arms around me, holding me to her. I pull back and begin kissing down the other side, drawing out the anticipation. Hers and mine.

When I come to her hip, I can hear her breath coming in quick, shallow gasps, similar to when she's about to come, and I know I've worked her into a frenzy. Just like I wanted her to be. My face comes right between her legs, and I use my tongue to flick her clit and she trembles. I do it again, and she trembles again. Finally, I suck her clit into my mouth and she stiffens, calling out my name as she unravels to my touch, but I don't stop, drawing out her orgasm. Her hands fist into my hair and she holds me there, grinding her sex against my tongue, and I lick and suck until she comes undone again.

While I've worked the woman I love to two orgasms that leave her eyelids heavy and unwilling to open, I've damn near exploded myself, but I take a deep breath, hoping like hell that I can calm down. I haven't been inside Cami for a long time and I want to savor this. I want to enjoy her, but I can't take not being inside her anymore.

I crawl up her body and her mouth is on mine. She's kissing away all of her own essence, and I'm not even inside her and I want to come. I gently line up my cock with her entrance and slowly slide inside of her. "Ah," I groan. "You're so tight," I say between kisses, but her hips come up, hungry for more, and I can feel her muscles contracting, sucking me inside her, and it's the most amazing feeling in the world. "I want to come," I breathe.

She stops kissing me and goes to my ear. "Come for me, Tristan." Then she sucks my earlobe into her mouth and I pull back and slide inside of her and explode, calling out her name. She doesn't come and I don't remove myself from her, which means I'm still hard as a rock. I immediately begin to move, slowly, in and out of her. Her hips come up to meet mine. It doesn't take long before I feel her muscles tightening around me.

"Wait for me," I whisper, and she moans. I speed up, and she moans again.

"Tristan, I can't.... It feels too good," she groans, and I'm almost there.

Her muscles clench and unclench along my cock and that's it; I'm there. Ready to let loose. "Come, baby," I say, and she comes undone, stiffening and trembling beneath me as she calls my name.

She falls asleep right after that, which is perfectly fine with me. I curl up with her and doze in and out. She sleeps a few good hours and I'm starting to get restless, thinking about dinner. She needs to eat, and she needs to get her strength back; I need my girl back. We haven't talked about what happened in the tub last night, and it bothers me a little, but I think I have the perfect idea about how to do it and do it right.

When I get down to the kitchen to start making dinner, I call Beau.

"How is she?" she asks me.

"She's good, been sleeping off and on, but she slept at least twelve hours at once."

"Good, she needs it."

"Hey, I called because I need your help."

"Sure, Tristan, what's up?"

"She said yes."

"Yes to wh— You proposed?" I can hear the shock, but she squeals into the phone, emphasizing her reaction.

"Yes, but I know what she wants and I need your help to make it happen."

After we hang up, I finish making a plate of Thanksgiving leftovers and put it on the tray. Just as I'm about to walk out and go upstairs, I catch her out of the corner of my eye. "How long have you been there?" I ask.

"Only a minute or so." Phew.

"I was just bringing dinner up to you."

She shakes her head. "I don't want to eat alone," she says as she comes closer to me. "I want to eat with you."

"Okay," I say and set the tray down. "Go sit." I nod toward the breakfast bar and watch as she climbs up onto the stool. She is back in my Ravens shirt, but now she has on a pair of shorts that barely peek out from underneath the t-shirt. I put her plate in front of her and set about making my own plate. "What would you like to drink?"

"Tea?" She says it like it's a question rather than an answer, and I look at her. I smile.

"Hot or cold?"

She smiles. "Hot, please?"

After we're done eating she starts looking a little tired again. "Want to go back to bed?"

She shakes her head. "No, I'd like to watch some TV or a movie. Down here."

"Okay. Everyone is planning on coming over for the game on Sunday. Is that okay?"

"What day is it now?" She looks positively puzzled, and I look at her.

"Are you okay?"

"Yeah, I've just been sleeping so much." She laughs a little.

"It's Friday."

She smiles at me. "That's what I thought, but you know. The last twenty-four hours are a complete blur to me. Well, most of it." I watch as a blush spreads across her skin. I finish putting the dishes in the dishwasher and I stalk toward her, and she laughs at the expression on my face. "Not that part," she says and smiles wider. I wrap my arms around her and hold her to me for a moment, and she just kind of sinks into me.

"Let's go watch TV," I tell her, and we go to the living room. As we're getting settled I ask her about yesterday. "Is that the way you normally spend Thanksgiving?"

"What do you mean?" She looks at me, curiosity in her eyes.

"I mean with Mick and Beau. The girls."

"Usually. Why?"

"I think it's a new tradition we need to start, having all of our friends together, if for nothing else than Thanksgiving every year."

Her eyes light up. "I think that would be a great idea." She leans over and kisses my cheek.

"What about Christmas?" She squirms a little bit. "What?"

"Um, I..." Her eyes dance, and the glassiness of tears forms. "Tristan, I've never celebrated Christmas." She looks at me. "At least not that I can remember."

I fight my own tears. Sure, since my mom passed away, Christmas has never been the same, but I've always done something to celebrate it. "That will never happen again." I wrap my arms around her. "I think we need to start our own Christmas tradition, and I have the perfect idea."

FORTY-ONE

"I'm laying ground rules, right now," I bark at Trinity. I'm standing in her office in Los Angeles, and she's just returned from her personal leave. Tristan filled me in on her "personal time" and when he went to Montana to confront Bobby about what he did to me and it turns my stomach. Though it doesn't take much to do that these days. Tomorrow I cross the sixteen-week mark of my pregnancy, and I've had to buy some new pants and have taken to wearing baby doll style shirts because hiding underneath is a bump that grows more pronounced with each passing week.

"What's that?"

"I don't want to hear about it. I don't want to know about it, and more importantly, anything that happens in this office stays in this office. There will be no reporting back to him." Because I know you will.

"Cami, I'm not sure what you're—"

"Trinity, I know you were in Montana with him. I know full well where you've been on your leave of absence, and I don't care. I just don't want to hear about it."

"Cami, he's gone."

"Wait, what?" I say.

"He left late last week. He left the country. Said that he had to leave because too many people knew where he was and that he wasn't sure about where things stood with the investigation, so he's left the country. I thought you knew?" I shake my head. "I could've sworn." She shakes her head too. "Maybe not. Look, he's gone again, maybe for good, I don't know. But it is better this way."

"Is it really?" I ask her, completely serious.

"I think it is. Yeah, it's fun for a while, but...meh," she says, like it's no big deal.

"Regardless, the same rules apply," I say to her and then leave, walking down the hall to Vinnie's office. I knock.

"Come in."

I take a deep breath before entering. The last time I was here, so was Bobby, and more importantly, it was the day I ran away from Tristan, and I don't want to get myself worked up like that again. I open the door and Vincent is alone in his office. Thank God.

"Hi, Cami."

"Hi, Vinnie." He smiles. I haven't called him that in a long time. I close the door behind me. "Listen, I need to—" He stands to come around his desk and gestures for me to sit on the couch. "No, I'm good. I need you to join me, along with Trinity and the board members, in a few minutes. But I needed to come in here first. Listen, I owe you an apology. I should've never reacted the way I did, and more importantly, I should've never blamed you for any of this."

I watch as there is a lost look of sadness in his eyes. "Your father was my best friend and I miss him dearly. Though I helped him, it killed me nearly every day. It tore me up for the longest time. Both because of what he did, but then because of what he was doing to his daughter. If I could've talked him out of it, Cami, believe me, I would have, but I tried and—"

"I know. But I needed someone to blame, and it was easier to blame you because I felt no attachment to you. But then I realized I was wrong. You've been there for me, and I treated you horribly and I'm sorry."

He takes a couple of steps closer to me, then pauses, then comes forward and gives me a hug. "I will always be here for you—" He pulls back. "What's that?" he says, looking down. Shit.

"Um..." I take a small step back and place my hand on top of my mound.

"No way, Cami, are you serious?" His face lights up like a kid's on Christmas. I nod and smile, and for the first time there is true excitement in my nod and in my smile. He hugs me again. "Congratulations."

"Shh. No one knows, and I want to keep it that way. At least a little while longer."

He makes a show of sealing his lips and he smiles. "I'm really happy for you and for Tristan."

"Speaking of Tristan, did you get that contract on that movie we talked about?"

He smiles and nods. "I did." He goes back to his desk and pulls a stack of papers from a larger stack and brings it over to me. "Take a look."

I look at it; it looks like a bunch of legal jargon, but something catches my eye. Something... "No way," I say, covering my mouth.

"Yes way. He's climbing the big leagues now, girl."

"Can I take this to him?"

"Please do. I need it back by the eighteenth," he says.

"Okay, I'll take it to him. We can courier it back as soon as we're done with it. I'm pretty sure he won't hesitate to sign it, he loves the script."

"Have you read it?" he asks.

"No." I look at him. "Why?"

"You should."

I cock my head at him. "Do you have it too? The complete script?"

He goes back to his desk and he grabs a very large bound book. "Don't open it. Take it home to him."

"Okay." I say, thanking my lucky stars he's here in L.A. with me. When I told him I was coming he refused to let me come alone, and I can't blame him for that.

"You said a board meeting?"

I look at him. "What? Oh, yeah, we need to go."

We step into the boardroom, and sitting there are Trinity and every member of the board, along with Bold's attorney. I take my spot at the head of the table, and Rayne comes in right behind us; she is carrying a large stack of rather thick packets and begins passing them out.

"Good afternoon, ladies and gentlemen." I get quiet greetings back, and I suddenly wish Tristan were here with me. He'd offered to come, but I told him no. "I'd like you to take a look at what Rayne is handing you. This is an updated business proposal pertaining to Bold and Bold's clientele.

"Starting off the package you will find a list of actors, athletes, and musicians. On this list you will also see who their agents currently are, and then next to that you will see the date that their contracts are expiring. We are going to begin by making contact and recruiting these individuals to bring them to Bold when their contracts expire." I look at Vinnie, who has a very 'Proud poppa' style look on his face, and I smile at him. But I continue. "On the subsequent pages you will find a list of agents and industry professionals who are either looking to get out of their existing agency or who are struggling under their own weight. With each agent there's also a list of their current clientele. We are going to enter into some negotiations and decide which of these seventy candidates have what Bold needs, and we're going to bring them, along with their clients, under our umbrella."

"When do you plan to start putting this into place?" Al Pierce, one of the board members, asks the question that I was expecting.

"Beginning January fifteenth. The day that I step into my role as full-time CEO." I look at Vinnie, who, like Trinity, is quietly applauding. "We are going to revitalize what we have and where we go from here. Bold International has been a staple in Hollywood for more than thirty years, and it is time that we turn that staple into a stamp. I want Bold back to the premier company our clients turn to for anything they need. My stepping up also means that Vincent and Trinity will no longer have clients under them, with a small exception of our two biggest clients, Tristan Michaels and one I am going to tell you about momentarily, whom Vincent will still continue to manage. Trinity is hereby relieved of her PR duties and will be in charge of Bold's PR Department, overseeing everything underneath her now, and nothing more."

"We are not staffed to handle this kind of client influx," Al says.

"You're right, we're not. But it is my goal, over the course of the next two years, to increase Bold's clientele by fifteen percent and increase its employees by at least thirty percent. It is time that we grow bigger and stronger, and these are the steps in the right direction to do so."

"How can you be so confident that this will work?" Al asks.

"I'm not." There is an audible gasp from everyone in the room. "Relax. But what I am confident in is Bold's longstanding reputation and its ability to hold some of Hollywood's finest in their arsenal. I want directors and studios to come to us first before running off to some little-known agency who got lucky with one good client, and that starts with recruiting. Bold has picked up another amazing contract from none other than Travis Jackson, bringing two of Hollywood's hottest stars under one roof. I will be holding a press conference in about an hour to announce my ascension into the CEO position, along with Bold's acquisition of Travis Jackson, which means that everyone in this room and in this building needs to be on their toes. I will lay odds that we receive at least five phone calls from that list of talent looking for new representation, thereby growing our reputation and expanding our business."

Vinnie stands up. "This won't be an easy road, and just like anything in this industry, we have to work for what we want. I believe that Cameron has given us the tools we need to make this happen and make it happen quickly. I'm very confident in the work she's done and will continue to do going forward. I think right now we need to give her our support and begin what will be the beginning of a bigger and better Bold International." I look at Vinnie and realize that either he is really good at blowing smoke up the board's ass or he really believes what he's just said, but either way, it works for me.

"Let's get to it," Al Pierce says, and the room applauds.

"Well done, kiddo," Vinnie says as he winks at me. Everyone files out and I plop down in my chair at the head of the table. I take a few deep breaths and then Vinnie comes back into the room. "I'm very proud of you."

"Oh." I jump. "I was scared shitless."

"You didn't show it. Never doubt what you're capable of. Are you sure this is the right time to step up?" he asks, but I can tell there is no malice in his voice, and he looks at my stomach and then back to my eyes.

"Probably not, but if I've learned anything from this whole damn mess it's that Bobby laid the groundwork of a great business, a business he trusted me to run one day, and I'd like to be able to pass that on to my child one day."

"This company tore your father apart."

"I understand that, and I won't let that happen. I will not allow this business to eat me alive, and I will be home every night for dinner, whether it is with Tristan or my family. I will be there and I will be the best damn mother I'm capable of being. This company has a strong foundation, and an even better structure. I have no doubt that I can run this business without allowing it to eat me alive."

"I have confidence that you can do that too, and I will do anything I can to help you with that." I stand and walk toward Vinnie.

"It won't be easy and I'll need your help."
"You have it, one hundred percent."

FORTY-TWO

I return to Tristan and my hotel room at the JW around five-thirty, and he is there with a table full of food for dinner. I smile, and he hugs me, kisses me, and then bends down to kiss my bump. "How'd it go?" he asks as he leads me over to the table. He pulls my chair out for me and I sit.

"It went amazing." I smile so huge, and Tristan's smile mirrors my own. "I spoke to Trinity and told her that what she and Bobby do is their business and that I don't want to know about it or hear about it. I also told her that what happens in that office stays in that office and does not go back to him."

His eyes widen fractionally. "How'd she take that?"

"She agreed, but then took it upon herself to inform me that Bobby has left the country."

"Shit, Cams, I'm sorry."

I put my hand up to stop him. "It's all right. It is probably better this way anyway. I don't need his influence over the way I run my company, and I know he'd do anything he could to keep up that pretense. So if he's gone, then he's gone." He frowns at me. "Really, I'm okay," I remind him. "I spoke with Vinnie too."

"Oh dear."

"No, nothing like that. I actually apologized to him. We worked through it. We reached a level beyond professional." Tristan's eyes grow concerned. "I think that if he'd known about me sooner, things between Bobby and us may have been different, and I think, along with the trickery, he holds that over his own head." I take a sip of the sparkling cider on the table. "He gave me a hug." I watch his face. "He felt my stomach and asked. He knows, but he's the only one, and I've sworn him to secrecy."

"What did he say?"

"To be honest."

"Uh oh." I smile at his expression.

"Telling Vinnie and seeing his excitement was...it was...I don't know, it was exhilarating. For the very first time I actually felt a large amount of joy and excitement over the fact that we're going to have a baby. It almost made me want to send out a memo." He laughs. "Then we went to the board meeting."

"Oh boy."

"I was nervous, and Al, the one I feared, was the only one asking all the questions, which I expected, but when it came down to it, Vinnie got them on board by telling them that he believed in me and my plan. So it was settled. After the room cleared out, I plopped into my chair and let out a huge breath. Vinnie came back into the room then, scaring me." I realize right now how much I am loving telling Tristan about my day, and I smile. "He asked me if now was really the right time, but his intentions were good. I told him what I told you, about how Bobby built it and left it for me, and how I wanted to do the same. I also told him that I wouldn't let Bold eat me alive, and he said that he'd be sure that never happened."

"Wow. I'm really impressed."

"Me too. The reactions I had out of Vinnie were...they were the types of reactions my father should've had to things, and I take a strange comfort in that. But I know it won't be all cupcakes and roses going forward. Eventually we will clash, and it will suck, but we can make it work." I take a bite of food. "Mmm, this is really good."

We both eat for a couple of minutes. He regales me with his exploits of boredom for the day. "I'm glad we live in Phoenix. I hate being trapped because I don't want to be seen."

"I know, I'm sorry. You could've stayed in Phoenix."

"Nope," he says through a mouthful of food. "Not a chance." He smiles.

"I have something for you," I say as I stand up, and I walk back toward my bag, which I dropped on the floor when I came in. I bend down and pull out the contract and the script. I turn back toward him and he is staring at me, watching me walk and move, and I love it. The only thing that has changed about our bedroom relationship is that he's more gentle now, despite my arguments about not being made of glass, and the fact that he worships my belly any chance he can get.

"What's all that?"

"A contract."

His eyebrows scrunch together. "For what?" I hand it to him. I watch as he looks at it. "Did you read this?"

"Not all of it."

"Come here," he says, and I go to him; he spreads his legs for me to take a seat on his lap. I do, and he hands me the contract.

I begin reading it. I see where it says Tristan's name, Vincent's and Bold's names, along with a bunch of other stuff.

For the role of Tyler Garrison, main character. "Additional contract attached."

I look up at him then flip the page.

Again, Tristan, Vinnie and Bold are named.

For the role of producer.

I squeal. "Ohmygod, Tristan! You got it, your first producing gig." I hug him. "Why didn't you tell me?"

"I wanted to surprise you. But they also didn't have much of a choice." I scowl at him. "You never looked very closely at the script. You, like me, became fixated on the date." He reaches for the thick stack of papers I'd set on the table. "Look at it. Very closely," he says, and I flip back the cover.

Finding Forever
Directed by Alexei Silverstein

I gasp.

Produced by: Tristan Michaels and Arnold Alberts
Written by: Tristan Michaels

I cry.

He doesn't say anything to me for a minute while I take in what I'm seeing.

"Baby?" he says.

I look up to him, our eyes meet, and I feel a swelling sense of pride wash through me, knowing that the man I love is seeing his dreams come true. "I'm so proud of you," I breathe, and I kiss him. "When did you write this?"

"A couple of years ago, but it holds a strange resemblance to the way things happened between us. So to see this—" He points to the script. "—just gives me the opportunity to portray how much I love you on screen."

We don't talk too much the rest of the night. Instead we wrap ourselves around each other and enjoy one another's company.

FORTY-THREE

******
Tristan
******

"Is everything all set?" I ask Beau on the phone.

"Yes, we're here and we will have the entire island to ourselves, excepting the staff, come the twenty-third, just as you've requested."

"Good. We're about to head to the airport."

"She still doesn't know?"

"No." I smile at my little secret. "I have to go." I hang up just as Cami comes out of the bathroom dressed in a blue sleeveless baby doll top and black cotton capris. I love her in the baby doll dresses and tops; I am so ready to announce this to the world, but it will have to wait until after we return.

She comes out of the bathroom, and sitting in the middle of the floor are all our suitcases. "What's going on?" she says, looking at me.

"You have a doctor appointment in thirty minutes. We need to get going."

"I know that, Tristan, but where did all these suitcases come from? We only came with one between the two of us. Tristan Michaels, what are you up to?" She smiles at me.

"Later, we have to go." *Knock, knock.* Saved by the knock.

Tyson stands on the other side of the door. "Ready?"

"Yep. Come on, love. We need to go."

"Tristan?" She scolds me with her eyes.

"Doctor appointment. Let's go."

"You're up to something, mister." Though she is trying to be angry, she is excited and I can tell.

We rush out of the hotel and we're off to the doctor's office. We get there with only moments to spare, and we get called back almost immediately.

Cami is up on the bed, naked from the waist down, and seeing her lying there, and her beautiful bump visible, is an amazing sight to see.

Dr. Burgess comes into the room. "Hello, Cameron, I'm Doctor Burgess," she says, and she extends her hand to Cami and then over to me. "Nice to meet you both. So, Cami, you think you're about sixteen to seventeen weeks along?"

"Yes," she says to the doctor.

"Is this your first time seeing a doctor?"

"No." She shakes her head. "I have a doctor in Phoenix, but when the time comes, we will be living here in Los Angeles, so I wanted to get a start on prenatal care here."

"Good choice."

We go through the initial exam, and then it comes time for an ultrasound. Dr. Burgess wants to take a look to be sure. She goes through the initial setup and gets

Cami ready, and my heart starts pounding. We haven't had an ultrasound since she was in the hospital and I'm excited to see our baby again. After a moment or two, Dr. Burgess asks us the all-knowing question. "Do you want to know the sex of the baby?"

"We've decided we'd like to wait," Cami says, but I secretly want to know.

"Okay, that sounds good. Let's take a look." She goes to work on the ultrasound machine and I can vaguely make out the grainy black-and-white images from the angle I'm at, but after only a few minutes Dr. Burgess turns the monitor in our direction. "It's got a great profile." She points out the features, which are a little easier to see this time around — more solid structure — and I wipe a tear from my eye. "Want to really see what your baby looks like?" Dr. Burgess asks us, and Cami and I both look at each other then back to Dr. Burgess.

"Sure," Cami says, and we watch as she moves the wand a little, and then all of a sudden the image changes from grainy black and white to a sepia-colored image where we can actually see the baby's eye sockets. "It's sucking its thumb?" Cami asks as we both watch the baby move.

"Sure is, did you feel that just now?" I look away from the monitor at Cami.

"No, I don't think so."

"Might be a little early, but sometime over the next couple of weeks you should be able to start to feel your baby move." Oh, wow. "I'll snap a couple of souvenir pictures for you to take with you." She does that and then leaves the room.

I stand up, kiss Cami on the forehead and put my hand on her belly. "That was...wow," is all I can say.

We're both fighting tears. "Are you sure you don't want to know?" I ask her. "We haven't talked about it, really."

"Do you?" she asks me.

"I want to know what you want to know. If you don't, then we will leave it a secret until it comes. If you want to know, then we can know." She smiles at me.

"You make this too easy sometimes." She smiles and sits up, sliding off of the table to get dressed.

After a few minutes we're back in the car and on our way to the airport. "Where are we going, Tristan?" she asks me as soon as we drive onto LAX property.

I smile. "It's a surprise," I say to her and smirk.

"We're going to Tarah, aren't we?" she asks, and I nod. She squeals and hugs me hard around the neck.

"Remember that new Christmas tradition we talked about starting?" She nods. "Well, this is the start of it."

"I love you."

"Ditto," I say, and she laughs.

******
Cami
******

We've been in Tarah about a week and the weather is perfect. Tristan has been amazingly attentive to anything I want. But I start to notice, when we go down for dinner or to Blu, that there are not a lot of people here. I'd expected so many more people. Spending the holiday break in paradise is the ultimate Christmas; but then again, that just might be my opinion.

It's Christmas Eve, and Tristan and I are going downstairs to have dinner. I'm very thankful that I was able to improvise on at least one of his presents. The

275

other ones are back in Phoenix and I had no way of getting them, at least not without him knowing. When we enter the dining room, it is completely empty except for a couple of servers. Then I hear a lot of commotion coming from behind a wall to the left, and I suddenly feel better about keeping the servers busy on Christmas Eve.

"Come on," Tristan says, and he leads me around the wall where the commotion was coming from a minute ago. We round the corner, and sitting there at a long table are Tyson, Jolene, Travis, Naomi, Mick and Beau.

My hand comes to my mouth, and I look at Tristan, then back to the table. "My God."

Tristan comes closer to me and whispers in my ear, "New tradition. Every year, regardless of where we all are, we come to Tarah for Christmas. We are our own family and we need to be with family for the holidays." He kisses me and then drags me over to the table.

The night is amazing; we have a great time together, talking and catching up. None of us have seen each other much, with the exception of Ty and Jo. We're all bantering and talking, everyone is drinking — except me — and having a good time, when the sound of silver on glass breaks us all up, and everyone looks to Tristan.

"Thank you, all of you, for being here and for helping Cami and me start a new tradition. I know you all have families outside of our little circle, but it means more to me than anything to have you all here." I take his hand and squeeze it gently as he looks around at everyone. "Now, for one of the real reasons why we're here." I see him wink to everyone, and he moves around his chair to stand off to my right and gets down on one knee and the waterworks start. From his pocket he produces a black box. "Cameron Celeste Enders, you've made me the happiest man on earth and I want to spend the rest of my life making you as happy as I am. Will you do the honor of becoming my wife?"

He opens the box, and inside is a beautiful heart cut diamond surrounded by no fewer than two dozen smaller diamonds that extend down to create the band. The tears in my eyes make it harder to see it, but I realize that he's waiting for an answer. "Yes. Absolutely yes." He comes up and he kisses me, and the rest of the world is gone; no one else is here but he and I.

Everyone at the table claps and there are girlish squeals of delight at Tristan's proposal. Tristan holds me close to him and he whispers in my ear, "Marry me on Wednesday."

"What?" I blurt, and he laughs.

"The island is empty, all of our friends are here. Marry me on Wednesday, at sunset on the beach."

"Tristan, I— What do you mean the island is empty?"

He laughs. "I reserved the entire hotel, the only people in it are us and a small amount of staff to service us."

"Oh my God, Tristan. I have nothing to wear."

He smiles again then looks at Beau. "I think Beau can help you with that?"

"Ohmygod, you're all in on this?"

The entire table erupts in applause and laughter. I look back at Tristan: His eyes are pleading with me, begging me to say yes. I would've said yes anyway, but it is fun to make him squirm. "Yes, Tristan, a thousand times yes."

His lips are on me in a nanosecond and he is kissing me with gusto, and I giggle, kissing him back, and again everyone erupts into clapping and hollering.

The rest of the night, I can't keep my eyes off of Tristan; I keep thinking about what he's done and is doing. He planned this whole thing and I should've known better, but I never expected this.

Christmas morning. Tristan is awake and looking at me when I finally open my eyes. "Hi, beautiful." I beat him to it.

"Hi beautiful yourself." He laughs, kisses my forehead. "Merry Christmas."

"Mmm, I like the sound of that. Merry Christmas, Tristan."

"Come on, get up. You have a lot to do today, starting with..." He produces a long black velvet box with a bow on it, and I smile.

"How long have you been awake?" I ask as I sit up.

He smiles. "Not long." Something tells me he's lying, but I don't care. I take the box from him, hold it between my fingers and lift the lid.

What's inside takes my breath away. It's a platinum band, a bracelet that has tiny links that are hooked on either side of an infinity symbol. One of the curves has the word *forever* spelled out. "Tristan, it's beautiful," I say as I try and remove it from the box. He takes it from me and unhooks it from its resting place. I hold out my left wrist and he clasps it. The platinum up against my sun-kissed skin is beautiful, and it sparkles in the light of the bedroom. I place my left hand on his cheek, catching the sparkle before I kiss him.

"There's more," he says. "Come on." He crawls out of bed and I slow him just a second.

"I need a minute," I say, and I go into the bathroom.

I feel really guilty that I wasn't able to get all of his presents here. He will have to wait until we get home and it breaks my heart. I try not to let it show when I come back out of the bathroom, but he catches that something is wrong. "What's the matter?" he asks as he wraps his arm over my shoulder and leads me toward the door.

I pause. "Tristan, I—" I don't quite know how to say this to him. "All of your presents are at home in Phoenix. I didn't know—"

"Shh. It's okay. This is a Christmas about you. Not me."

"That's hardly fair," I say, and he leads me to the door anyway. He opens it up, and sitting in the living room of our penthouse suite is a Christmas tree, completely decorated, and around the bottom is a massive pile of presents. But I also notice that there are several presents wrapped in the paper I used back home. "How?"

"Beau. She found them in the condo and brought them with."

"Oh, for hell. You guys are too much to take sometimes." He laughs as I roll my eyes. "Now at least I feel a little less guilty."

"Good. Come on, sit down in your favorite chair." He leads me to it and I sit down. The chair isn't as comfortable as it once was, and I think I have this growing bump as an explanation for it. I can no longer pull my knees to my chin. Tristan laughed when I realized I couldn't do it anymore, but dang it, that's my most comfortable position. He reassured me that I'd be able to do it again...one day.

I watch as he rummages through the packages, but I can see that he's extremely excited about making this day about me and I take great comfort in that. He walks toward me with a small box, similar to the one with my bracelet in it but a little bigger. He hands it to me. "Go ahead, open it," he says, and he sits on the edge of the coffee table.

I smile and tear into the wrapping paper. There is a plain white box and I pull the lid off. Sitting inside is a desk plaque.

Cameron 'Cami' Michaels
CEO

"What would you have done if I'd said no?" I laugh. He smirks his all-knowing grin. I shake my head at him. "You are too much sometimes. And I love you like crazy for it." He kisses my forehead as he stands up and goes back to the tree. "Open one of mine to you," I say, and he shakes his head.

"You get to go first," he says as he brings me another package. This one is bigger and I can't quite tell what it is. "You're really hard to shop for, especially since I know you buy the things you want. So this is a little something for me, too."

I smirk at him — the only thing that could possibly be for him too is lingerie — but like any kid on Christmas I tear into the package and open the lid of the box. Inside are twelve barbells tucked into a card. I cock my head at the package and he explains. "A couple of weeks ago, you said that putting ribbon in your back tugged more than you were comfortable with. So I thought maybe if you had barbells to replace the hoops, you wouldn't feel so obligated to lace them. And I wouldn't be worried about snagging them so much."

I smile up at him. "That's a great idea. Thank you for thinking about it." I never thought about replacing the hoops, and I'm not sure I want to, but this might not be a bad idea. At least right now.

"Lift the card," he says, and I do.

Underneath is a bellybutton ring, but this one is different; it's... "Stretchy?" I ask him.

He nods. "I read online that if you're pregnant with a bellybutton ring, one of two things will happen, either it will close or there is a risk of it tearing. I didn't want to see either happen, so I found this. It is designed to stretch and give as your belly expands." I smile at his thoughtfulness, and I'm glad he's thought about it because I certainly haven't. "There's one more."

"My nipples?"

He grins. "These, though, are for me." I blush slightly and lift the card with the bellybutton ring, and underneath are two circles that are inlayed with diamonds and with barbells running through the centers. I smile. "You can wear them whenever you want, but I'd like it if you wore them tomorrow."

I blush a little and nod. "They're beautiful, of course I will."

Of all the things in the world he could get me for Christmas, he's bought me a massive amount of jewelry — but all with my own comfort in mind, and I can't help but let my heart be filled with warmth at his thoughtfulness.

FORTY-FOUR

Over the course of the morning, I open up another fourteen presents from him. Everything from a beautiful Gucci dress to Jimmy Choos to a new swimming suit. And of course, as I figured, lingerie was included, but I'll keep that to myself.

The last present he brings over is one similar to the birthday present I gave him and I scoff at him; we already have two houses, for crying out loud, but I dutifully open the present. Sure enough, it is a locked tube, and I look at him. "Open it," he says, and he is bouncing up and down. I look inside and there are three sets of blueprints. I get down on the floor and spread them out on the coffee table. The first set has a picture of our house in California. I look up at him. "The house wasn't originally designed to accommodate a nursery on the main floor next to our suite. So, I had them redesign the plans a little bit. We're still maintaining the same structure, just changing the layout a little."

I flip to the first page. It is the ground level, and where our master suite was supposed to be there are now three rooms: one labeled *Cami's Office*, another labeled

Tristan's Office, and finally the last room, which is tucked into the back corner of the house. It says *Nanny Quarters*. "Tristan, I—"

"Listen. I know that we haven't talked about it yet. But I thought that the house needed a redesign, just in case. I think — and obviously it is up for discussion later — that we need to consider that option. If I am going to continue to act and produce and things of that nature, I won't always be able to be home. You will be in L.A. or in Phoenix alone, and you will need to work too. The condo is already equipped with a servant's quarters, so I didn't do much with that."

"Okay, I'm open to a nanny discussion. Another day." I smile at him then I turn the page. Upstairs has been redesigned, taking two of the original bedrooms away and creating a master suite while maintaining the other two rooms, one of which is right across the hall from our room. "That's a brilliant idea, Tristan. I love it." He leans over and kisses me.

"You can flip to the next set. The rest in that one are just some general design changes that they sent along with my changes." I flip to the next set. It says *Tarah* across it. "These are temporary designs, and they come from Beau."

I flip the page, taking one quick look, then I look at him. "The bar?" He nods. "Blu Phoenix?"

"That was Beau's idea. She thought it would be fun to have our own little piece of paradise in Phoenix."

"I like it," I say as I flip the page. The first page is the bar's layout, which isn't a whole lot to get excited about, at least not yet. The bar itself has a wide open space and floor plan. It was once a country bar, after all. He stops me from turning the page, and he does it himself.

"This goes backwards. See — the blank layout, like the previous page." He flips back one of the pages in front of it. It is transparent, and I can see it; it almost becomes three-dimensional. First comes the main bar. Off to the right of the door, behind the bar, is a kitchen and office space. The bar spans the entire length of the east wall of the building, and the kitchen and offices behind it do the same. He flips the next page, and a stage appears along the back wall, along with an extension to the building onto the back patio. A dressing/waiting room, then there is a doorway that leads to the stage. Then, finally, the last page comes down, and appearing to the left of the door is another small bar, tucked back out of sight of the doorway, with a couple of bar-height tables in front and then lining the wall back toward the stage. To the right of the door, there are a few more tables that lead to a larger group of tables that surround a massive dance floor in front of the stage. "The stage is big enough that we could host a good sized band, but the bar maintains that intimate viewing experience."

"It's amazing, she's done a wonderful job." He turns back the transparent pages and the blank one. Behind it is the layout of the back of the property. "The old arena?"

"Yup, she wants to turn it into an outside concert area, allowing for two more bars, a few tables, more patrons and a bigger stage."

"So, turning it into a small concert venue. Oh my God, that's genius. I never even considered that."

He smiles at me, and it's warm and inviting. "She's done a wonderful job and she's excited to get started. I am sure sometime over the rest of our stay here, she will badger you about it." He laughs.

"Just how long are we staying?"

"As long as you want. Or January tenth. Which would give you enough time to get back to Phoenix and get ready to start up at Bold."

"Sounds great." I stand up and kiss him.

"Oh, you're not done yet." He gives me a wicked grin.

"Dang it, Tristan, what else is there?" I laugh, and he pulls up the bar's blueprints to reveal another set of blueprints. "Ah hell, Tristan. We have two houses."

He laughs harder. "We do, but we needed something else. But this isn't your Christmas gift, this is a wedding gift. For both of us."

I look down and read the lettering across the top. *Michaels Vacation Home*. I turn the page and it's an island. "You bought an island."

He snorts. "No. I bought a plot on the island. About a three-hour boat ride from here. We love to come here so much, but we spend so much money. When I weighed that against buying and building, this came out ahead in the long run."

I can't help the tears that escape my eyes, and I turn the page. Laid out are three domed buildings, all connected together by what appear to be suspended walkways. The houses are on stilts, and I immediately see why. They are over the water, like the place we stayed at in Bora Bora. But beyond that, on land, is another, larger house — but it is not huge, by any means. I flip the page and it is the layout design of the huts. They are small, but still two-bedroom with a sitting room. Then I come to the house. It is a quaint little oceanfront house, typical of this part of the South Pacific, and it is beautiful.

Three bedrooms, kitchen, dining room — the works. I flip the page again, and there is a massive patio and pool, and it is simply stunning. "Tristan, I don't know what to say."

"Thank you?"

"Thank you, thank you." I smile and kiss him more than a few times. Then I remember his own presents. "You have presents, too." I say, and he scowls.

FORTY-FIVE

"They can wait," I tell her. My presents, no matter what they are, are unimportant. Today is for Cami and no one else. But I can see she won't let it go, so I dutifully go back to the tree, grab my presents and bring them back to the sitting area we're in. I worried and worried over all the blueprints; the other stuff was minor, but the house — especially the house — was freaking me out for two reasons: one, how she would react to the amount of money; and two, because she'd done the same for me for my birthday a few months ago.

I sit down and ask her, "Which one?"

She shrugs. "Pick one." So I do, and she blushes bright red.

"Hmm, wonder what's in here?" I tease her, and tear into the paper.

"More for me than for you." She smiles and I open the box.

"Hmm, to use on me or for me to use on you?" I ask her.

She shrugs again. "Either, or." I like that idea. Inside the box are a pair of leather cuffs and a blindfold. We've played around with restraints before, but not recently, and I rather like the idea of restraining her, especially with the blindfold. The idea stirs my cock awake. "I can see your wheels turning," she says, and laughs.

"Oh, of course." I put the lid back on and pick another one. I made her wait patiently for each gift, but I know this is a little different for her and it's not about me, so I move on quickly. I tear open the paper, and it is a sleek black box. I already have a watch. I open the lid, and lying on some black tissue paper is a key. A car key. I smirk. "What is this to?" I ask her.

"The R-eight."

"No way," I say, very excited. "Why?" I ask her, and she doesn't say anything; she doesn't need to. She just brings her hand to rest on her bump. "It's still your car," I say.

"Lift the paper," she says, and I do; underneath the paper is the title to the car, transferred from her name to mine. "No, it's yours. It is practically brand new, I couldn't part with it because it is my favorite car, so I thought that you might like to have it."

I smile and shake my head. "I love the crap out of you," I say, and she busts out laughing.

"Go on, you have more to open," she says as she watches me. I grab another package; this one is smaller, more gift card size than an actual present. I open it.

Inside is a gift card. "Skeleton Key?"

"It's to X, my tattoo goddess. You once talked about getting a tribal done on your shoulder. I can't take you to get it now, since we're here, but I thought maybe you'd like to get it done another time."

"Cami, it's perfect. Thank you." I hadn't actually thought about it in some time, and it's not that I couldn't afford it on my own; she wants it to come from her, and I love that about her.

I finish with my presents: some clothes — well, more specifically, Ravens gear. I think we both did really well, considering neither one of us said anything about what we wanted for Christmas.

The rest of our friends join us early in the afternoon. Travis, the one man I never thought would settle down, has decided to move to Phoenix with Naomi — at least until the houses in L.A. are done. It makes me happy to see that he's making a commitment to her, and that was his big gift to her for Christmas. Cami and I had gone together and gotten something for everyone, though it wasn't anything huge because the trip is on me; well, after Cami and I talked, we decided that we're going to split the cost. She said it was important to her.

The girls all disappear around four and are gone until dinner arrives in the suite and is set up at the big table outside at six. When the girls come back up, they join their men, but Cami isn't anywhere to be found. "Where's Cams?" I ask.

"She said she needed a minute." Oh. I give her a few minutes, but she doesn't come out to join us, so I go looking for her. I knock on the bedroom door.

"Come in," she says, and I open the door, step inside and close it behind me.

"Hey, sweets, you okay?"

"I'm freaking out a little bit." I look at her then: She has her shirt pulled up and her pants rolled down slightly, and her hands are on her belly.

"What's wrong?"

She looks up at me and smiles. "Come here." I take the few steps toward her. "Feel." She takes my hands and places them on her belly.

It takes a moment, but then... "It feels like popcorn."

She laughs. "I thought maybe it was either that I was hungry or had to go to the bathroom. Neither seemed to be the case, so I just sat here. I couldn't take my hands off."

It stops when she stops talking. "Say something else."

"Like what?" And it happens again. It is the most beautiful feeling in the world, and I feel her thumb wipe away a tear before I even realize I'm crying.

"You're so beautiful," I tell her, and she smiles.

"So are you." I lean forward and kiss her, keeping my hands on her belly. After a couple more pops it stops. We both wait anxiously for a few moments and decide that there is plenty of time to feel it again, and we join our friends.

Beau tries to convince Cami that she can't see me tomorrow, and she refuses. "I've never imagined not seeing my husband-to-be on my wedding day. So forget it," she scolds.

"Okay, fine, you can stay with him tonight, but come noon tomorrow, you're mine," she says as she and Mick leave our suite. They're the last to leave for the night, and Cami and I fall into bed, exhausted, but that doesn't stop us from enjoying each other one last time as boyfriend and girlfriend. "Mrs. Michaels. I love the way that sounds," I tell her, and she giggles.

"Mrs. Tristan Michaels. That does have a nice ring to it.

I fall asleep playing her name over and over in my head. Cameron Celeste Michaels. Cami Michaels. It sounds so perfect.

I am kicked out of the suite promptly at noon. I'm trying desperately to figure out what they need seven hours for, but I decide not to argue when Beau tells me that she will be ready by five, at which time I need to be ready and she will find me, and I'm okay with that. I go downstairs to Travis's suite, thankful that the girls are all upstairs doing their girlie things. Trav and I hang out, talk about anything and everything. I come to find out that Trav is completely in love with Naomi and that he's been doing everything he can to prove to her that he's committed to her. Short of putting a ring on her finger. He hates that she doesn't travel with him, but I told him that could be arranged. He just needs to hire her. But he made a few good points about them working together. He's afraid he will grow tired of her. But in reality, I think it is just Trav being a man and wanting something that is his own.

I am eternally grateful that Cami likes to travel with me, though in the coming months that will become harder for her to do and it makes me sad. But, while I'm filming, she does other things. She's not hanging around the set bored or anything along those lines, so I have mine and she will soon have hers.

Three o'clock rolls around, and Mick and Ty show up in Travis's suite. Mick has my outfit for today: white linen pants and a matching short-sleeved shirt. He says that it will go great with what Cami is wearing, and it is perfect for a beach wedding. We all finish getting dressed and the room phone rings. I answer it because I'm closest to it. "The photographer is ready for you guys. On Blu's deck."

"Thanks, Beau. Am I still to come up there at five?"

"Sure, or when you're done with pictures, whichever comes later." I roll my eyes.

"All right."

"Bring the guys too."

"Okay." She hangs up.

Cami and I have agreed that we won't officially have anyone standing with us today but that, because they're here, they are automatically part of the ceremony. The girls will be walking down the aisle before Cami does.

When we get downstairs and onto Blu's deck, it dawns on me that not only will Cami and I be getting married on the beach on the same island where we met, but that we literally will be getting married in the exact spot where we first met. It seems like a lifetime ago, but yet not all that long ago, either. She is who I want to spend the rest of my life with, no one else.

FORTY-SIX

Knock, knock. "That's probably Tristan," Jo says as she goes to the door. She opens it. "Or not. What are you doing here?"

"Who is it, Jo?" I ask from the living room.

"Um." She doesn't answer, and I look toward the door.

"Prime time for you to show up," I snap.

"Please don't be like that, Cameron. Girls, can I have a moment alone with my daughter?" All eyes snap to me and I nod. I'm sitting on the couch, turning over the sofa to look at him; he can't see all of me. The girls leave the room for the foyer. I have a feeling Tristan will be up here in no time flat, and I'm okay with that.

"What are you doing here, Bobby?"

"Please, don't be angry with me."

"How did you even know where to find me?" I don't want the answer to that question.

His answer surprises me. "Tristan."

I gasp. "What?"

"He sent me an email. Told me where and what time. Told me that this was going to be the biggest day of my daughter's life, a day that I would miss if I didn't come." I watch as the tears form in his eyes. I've never, ever seen Bobby cry. "I couldn't miss it and I couldn't watch it from afar."

I stand up. I'm still facing away from him. My dress is a white linen halter top dress with a plunging neckline that meets a band that runs under my breasts, and it's open in the back. My hair is up in a very beautiful, messy 'do, and I have a purple flower over my right ear. There are three things happening here. One, I am not wearing a bra and my breasts have grown a full size since the last time I saw Bobby. Two, every inch of my back and my shoulders is exposed, showing off my wings as well as my shoulder tattoos. And lastly, even with the wide, flowing skirt, I am very clearly showing.

I hesitate too long, and I know that Bobby is getting a full view of the ink on my body and I am certain that he is not pleased. "Cameron, turn around, please." Nope, not pleased at all. So what. I turn around, and as I do I hear his sharp intake of breath, but I can't bring myself to look at him. I feel like the six-year-old who stole a cookie from the cookie jar and I'm going to have it ripped out of my hands. "Please tell me—" he starts, and panic washes through me. "Please tell me that you are marrying him because you love him." My eyes meet his, which are alight with curiosity and emotion, and a smile spreads across his face.

"Yes, I am marrying him because I love him. I am marrying him right now because he's asked and surprised me with this whole thing. Not because I am eighteen weeks pregnant with his child."

Relief washes over his features, and I stand there staring at him, waiting for the anger to set in, but he surprises me still. "I'm a horrible person for everything I've done to you. I don't deserve to be here on your special day. But I am asking you to please, find it in your heart to forgive me for the God-awful mistakes I've made." He takes a deep breath. "I can't right the ship, I can't make it go away, and as much as I want to, I won't be able to fight to have a relationship with you because I can't be there for you in a way I know you want me to be. Not because I don't want to, but because I can't."

"What do you mean?"

"I've had to leave the U.S. I can't go back, at least not until I testify, which could take years. Even then, once I testify, I will likely never be safe again. Just because they've managed to take down the one person they needed to.... These rings are complicated, and just because the big guy is gone doesn't mean there isn't someone else waiting in the wings."

I try hard not to cry because of my makeup. But it's very hard. "So I'll never see you again after today?" He takes a step in my direction.

"Oh, I wouldn't say that," he says as he draws closer to me. I hear the door click closed and Tristan comes into the room. "You see, your soon-to-be husband has acquired a piece of property on an island here in the South Pacific. An island that belongs to me." He reaches me then, and I wrap my arms around him. "But that is our secret, between the three of us here and no more. No one else can ever know either that I own it or that I have a home on it. If you decide to visit and you're alone — no friends, no staff, no nothing — I will come and visit you.

But only I will come to you. Tristan knows how to reach me."

"What about today?" I ask.

"Today is your day. Your friends here all know the truth — they know that I'm alive, which is fine — but by the time anyone knows I've been here, if at all, I will be long gone, disappeared over the horizon." The way he says it sounds so mysterious and James Bond-ish. But I understand. I pull back from Bobby to look at Tristan.

"Did you know?"

He gives me a small smile. "I had a feeling when an anonymous email appeared outlining a listing of sorts. I put two and two together when I only paid fifteen grand for the property itself."

"He's a smart one," Bobby says, and he puts some distance between us. I look at Tristan: his tousled blond and brown hair, his beautiful white linen shirt and pants. Even in the light coming in from the patio, I can see through the shirt and see his dragon. He is wearing sandals, but I believe those will be ditched before the actual ceremony begins. He looks beautiful. He takes in the sight of me in my dress, then he comes over to hug me.

"You look amazing," he says as he kisses my forehead. We agreed that, other than for the pictures we're supposed to take, we wouldn't kiss between when we separated at noon and the ceremony.

"Thank you, Tristan." He pulls back from me and holds his hand out for Bobby to take, and Bobby does.

"Thank you for being here."

Bobby smiles. "I wouldn't miss it. Never have, never will."

"Dad," I say before I realize what I've called him, but I don't care. "Will you walk me down the aisle?" My voice is full of emotion and Tristan looks at me, testing to make sure this is what I really want.

"I would be honored," he says to me, and he smiles.

I suddenly feel a twinge of guilt run through me. Tristan's mom. She isn't here and I feel awful about it. I look at Bobby. "Thank you," I say. "Tristan and I are going to do some pictures up here, then we will be downstairs, on Blu's patio. Can we meet you there?"

"Absolutely," he says, and he departs. I know I only have a few minutes before the photographer shows up and I want to say something to Tristan.

"You look amazing," he says to me, and he smiles. I smile back at him, but it is guarded.

"Tristan?"

"Yeah," he says, knowing something is playing on my mind. "If you don't really want him here, he can leave."

"No, it's not that, and I thank you from the bottom of my heart for letting him know, but it made me think of something and it's not something I want to bring up..."

He takes a deep breath, almost a sigh. "You're referring to my mum." I look at him then. "Sure, I wish she could be here to see you, to meet you, to meet our baby and to be a part of my life, but her passing is a reality I accepted a long time ago. And when I accepted that reality I understood that she'd never be at my wedding." He takes another deep, long, shuddering breath. "It still hurts that she isn't here, but your father being here does not make me wish she were here any more." He starts to unbutton his shirt, and I watch as his dragon's head appears. His hand rubs at it. "She is always with me." He points to the dragon's eyes and the dermal studs there. "You see, his eyes — those are made from earrings that she wore every day."

He begins to button up his shirt, and I can't stop the tears from sliding down my cheeks. "God I love you," I breathe.

"I once had a dragon tattooed on my body, missing its heart because I always thought that my mum had taken it away from me when she left, but she put my heart in your hands to make me whole once again."

FORTY-SEVEN

******
Tristan
******

"Do I wish she were here? Absolutely," I breathe, and Cami comes closer to me.

"She's here with us, Tristan, never, ever doubt that." She puts her arms on my shoulders. "Everyone who is here with us, they are the people who matter. Today, and they matter tomorrow, and next month or next year. Your mom is here in your heart." She places her hand on my chest over my heart. "And she is in here." She places her hand on her own heart. "I'm sorry if I made you sad, it was not my intention."

I smile at her. "Cams, nothing on this day can make me sad. This is our day." I lean down and kiss her.

The photographer comes into the room, followed closely by Beau. "Hey now, no kissing," she says.

"But the photographer is here," I say through clenched teeth for interrupting my kiss with Cami.

"He wasn't when you started." I look at her and she sticks her tongue out at me. Cami busts into a fit of giggles at our exchange and all the heaviness of our conversation is washed away, just like that.

Cami and I are posed and photographed over and over again. As we head downstairs to everyone else, Beau and the photographer leave ahead of us. I turn to Cami. "Do you have any idea how much those pictures are now worth?"

She laughs. "Yes, I have an idea, but what makes them more expensive is the bump. Nothing fires up the paparazzi more than a bump watch." She smiles at me.

"How much longer can you wear baby dolls?"

She lets out a carefree laugh. "Not too much longer, it is going to come out."

"Awards season is coming. Let's try and hold off until then."

"It's time," Naomi says, and she shoos me and the guys out of Blu and onto the beach. The girls are dressed in short sundresses; they don't match, but they are all similar in design and color. We'd decided that no one was officially standing with us today, but our friends are still part of our ceremony.

Out on the beach is a beautiful white lattice that is wrapped with tropical flowers. There are only a few chairs in front of the altar set up. Seven to be exact. One for each of our friends and Cami's father.

I was so worried that she'd be angry with me for inviting Bobby, but it seems it was a good choice and I'm happy I did it.

The four of us walk toward the altar, and standing there is a gentleman — I'm assuming he is our minister —

and I walk toward him to shake his hand and thank him for being here. I turn back, and my best friends are sitting from right to left with a chair in between them. Tyson, then Travis. Across the aisle are two empty chairs and then Mick. I stand there for a few minutes, waiting impatiently.

The doors open up, and standing on the other side of them is Naomi; behind her is Jo, then it goes dark. A guitar starts playing, light and soft. Naomi begins walking toward me; then the most beautiful voice begins to sing.

Naomi comes forward, and just as the song registers, Jolene steps through the door.

It's "I Won't Give Up," but Jason Mraz isn't singing it.

Beau starts walking just as the chorus picks up.

I see Cami stepping into the doorway, her arm through her father's.

She's singing. I start crying.

She's walking toward me.

She finishes the song and tears streak down my cheeks.

The girls are now standing in front of their chairs, turned toward Cami.

It's just she and her father walking toward me in step to the music.

She and her father are standing right in front of me. Bobby has an awed look on his face, and the song picks up in tempo.

She smiles at me as I wipe away a tear.

She wipes away her own tears before finishing out the song.

Bobby removes Cami's hand from his arm. "You're beautiful," he says to her, and she smiles at him. He kisses her cheek and places her hand in mine. I want to kiss her so bad for her beautiful song, but I behave myself at least for a few minutes.

The sun is setting, and high clouds begin to dance with beautiful oranges, yellows and reds. The backdrop is gorgeous and I've never wanted anything more than the woman standing next to me in this beautiful and perfect setting.

I wait very impatiently for the best part of this service, but before that, we exchange our rings, and the ring she's given me is beautiful and simple: black gold surrounding a wide platinum band. I slip her ring on her finger, and it's platinum, to match her engagement ring, and it locks under the heart that she's already wearing.

"I now pronounce you husband and wife."

That's my cue and I grin. I pull her close to me, and I spin toward our small audience and dip her. She squeals. "I love you." And I kiss her, hot and needy, in front of all our friends.

FORTY-EIGHT

We spend the rest of the evening with our friends inside of Blu; everyone is having a great time. It is a surprise to see Jessie behind the bar, and it is good to see him again.

We spend the evening dancing, including a dance with Cami and her father, and for our dance, she serenades me with her own acoustic rendition of "When I Look at You." And I have to admit, she sings it far better than Miley Cyrus. Throughout the night I notice that she seems happier than I've ever seen her, and I'm so happy he came — for her if no one else.

Bobby is the first to leave.

"Take care of my girl," he tells me as he takes my hand.

"I intend to." He pulls me into a hug and I'm surprised by it.

"I'd always hoped you two would find each other. I knew from the moment I met you that there was something special with you."

"Thank you, sir."

He pulls back and embraces Cami. "I should've never stifled that beautiful talent you have. You're beautiful and I am so honored to have been here today."

"I'm glad you were here too. Thank you," she whispers, and I can see that this is a very emotional goodbye for her. She knows that she can see her father again, but there is always that chance that she never will.

After Bobby leaves, I take Cami into the lobby of the hotel.

"Are you okay?"

She smiles through her tears. "I will be. I didn't know that he'd attended my graduations, and more importantly, I was angry that he was there and I didn't know it. But today, having him here makes up for all of that. Thank you, Tristan, for telling him. I know you couldn't make him come, and if he hadn't shown up, I'm not sure I would've missed him. But having him here means a lot to me." She hugs me.

I use my hand to lift her chin. "Anything for my wife." She smiles and blushes as I use a new term. My heart fills with pride and joy, knowing that this woman is mine forever.

It is nearly midnight before Cami and I escape to our penthouse suite. "How are you feeling?" I ask her. I noticed a little while ago that she was a little restless.

"I feel amazing," she says, and she comes toward me. "Now I want to feel even more amazing." She pushes me back on the bed, but she's not satisfied to have me sitting and she pushes me back. She hitches up the skirt of her dress and straddles me. She brings her lips to mine, and her kiss has my head swimming. She smells amazing, like the ocean and Cami. A scent I've come to love, especially when we're here.

304

I feel her hands move along my chest, and the cool air of the room comes through as she unbuttons my shirt. When she's reached the last button, her lips come away from mine and she begins kissing down my neck to my chest. Her tongue flicks across one of my nipples and the small barbell running through it warms and cools quickly. She kisses her way to the other and does the same thing.

Then she moves up my chest and kisses my dragon, and I can't take it anymore. I begin pulling up her dress and find no resistance – she's been careful to pull it up so she's not kneeling on it — and I love that. The dress clears her body quickly, and I am met with her beautifully full breasts. "No bra, Mrs. Michaels?" I tease — I knew she wasn't wearing one — and she smiles, then kisses me. I kiss her back, but I want to enjoy the view a little longer so I push her back and up.

She is wearing the nipple rings I gave her. The diamonds are surrounding her nipples and the rings are helping to keep her nipples hard, and I love it. Though the rings are a little small, when my tongue grazes one she trembles, and I know they're super sensitive and I like it, and I'm glad she does too.

She arches her back so that her chest is thrust forward, and I take that as my cue to continue. I take ahold of both of them and bring her to me, licking, kissing and sucking. She moans, and my erection strains against my pants.

My hands come away from her breasts and slide along the soft skin of her body, and she shivers and I can feel the goose bumps rise along her skin. My hands slide around to her back, and I feel a very soft ribbon along her back and my finger traces the line. "Something blue," she breathes.

"Something borrowed?" I ask.

"The comb in my hair."

"Something new?"

"My ring, my dress, my panties." She smirks and kisses me.

Our dance of kisses and tongues continues until I can't take it anymore and I need her, so I roll her over onto her back, and now I am hovering over her, holding my weight above her, and she arches her back, desperate to feel me against her. I look down the line of her body, beautiful and glowing. Her bump is more pronounced, sexier than anything I could've ever imagined, and I begin kissing my way down her body until my tongue finds her warm, wet center, and she comes apart under my tongue.

I roll her over slightly and bend her leg so she can brace herself, and I begin kissing along the curve of her hip, down along her back, until my mouth finds the end of one of her ribbons and I pull. The ribbon comes undone, and I take it in my hand and gently pull, watching as goose bumps form again as she feels the silky ribbon sliding along her back. She moans, and my hands begin to glide along her body and I roll her back over. She props herself up on her elbows. "You're wearing too many clothes," she breathes, and I stand up, unbuttoning my pants and finally freeing my straining erection. I lean over her and hook her white lacy panties in my hand, and she lifts her hip. I slide them down her legs and add them to the growing pile of clothes on the floor.

She slides up the bed and I watch her move. She is so beautiful and it's hard to believe that she's my wife. These last six months have been a whirlwind of ups and downs. But the ups definitely outweigh the downs, and I love her more every day.

Soon we will be parents and will be living lives with careers and a family, both of which I never imagined I'd

306

have in my life, but now that I do, it's heady, overwhelming, but oh so amazing.

I climb up onto the bed between her waiting legs, and in a matter of moments, I am sliding home. "You're my life. You are my everything. You are my wife and I have never felt more complete. I love you, Cameron Michaels." I kiss her slowly, full of passion and needy desire. Her answering kiss is just as strong and powerful, and I am lost to her, lost in her, and I never want to be found.

FORTY-NINE

May 28th, 2013
Five Months Later

The last five months have been pure bliss. Tristan, my husband — that still sounds strange, but it is a very good strange to hear — has been my everything. He's been there every day, and in everyway possible, and we've never had a fight that we haven't bounced back from stronger.

I'm a whale — or at least I feel that way, and for good reason. Yesterday was my due date, but nope; this stubborn little one is deciding to hang out a little longer. I was relieved when I didn't go into labor yesterday, if only for the reason that I didn't want a beautiful day to be tainted by the memory of two years ago. The day that Bobby, my father, disappeared from this world. Sure, if you would've asked me back in December how I felt about it, I'd have told you I didn't care. But since Tristan and I were married on Tarah's beach five months ago, Bobby and I have grown closer than we ever were.

Though our communication is severely limited and consists of emails, we communicate nearly every day, and it is an amazing feeling.

Life around us is blooming and blossoming. Mick and Beau were married on Valentine's Day, just like they wanted, and what made it even more special was that they were married at Blu Phoenix, our jointly owned bar that is now open and booming with business. Tristan arranged to have two private shows play opening weekend with two of Nashville's biggest stars. It was perfect and beautiful, and ever since then we've had artists dying to play our intimate little venue, and Blu Phoenix is turning a major profit.

Tristan and I now live nearly fulltime in Los Angeles. Though I'm not a fan of it, our house is nearly done, our baby is almost here, and he is busy acting in and producing *Finding Forever*. Complements of a great working relationship with the writing staff on the movie, he's made some changes to the script, changes that are more like our own life than they were before. Though I have to admit, the original script was pretty damn close. After I read it, I understood a lot more about Tristan and how he feels about me and why things were and remain so important to him.

We were able to wait until award season to announce our marriage and pregnancy, and since then I've gained my own celebrity, both in fashion and in the fact that I'm Mrs. Tristan Michaels. Quietly leaving the house we're renting has been more of a challenge due to the impending "baby watch."

"Oomph," I groan as another contraction strikes. I check my watch, a beautiful Rolex given to me by my husband on our one-month anniversary and also as a first-day-on-the-job gift. Eight minutes. It might be time to start making some phone calls.

I click the intercom button on my phone. "Rayne, can you come in here, please?"

"Yes, ma'am." After two heartbeats, she is in my office.

"I need the car," I say to her.

"Is it time?" I nod. "Yes, ma'am. Do you need help?" I shake my head and she leaves. I stand, grabbing my phone, and I dial Vinnie's extension.

"Hello, Cami."

"Hi, Vinnie, can you grab Trinity and come into my office, ASAP?"

"On our way," he says, and he hangs up.

It doesn't take but a couple of minutes for them to arrive, and when they do, I am leaning over the desk, breathing slowly through another contraction.

"You all right?" Vinnie asks.

I nod, rather dramatically, then look at my watch. Still eight minutes. Good.

"The car is here," Rayne says as she comes into my office.

"Thank you," I say as my contraction calms down.

"You two are in charge. I'll let you know what happens, or at least after it's happened. But don't expect me back until at least August."

"Absolutely. You need some help?" Vinnie says, concerned. I look at my watch.

"Nope, I have about six and a half minutes before another one strikes and I'm sure Rayne is holding the elevator." I grab my bag from the table behind my desk and walk toward them. "I'll let you know when I'm available for emergency situations, and you can draw up a press release once Tristan, the baby and I are at home." I look at my watch. Less than six minutes now.

"Good luck," Trinity says, and I smile at her and Vinnie as I leave my office. Rayne, as I expected, is holding the elevator for me.

"Are you sure you're alright?" she asks when I step inside.

"I'm great, and going to have a baby. But I don't need a scene outside."

She nods and the doors close. I pull my phone from my purse and check my watch. Four minutes.

I clear the elevator, walking as quickly and as tall as I can manage. I don't need anyone in the lobby or out on the sidewalk to suspect anything other than that I'm leaving the office. It's three in the afternoon.

I climb inside the car. "Cedars-Sinai," I tell the driver, and I look at my watch. One minute.

I look at my phone and the picture of Tristan and me on our wedding day. It's one of our shots from the penthouse. Tristan is down on his knees, holding my belly in his hands, looking up at me as he kisses my bump. Breathe, Cams.

Eight minutes.

The contraction passes a little faster than the last one did. But I keep an eye on my watch, concerned the next one might be coming faster. I press Tristan's name, and the phone starts to ring. No answer, as I expected. He is deep in filming *Finding Forever*. I try Travis, who is also in the movie. No answer. "Oh, for hell." Now Tyson.

"Cami, are you all right?"

"Nope, I'm headed to the hospital now."

"How far apart?"

We've practiced this a million times. "Eight minutes, but getting stronger. Where is he?"

"He's filming, but he saw me answer the phone. I'm looking at him now."

"What's he look like?"

"Total panic mode." He laughs and I join him.

"No panicking, it's not allowed."

"Good luck with that one, darlin'," he says. "We will be on our way."

"See you soon."

We hang up. I call Beau.

"Finally," she says into the phone, and I laugh. I look at my watch, and nearly five minutes have passed already.

"Forgone conclusion."

"So you're not in labor?"

I laugh. "Yes, I am."

"Yay!" she shouts. "We're on our way."

We hang up.

Mick and Beau are in Phoenix, but a flight leaves Phoenix like every half hour, so I have no doubt they will be airborne within the hour and at the hospital within three. Which should still be plenty of time.

Tristan and I still do not know what we are having. We both decided that there are very few surprises in life and that this should be one of the few we keep ahold of. Breathe.

I check my watch: six minutes. I breathe through the contraction, which is stronger and more painful than the last.

The car pulls up in front of the hospital and I can see photographers off in the distance. "Shit. Can you go inside, act normal, and grab a nurse or three?"

"Yes, ma'am." He climbs out of the car. This baby is the hottest ticket in Hollywood right now and I'm hoping like hell we can get inside quickly.

My driver returns with three nurses in tow. I open the door. "Are you all right?" the nurse asks.

"Yes, I'm in labor, but I need a screen. I don't need the paparazzi catching this."

"Yes, ma'am," the nurse says. They are well-versed in celebrity arrivals and they manage to extract me from the car and get me into the wheelchair without alerting the press. We're inside and on our way to Labor and Delivery in no time flat.

******
Tristan
******

I'm wringing my hands together as Tyson drives to the hospital. To say that I'm freaking out is probably an understatement. It's time, it is finally time to meet my son — or daughter — and... "Oh my God, I'm freaking out."

Tyson laughs. "She'll do great, you'll do great. Just relax."

I start to think about all the things we're not ready for. The house isn't done; the nursery certainly isn't done. But our rental is well-prepared for Baby Michaels's arrival, and I relax a little.

We've been filming my scenes nonstop since we got here. I made it very clear to them that I would be taking off for a few days when the time came, and they were understanding and made some adjustments. We finished nearly all of my scenes, and I wasn't on set when Tyson got the call, but I didn't have my phone.

"We're almost there," Tyson says. "I'll pull into the parking garage. Best chance to avoid a scene."

I nod and hope that Cami got in without one too. My phone doesn't go off with any new alerts, so I'm assuming we're still under the radar for now.

We finally arrive and Tyson leaves me to go park the car, and I practically run to the third floor nurses' station. "Mrs. Michaels?" Both of the nurses stare at me; they know exactly who I am, and I am extremely thankful for patient confidentiality and the fact that they can't go running to the press.

"Room three," the one says, and points to my right. I move quickly to the door of the room and I hear some commotion inside; I open the door and Cami is there on the bed. Her knees are up and there is a nurse between her legs.

"Cams?"

"Hi, beautiful," she says, and I want to cry. She's in labor and calls me beautiful.

"Hi beautiful yourself." I come to stand next to her, opposite the nurse, and she's pulling her hand out and removing her glove.

"You're about five and half centimeters," she says as the glove snaps, and I jump. I feel Cami's hand on mine. Then the sound finally registers: I can hear a heartbeat. It's quiet, but still there.

I look at Cami and give her the best half smile I can manage. "How are you doing?" I ask her.

"I'm better now."

"Oh."

She smiles wide. "Epidural."

I laugh. "Well okay then." She looks to her right.

"Watch the top line." I do, and it is nearly peaked at the top. "That is a contraction, and I am feeling nothing except a little pressure."

"How far apart?"

"About three minutes."

The nurse comes over to the bed; she is holding something that looks a little like a crochet hook. "I'm going to break your water. You won't feel too much, but the contractions should increase in frequency and they will intensify." I watch as the nurse goes back to where she was when I came in and does something, then I hear a popping sound of sorts. "Nice and clear. Don't move, we'll change the sheets under you."

Cami grunts a little and I look at her. "She wasn't kidding. Feel?" she says, taking my hands. She places them on her belly, and it is hard as a rock. But after a few heartbeats it softens a little. I don't remove my hands because I'm looking at Cami; then suddenly her belly hardens again and I look to the contraction monitor and, sure enough, she is peaking again.

"You're about a minute apart." The nurse sets about changing Cami's sheets and then she leaves, saying, "I'll be back in a few minutes. We will check your progress again and go from there."

The nurse leaves, and Cami and I are alone.

"Push, baby," I tell her, and she looks at me; she's scared. "You're doing great." No need to tell her that I'm my own mess right now. We're so close, but we've been so close for over an hour. It's now nearly two in the morning and she's been here since just before four.

"You're doing great, Cami," Dr. Burgess encourages her. "You're almost there."

Cami pushes again, and I see Dr. Burgess get a little more excited.

"Tristan, do you want to watch?" I look at Cami and she nods. I take a step toward the end of her bed, closer to her knee, and I look over. "Okay, Cami, push again. Let's show Tristan your baby's head. Ready?" Cami nods and braces herself to push harder. I can see the determination in her eyes. "Push."

Cami grabs her thighs and pushes with all her might, and I watch as a messy yet hair-streaked head slowly appears, and I'm overcome. "Again, Cami, just like that one," Dr. Burgess encourages her again, and she does, putting everything she can into it, and our baby's head descends a little further. When Cami relaxes, though, the head doesn't go back in. "Cami, one more push and we should see a head." Cami catches her breath and her might, and she pushes, and out comes our baby's head. "Hang on, Cami." I watch as Dr. Burgess goes to work with one of those ball suckers, clearing out mouth and nose. "All right, Cami, one more push and you'll be holding your baby in your arms. One, two, three."

She musters up any strength she may have left and pushes hard, and just like that our child is born and the room's silence is pierced by a screaming wail. I look at Cami and we're both in tears.

"Congratulations, you have a baby boy."

Dr. Burgess places our son on Cami's chest. The nurse puts a light blue cap on his head and wipes him down. "He's perfect," I say to Cami, who can't pull her eyes away from him. I kiss her forehead. "I'm so proud of you."

We take a moment to enjoy him in her arms, just for a few minutes, then the nurse takes him away to clean him up. I kiss Cami and we put our foreheads together, staring into each other's eyes, lost in our little miracle moment.

"I love you. So much." I kiss her.

"Ditto."

CHASING LOVE'S WINGS

My heart is swollen so large I feel like it will burst with the unconditional love I feel for my wife and for our son. The last year has been a crazy rollercoaster that has become the start of something beautiful. I'm no longer seeking, finding, or chasing love's wings. They are here with me, now and forever.

FIFTY

******
Bobby
******

It's just after one and I need something to do. I thought for sure this self-imposed sentence on a remote island would be better than this, but there are days where I really go stir crazy. Today is one of those days. It is the middle of August, and I haven't heard from Cameron since the middle of May. I gather that things are going well because Tristan has been lighting up the headlines. There is a lot of praise coming to him for his upcoming movies. But I'm interested in the one that he's finished filming recently.

When I saw the information I was floored. I had no idea he was interested in producing or in writing. But this one, *Finding Forever*, seems to be one for the ages. The release date is scheduled for later this year. But I have no doubt that all of this attention is keeping Cameron busier than she was before.

I'm saddened by the fact that I haven't heard anything in regards to Baby Michaels.

I hear Alfred open the door.

"What is it, Alfred?"

"A package, sir." A package, that's odd. Not something he's received since moving to Carnealeon.

Alfred brings the envelope into the living room where I'm sitting. I take a look at the address and then at where it comes from. It just says Los Angeles, and it is addressed to Bob.

I tear back the perforated tab to open it. It's a flat, eight-by-ten size envelope, and I look inside. There is an envelope inside. Removing the envelope from the larger one, I notice handwriting and I look at it.

Grandpa Bobby.

I lift the lip of the envelope to find a card.

Birth Announcement
Mr. & Mrs Tristan Michaels are proud to announce
the birth of their son
Jaden Robert Michaels
born May 29th, 2013, 1:56 a.m.
weight: 7lbs, 8oz
21.5 inches long

There is a pictures included on the card, and I stare at the beautiful baby boy. He looks a lot like Cameron did when she was born. I look again at the date. That was more than two months ago.

"How did I not hear about this — in the news, at the very least?"

"Because we're good at keeping secrets." I jump and stand up. Standing at the entrance to my living room is my daughter, holding onto a small blue bundle. Her husband, Tristan, is standing behind her.

"I told you not to come here."

"I know, but I thought that you might like to see your grandson, and the house is not yet finished." She takes a few steps in my direction and I meet her halfway. I kiss her forehead, and she hands me her son.

I take him in my hands and I immediately start humming; it's the same tune I hummed for Cameron when she was born. I look at Jaden and he is beautiful. I can see both Tristan and Cami in him and he's so precious. I kiss his forehead.

"I've been wondering where she got that song." I look at Tristan. "Now I know."

I look at Cami and then back to Tristan and then to my grandson. My heart swells with the love I've missed, the love I've always thought I needed to feel when it came to my daughter, and she, along with her husband, have given me that unconditional love.

The End

About Zoey

Amazon and iTunes Best Selling Author Zoey Derrick comes from Glendale, Arizona. Zoey, was a mortgage underwriter by day and is now a paranormal, romance and erotica novelist full-time. She writes stories as hot as the desert sun itself. It is this passion that drips off of her work, bringing excitement to anyone who enjoys a good and sensual love story.

Not only does she aim to take her readers on an erotic dance that lasts the night, it allows her to empty her mind of stories we all wish were true.
Her stories are hopeful yet true to life, skillfully avoiding melodrama and the unrealistic, bringing her gripping Erotica only closer to the heart of those that dare dipping into it.

The intimacy of her fantasies that she shares with her readers is thrilling and encouraging, climactic yet full of suspense. She is a loving mistress, up for anything, of which any reader is doomed to return to again and again.

Zoey Derrick

Stalk Zoey
On Twitter: www.twitter.com/ZoeyDerrick
On Facebook: www.facebook.com/Zoey.Derrick.1 -
Personal
www.facebook.com/Zoey.Derrick (Author)
On Her Website: www.ZoeyDerrick.com
Email Her: Zoey@ZoeyDerrick.com